UNQUIET
GRAVE

UNQUIET GRAVE

Janet LaPierre

ST. MARTIN'S PRESS
NEW YORK

Design by Design Oasis

Library of Congress Cataloging-in-Publication Data

LaPierre, Janet.
    Unquiet grave.

    I. Title.
PS3562.A624U5   1987   813'.54   87-16453
ISBN 0-312-01102-4

First Edition

10 9 8 7 6 5 4 3 2 1

This book is for my dear husband, who never once pointed out to me that most of his friends have working wives.

AUTHOR'S NOTE

Port Silva, California, is an imaginary town. Stretch the
Mendocino coast some twenty miles longer, scoop up Mendocino Village and Fort Bragg, toss in a bit of Santa Cruz.
Set this concoction on a dramatic headland over a small harbor and add a university. Established 1885. Elevation 100.
Population 24,020, a mix of old families, urban escapers, students, academics, and tourists in season.

UNQUIET
GRAVE

Prologue

The bending line of clear, sweet sound had sung the moon down and now beckoned the hovering fog. Come in, come in, urged the flute. Come cradle the nodding boats, shroud the fierce black rocks, smooth the waves. Sweep up and over the headlands, blot out the brightness threatening from the east, keep the world gray. And soft. And secret.

The old bull raccoon hesitated, tucking a crippled forepaw against his chest as his pointed nose tested the air. His belly was still half-empty after long hours of hunting, but that odd noise was between him and a favorite fishing spot, just beyond the road where the creek grew wide and shallow.

Heavy footfalls and a faint groan of timbers as a high black shape moved across the arching bridge and then stepped seaward along the creek; the music swooped lower, throaty and hollow. The raccoon dropped to all fours, shook himself, and began to shoulder his way south through scrub brush and long grass, toward the headland and its scatter of houses and garbage cans.

Screened from the road by a stand of young redwoods, these dwellings were purposefully separate one from another, hunched gray shapes with sleeping faces turned to the sea. Curtains were drawn, garage doors closed tight against salty moisture. When a motorcycle roared over the bridge it disturbed only a lean gray cat, which froze belly to ground, growling a soft, muffled growl around a struggling mouse. The engine shut down with one last cough, and the machine glided silently to rest beside a silent house. The cat dropped the mouse, snapped its spine, and crouched to feed.

From the harbor to the north a foghorn began to call its mournful oooo-aaah, familiar background to the dreams of coastal folk. The fog crept up and over the headland in clots and wisps, engulfing this building, missing the next, gathering on roofs to drip to decks like slow rain. In the brushy field between road and highway a rabbit screamed and died in the claws of a swooping owl.

On a deck above the sea a small light bloomed and voices murmured, barely discernible from sea-sound. After a time the light went out and the voices grew louder; there was a scream, a flurry of scrapes and thumps. Boards clattered, a cry rose and was cut off; then came a crunching thud, and another, again and again.

Many minutes later, the only sounds were harsh breathing and the slow thunk of trailing heels as a bent figure dragged a long, limp form to the edge of the deck. He planted his feet, shifted his grip, and with a grunt of effort heaved his burden over the waist-high railing.

It hit and bounced and began to roll down the slope in a rattle of small stones. Over it went and over, loose-limbed, a leg flung forward from a bending knee, an arm sketching a languid gesture in air as it followed the pull of a shoulder. The body jolted against a protruding rock, jackknifed and held around a larger one, slid slowly free. It rolled once more, to sprawl facedown on the wet sand of the beach, long pale hair colorless as sea-foam in the gray of approaching dawn.

CHAPTER 1

Just about the color of Ilona's hair, thought Joe Mancuso sourly, and he yanked the heavy curtains tighter, cutting off the shaft of pale morning sun. She'd tossed that shimmering mane back in a "you'll be sorry" gesture as she stalked out Saturday night. And so he was, sorry or guilty or something. He squared his shoulders, punched the phone buttons, was clearing his throat as his brain finally registered what his ear was hearing: blat-blat-blat-blat.

Busy. At what, eight-thirty of a Monday morning? Ilona must be working from home. Joe unclipped the jack from the telephone and connected it to the modem of his AT. The thing to do was return this relationship to its proper, professional basis, teacher to student. He would send a polite inquiry—and a few words of encouragement—via electronic mail, and she could reply or not as she chose. He flipped the computer's power switch and turned on the monitor, wondering if he might be getting too old to shepherd the hackers and baby geniuses. Especially when they were blond, beautiful, and rich.

Amber shapes glowed: date, time, >C. He bent over the keyboard, entered "callvera," and listened to the modem dial, watched the prompts and responses appear on the monitor as his program connected him to the VAX 11/785 at UC Port Silva. Welcome to VERA. Log in: JOMAN. Password.

Click buzz buzz. Bulletin board: Machine will be down Tuesday from 6 to 9 A.M. for preventive maintenance. Then his own system prompt: Hi, Daddy.

Leaving the machine on and the door open, he moved down the hall, skirted the living room, and pushed through a swinging door to stand blinking in the uncurtained brightness of his spacious kitchen. He yawned a jaw-cracking yawn, finger-combed his damp hair, linked his hands behind his neck, and stretched. Then another yawn, and a grin of well-being as he noted sun-dazzle on French doors, varied greens of garden and trees beyond. When he'd moved north from San Francisco five years earlier, a new assistant professor at the newest and smallest campus in the University of California system, he'd spent nearly half his salary to rent a weathered cottage perched on a fog-bound cliff above the Pacific. Now he owned a nice solid house and nearly an acre of nice flat land on the very eastern edge of Port Silva, and he visited the ocean when he felt the need.

No ocean today, gardening today. After breakfast. He took a slab of bacon from the refrigerator, and a carton of eggs. He set these on the worktable, added a bunch of green onions, two cold baked potatoes, a covered bowl of grated Parmesan cheese.

He filled the kettle, set it on the stove, then returned to the sink to peer out the window. The front door of the tiny cottage was still closed tight, the curtains in the side window drawn. Last night, Sunday night, his young tenant, Cat Smith, had gone off in an ancient Volks van with the crew Joe always thought of as the Bremen-town musicians. It was probably late when she got home.

He pulled a big chef's knife from its slot at the end of the worktable, cut three slices off the bacon slab, then shrugged and cut three more. If she woke up hungry, he was cooking anyway and she knew she was welcome. Otherwise, Arthur could have a feast. Joe diced the potatoes, skin and all, chopped onions, turned the browning bacon.

"Smells awesome, Joey!" Spatula clattered on stove-top as Joe spun around to face the figure looming in the doorway.

"George! Where the hell . . . ? I didn't hear you come in."

"Last night, big brother, very late and quiet as a mouse. I slept on the couch." With a grin and a shrug George ambled into the kitchen to survey worktable and stove. "How long till we eat?"

In the clear morning light the two made an unlikely pair of brothers. Joe, the elder by ten years, was five feet nine, with powerful arms, a thick torso, and a butt so flat that even Levi's hung loose behind. Coarse, densely black hair framed a round, swarthy face; heavy-lidded brown eyes tipped sleepily away from a thrusting Roman nose.

If Joe was a teamster, or maybe a plumber, George was a tennis player or a first baseman, a Yankee. Six feet two, rangy and broad of shoulder, he had tanned fair skin, longish sandy hair streaked from the sun, wide gray eyes fringed with curling dark lashes.

Joe glanced out the window once more, but was unsurprised to find that the cottage remained closed and silent. Cat was as solitary and reserved as her namesake; she wouldn't come to the house while George was here. "Maybe ten minutes," he told his brother. He cracked six eggs, stirred in a handful of cheese, added the green onions and a bit of dried basil. "You can make some toast," he said as he poured the mixture slowly over the bacon and browned potatoes. "And set the table."

"Did I hear you at the terminal already? On your day off?" George spoke over his shoulder as he set out placemats and napkins.

5

"I was sending mail to Ilona," Joe told him. "I more or less brushed her off Saturday night, after the rest of you had left; told her I didn't have time to work right then and she should call me the next day. Which she didn't. You probably didn't notice," he added, "but all evening Ilona seemed to be, well . . ."

"Coming on to you. I noticed," said George with a grin. "In today's world, Joey, you gotta have a graceful response ready when a woman lets you know she's got this incredible lust for your bod."

"There hasn't been a whole lot of demand for mine," Joe told him. "And I don't think . . ." He stared at the spatula without seeing it. "I think Ilona Berggren is trying too hard to be her father's daughter. You know, win all the medals, make a million dollars, fuck anything that'll stand still long enough. Used to be only guys got caught in that trap."

The round oak table stood at the east end of the room before the French doors; as Joe set the hot plates down, he really looked at his brother for the first time that morning. George settled into his chair with some delicacy; the hand reaching for the saltshaker was scabbed across the knuckles, and there was a dark bruise just above his right eye. "It doesn't need more salt," Joe said automatically. "Uh, George, your BMW—?"

"Hey, I promised Mama, remember? That bike's cherry, not a scratch on it."

"Seem to be a few on *you*."

"Oh, well." George looked at his hand, flexed it. "It's kind of embarrassing. My, um, landlady, she and I had a little disagreement over the rent. I thought she was kidding—about evicting me, that is. But when I got home last night, or this morning actually, she wouldn't let me in. In fact, she shoved me and I sorta fell down the porch steps."

"She wanted to raise your rent?"

6

"That, too," said George, and paused to take another mouthful. "Really great, Joey, I sure wish I could cook like this. The thing is, that night security job at the computer science building doesn't pay a whole lot, and I keep coming up short. But I've been doing things around the place for her."

"I'll bet." Joe reached for another piece of toast.

"Anyway, she really wants a roomer who's there more, not some guy with a night job and an active social life. And I sure need to save some money. That's why I was wondering about here." George put his fork down and smiled a hopeful, winning smile.

"You're welcome to the living room sofa for a day or two, George. You know the back room isn't a bedroom anymore; it's my workroom."

"I was thinking about the cottage, Joey. You know, if I had a place of my own for a while I could probably get it together, go back to school or whatever."

Mostly whatever, Joe thought sadly. He shook his head. "Sorry, I have a tenant."

"That street kid? Seriously, Joey, I've been meaning to talk to you about that." George pushed his chair away from the table and tilted it up on its back legs. "I mean, you found her going through the garbage behind Silveira's, right? She's gotta be carrying TB, herpes, who knows what? And you've got a houseful of very marketable gear. One of these nights she'll hit you over the head and clean the place out."

"Cat probably weighs ninety pounds," said Joe, rising to refill his coffee mug. "Dr. Brodhaus said she was undernourished and had been beaten up, nothing else. And she hasn't stolen one damned thing in the six months she's been here," he added. "Cat's no freeloader; she works hard."

George's eyes narrowed at this last remark. "I guess she does, if she keeps you so easy you can walk away from Ilona

7

Berggren. And here I thought you were being the big altruist— Hey!" he yelled, as Joe hooked one foot under the front rung of his chair and sent it over backwards.

George hung up the dish towel and leaned over the sink to watch a big orange cat with a white chest and a stub tail come down the front steps of the cottage. Head low, ears flat, the cat put one foot in front of the other with precise grace as he moved around to the back deck, where Joe was setting out the remains of breakfast.

"A girl named Cat, and a cat named Arthur," George muttered. He shook his head, then winced and touched the back of it gingerly. "Hey," he said, leaning closer to the window to peer toward the street. "Joey, you've got company. It's Ed Berggren, and he looks seriously pissed off."

"Ed?" Joe was frowning as he stepped back through the French doors. "He should be busy as hell on his boat, he's sailing for Puget Sound tomorrow." The key-twist doorbell shrieked, and Joe said, "Let him in, will you?"

Ed Berggren surged into the kitchen like a board chairman who'd come from his yacht to foil a takeover. His short-sleeved plaid shirt was neatly tucked into tan wash-and-wear slacks, his Topsiders had a well-oiled gleam; but a spot of red marked each cheekbone, and his breath came fast and shallow. "What the hell!" he barked at Joe. "Don't you ever answer your goddamned phone?"

"On Mondays it doesn't ring," replied Joe, "because it's not plugged in. George, get out a couple of beers and that jug of fresh tomato juice. You'd better sit down," he told Berggren.

Berggren wilted into the nearest chair and watched Joe pour beer and tomato juice at the same time into the same glass. "Christ, Mancuso, I haven't drunk that foul-looking mix since I was a starving assistant professor and you were a pissant undergrad."

8

"Pretend it's Dom Perignon and orange juice," suggested Joe. "What's happened, did you try to hire one of our baby geniuses and get a rude turndown?"

Berggren sipped the murky fluid, then sipped again. "Ah. That's good." He sat straighter, calling himself back to order. "No, I'm afraid this is personal. I can't find Ilona. I thought she might be here."

Joe stopped his own glass halfway to his mouth. "Here?"

"You and my daughter got pretty friendly Saturday night," said Berggren. "She was still here when I left. When she didn't show up for Sunday supper at the boat, I thought the two of you had made a weekend of it."

"I don't seduce students." Joe spoke each word with separate force. "Especially a student I knew when she was in pigtails."

A snort from George, and a sardonic look from Berggren. "*I* can appreciate such delicate discrimination," the older man murmured, "but I doubt that Ilona did."

"Are you sure she's not working from a terminal at home? I called her earlier this morning," Joe explained, "and got a busy signal. So I sent her mail, asked her to bring me up to date when she had time."

Berggren shook his head. "I just came from her apartment. The phone's hooked up to her micro, all right, but Ilona's not there. Place was full of . . . dead air, as if no one had ever lived there." He shivered and took a gulp from his glass.

"The shop?" Joe suggested, meaning CS 100X, the terminal room used solely by computer science students.

"Hah!" The bloodshot blue eyes narrowed. "I called there and got some snippy bitch of a secretary who told me she hadn't seen Ilona and hung up. And when I called back no one answered."

"No secretaries, just grad students and researchers. Come on, we'll check to see if she's logged on." He led Berggren

9

to the workroom, George trailing along. The three of them breathed shallowly, listening to clicks and beeps, watching letters form.

Ilona's name did not appear. Joe frowned at the screen, then made an effort to ease his expression as he turned to Berggren. "Ed, Ilona's a big girl; are you sure—?"

"I'm not sure of anything except that this feels wrong. She knows I'm leaving tomorrow and she'd normally be in touch. What the hell did you *say* to her Saturday night?"

Joe stood straighter. What were the rules for explaining to a father that you had chosen not to go to bed with his daughter? "Everyone else had gone, and Ilona was helping me clear the table. She said that one of the hackers was putting bugs in her program; why didn't we open another bottle of wine and work out a plan for getting the guy? I told her I couldn't right then; I'd promised Alice that I'd come by her house after I finished cleaning up."

"Alice?"

"Joe's friend Dr. Alice," offered George. "I think she sat across the table from you. Reddish hair, tits out to here?"

"I'd promised Alice," Joe repeated, directing a quelling look at his brother. "So Ilona said she'd handle it herself, and she drove off. I'll bet she's still there; those kids sit at a terminal until their eyes glaze and then they crawl into a corner for a nap." He pulled his chair up to the computer desk and sat down. Berggren came to stand at his shoulder.

Joe scanned the logged-in names once again, said, "Let's try Jason," and began to rattle the keyboard. "Epstein, this is Mancuso. Is Ilona Berggren in the building?"

There was a beep, and then the answer appeared. "Hi, Joe. No idea."

"Go look," Joe commanded.

"Hey, I'm in the middle of some serious stuff here, I'll be through in about half an hour."

10

"EPSTEIN!"

"Yessir."

"Okay. Pay attention. Check out the whole floor; she's probably sacked out in one of the lounges. And send somebody out to the parking lot to look for her car; it's a little red Alfa."

"Here," said a voice from behind them, and Joe and Berggren swung around to find George holding out refilled glasses. "Beer was open," he explained, "so I figured we might as well finish it."

"Thanks," muttered Berggren, and he drank deeply. "Joe, I want you to know I appreciate your help."

"That's okay," Joe replied absently, his eyes on the monitor.

"I guess I'm acting like an idiot, but there are always kooks around a college, and sometimes Ilona has more nerve than sense. Goddamn!" he said through his teeth, "I'm going to read that kid the riot act, even if she is almost twenty-one."

Breathing. The click of glass against teeth, audible swallows. The creak of Joe's chair. A sigh from George, a floorboard squeak as Berggren shifted his feet. Then a beep from the machine, and all three of them leaned forward to watch the amber letters appear.

"Joe, Jase here. Ilona Berggren is not in the building, and no one has seen her recently. Just a minute."

Long silent seconds; sharply drawn breaths as new words flickered into shape. "But there is a red Alfa in the lot, a sports job, license says IBERG."

11

CHAPTER 2

Maybe they'd left and she hadn't heard them. Cat knelt before the front window, parted the curtains slightly, carefully, and peered out. "Shit!" she muttered. Cycle beside the house, Mercedes convertible in the street, both of them chromed and polished and reflecting hundreds of little suns.

If it were just Joe, she'd chance it and ask him for help. But that silly prick of a brother would give her trouble for the fun of it, and the convertible man walked like somebody who thought he owned the world.

She stood up, brushed off her bare knees, tugged her T-shirt down over her panties as she moved across the room to stand beside the narrow bed. Too small to warm his gaunt six-and-a-half-foot frame with her own body, she'd piled on all her blankets and turned the heater up high. And still he'd shivered for hours, clenching his teeth as if their chatter might reveal his hiding place to whatever shadowy things were pursuing him this time.

Now he shifted, straightening bent legs; the bed creaked and he groaned as if in response. "Sshhh," she whispered, and stroked the bushy light brown hair, finding it damp at the temples. Probably be a good idea to take off one of the blankets.

She eased the blanket free, folded it, dropped it on the

12

redwood garden lounge she'd slept on last night. Antelope's shirt was dry, she noted, and so were his undershorts; she tossed the two garments after the blanket and hung the still-damp army surplus trousers back over the kitchen chair that stood before the glowing electric heater. Indecision caught her for a moment . . . thumb between her teeth, eyes on the red-orange bars, head tilted as if to hear the faint thrum. What had set him off? And what was she going to do with him? She sighed, and was offended by such a raggedy, hopeless sound. A shower, and a pot of tea, and then she'd think of something.

In the tiny bathroom she dropped her clothes in a corner, turned on the shower, then moved back to the doorway to make sure he was as she'd left him. "Sshh, everything will be okay," she said softly. She showered with the bathroom door open and the shower door not pulled tight.

Sgt. Duane Mendenhall took the corner in an acute lean, gunned his black Kawasaki one last time, and slacked off to a more decorous speed. Goddamned people-mover and hand-holder, that's all he was these days. Never should have left the big city.

He ran the bike smartly to the curb behind a Mercedes, stepped off and set his helmet on the seat, and turned to glare at the house, an ordinary stucco building flanked by a lot of new and expensive deck. First a bunch of animal rights creeps who thought they were entitled to parade up Main Street during morning traffic, and now some rich bastard who couldn't keep his kid in line. With a muttered "Yessir, Chief," he straightened, mentally clicked his boot heels, and strode up the walk.

The rusty caw of the doorbell brought instant response. The man in the doorway was short, stocky, sleepy-looking. "Edward Berggren?" Mendenhall snapped.

The other man shook his head and stepped back, pulling the door wider.

"And who're you?" demanded the policeman.

"Joseph Mancuso. This is my house." Deep voice, with a hard edge. Mendenhall's glance moved from the hint of a gut to sloping muscular shoulders, a thick neck. "If you're here to speak with Mr. Berggren," Mancuso added, "you'd better come in."

The policeman stepped through the door, pulling off his motorcycle gauntlets and ramming them into the pockets of his jacket. Living room about fourteen by twenty, ordinary furniture, Mancuso and two other men. No, one other man and a tall kid with a smirk. "Sergeant Duane Mendenhall," he said with a slight inclination of his head. "According to Chief Gutierrez, an Edward Berggren says his teenage daughter took a walk."

"My daughter is no teenager, she's twenty years old and a college graduate!"

Mendenhall surveyed the speaker: just under six feet tall, ramrod straight and high-shouldered, electricity in the stance and sparking from bright-blue eyes. Kind of man could chew up and spit out a small-town cop. "Which means she's of age and can go where she wants," he told the worried father, but in mild tones. "How long's she been gone?"

"I last saw her Saturday night, one A.M. or maybe a little before," said Berggren. "And Joe says she left here shortly after that. So far as I've been able to learn, no one has seen her since."

"That's less than thirty-six hours," suggested Mendenhall.

"The hell you say! Look, Sergeant—"

Joe interrupted, putting a hand on Berggren's shoulder. "Why don't we all sit down? The deck would be the best place." He turned and set off through the kitchen, and after

14

a moment Berggren and Mendenhall and George followed, single file.

Outside, the policeman swallowed his disbelief, took out his notebook, asked polite questions, and wrote down particulars. Listening to Berggren's clipped voice, noting the set of his shoulders and the forceful thrust of his jaw, Joe wondered how a father and daughter so similar in temperament could have tolerated each other. Perhaps in fact they hadn't always. Ilona would not have disappeared merely to make him, Joe Mancuso, uncomfortable; but her absence could be a calculated shot at her father in some war Joe knew nothing about.

"You say you were planning to take your boat north tomorrow. Was your daughter sailing with you?" Mendenhall asked.

To Joe's astonishment, Berggren reddened slightly as he shook his head. "No, I have a crew. An associate of mine is driving up from San Francisco tonight, and he's bringing two friends with him, people Ilona doesn't know. All experienced sailors, of course," he added quickly. "But Ilona always sees me off, or at least calls me."

The policeman's expression remained unchanged except for the briefest twitch of one eyebrow. "Okay. Now, you and your daughter were here Saturday night. What was the occasion?"

"A dinner, mostly old friends. Joe was my student years ago, and he likes to cook."

"Who else was present?"

Berggren crossed his arms on his chest. "George there, Joe's brother. Mal Burns, we were in grad school together and he lives here now. Mal's son, Aaron, he must be twenty-one, twenty-two years old.

"Then there was Alice somebody, Joe's friend," Berggren

15

went on, and Joe added, "Dr. Alice Magruder, she's a partner in the Family Practice Clinic downtown."

"And Mike Renfrew, another student in Joe's summer program, and his new girl, Randy something."

"*New* girl?" Joe looked at Berggren, but it was George who answered.

"Ilona was Renfrew's old girl. I got the feeling she wasn't too thrilled to see him here."

"Well, nobody told *me*," said Joe. "And I don't keep track of the kids' love lives. I like Renfrew; he's bright and he's more mature than some of the others in the program."

"What is it, this program?" Mendenhall inquired.

"The computer industry has set up a national network of scholarships for brilliant math or physics graduates who want to work in artificial intelligence. Ilona is part of the group here that is headed for San Diego in the fall." Berggren's voice was full of pride.

"Artificial intelligence?" Mendenhall's nose twitched, as if he smelled something suspicious. "What the hell is that, artificial intelligence?"

"It's a different, faster kind of computing," Joe said. "But that's for San Diego. What they're doing here is playing with programming, designing languages. I watch and advise, mostly watch."

"Designing languages." Mendenhall wrote that down carefully. "Okay. When you left here Saturday night, Mr. Berggren, were you and your daughter on good terms?"

"Of course we were!" snapped Berggren.

"And who saw her last?"

"I did," admitted Joe. "She stayed to talk to me for a few minutes, after everyone else had left. She thought we might work for a while, but I had other plans."

"And?"

"And she left, and I went to clean up my kitchen, and that's it."

16

"Now look, I don't want to make anybody mad," said Mendenhall. He lifted his dark glasses off the top of his head, ran a smoothing hand over his hair, set the glasses back in place. "But this girl . . . this young lady has just spent the evening watching her former boyfriend with his new girl. And she knows Daddy . . . she knows her father is off the next day for a nice long sail with a friend and a couple of young ladies, is that right?" When Berggren didn't reply, he went on. "And when she looks for a little consolation from her professor, he's busy, right? Gentlemen, my best cop's guess: Miss Berggren is someplace sulking and she'll turn up when she feels like it."

"Then why didn't she take her car?" asked George.

Mendenhall stared at him, then at Berggren. "Nobody mentioned her car; what about her car?"

"We called the campus and had some students check the computer science building for Ilona," Joe said. "She wasn't there, but they found her car in the parking lot."

"Oookay." The policeman drew the word out long, as he pulled booted feet closer to his chair and straightened his back. "See, that kind of puts a different complexion on things. Um, dependable car, is it? I mean, you don't think she maybe couldn't start it, so she decided to hitch a ride?"

"It's an Alfa Romeo, and she keeps it in top shape. Ilona has no patience with machines that don't perform," said Berggren. "And she wouldn't in any case have hitched a ride; she'd have gone back into the building for help, or for a telephone."

"Okay," said Mendenhall again, rising from his chair. "Mr. Berggren, I still think your daughter took a walk. But it wouldn't hurt to have a look at the car, maybe talk to some of the people there at the university. Best thing for you would be to go back to, where is it you're staying, River's End? Go back there and see if you've had any calls, then maybe hang around in case one comes."

"You're thinking kidnapping?" Berggren spoke slowly, and a line of white showed around his lips.

Mendenhall shook his head. "I don't think anything, but people with money, they catch some bastard's attention and there you are. Chances are your daughter will call you any time now, let you know she's spending a few days with a friend. If she doesn't, why don't you make me a list of special friends she *might* call? And maybe a list of people who might not like you."

Berggren got to his feet, moving stiffly. "Yes. I'll do that. And I'll be hearing from you?"

"Yessir, from me or from Chief Gutierrez."

Berggren hurried away with no further words. Joe's gaze followed him for a moment, then settled on Mendenhall. "Would you like me to go to the campus and talk to the kids?"

The policeman shook his head. "I'll probably do that myself, after I have a look at the car. *After* I check with the chief. Did you see her drive off Saturday night?"

"Sorry, but no. She was annoyed with me; she stalked out and slammed the door and I thought following her would just make things worse. No, I went into the kitchen and turned the water on; I didn't even hear her car start. This street isn't heavily traveled," he added, "and the neighborhood is quiet. The possibility of trouble just didn't occur to me."

"Well." Mendenhall looked out at the street: old trees, thick shrubbery, houses set well back on large lots. "I don't suppose the neighbors noticed anything, but we'll check. What about that cottage?" he said suddenly, and turned to George. "Or is that where *you* live?"

"I have a tenant," Joe began, but George interrupted.

"Just a street kid; my brother is a soft touch for strays and misfits. Chances are she was too spaced to notice anything."

18

George the mischief-maker, eight years old forever. Joe fixed cold eyes on his brother, who had the grace to look briefly shamefaced. "A young woman rents my cottage," Joe told the policeman. "I don't know whether she was at home Saturday night. In fact, I don't know whether she's at home now."

"Might as well go find out," said Mendenhall, thumping down the deck steps. Joe followed, irritated by his own reluctance. Cat was merely small; she wasn't frail. And she certainly wasn't timid.

George hesitated at the edge of the deck, caught Joe's glance, and stayed there. Mendenhall strode around to the front of the cottage, stepped up onto the small porch, and rapped on the door.

Cat was waiting inside; she'd been waiting since the policeman arrived. She'd flown around the room like a silent fury, adjusting the heat and arranging the blankets so that Antelope wouldn't suddenly waken because he was too warm, wishing that this once she had some kind of pill to feed him, any kind, something to keep him safely out. Even at his best Antelope was terrified of anyone wearing a uniform; in his present state, he might . . . She had no idea what he might do.

Out the back, she'd thought at first. If the cop looked like staying, she'd coax Antelope out the back door and around the far side of the house. But then they all settled out on Joe's deck, which meant neither door could serve for escape. So she'd sat beside the bed singing low soft songs, willing him deeper into sleep.

At the sound of steps on the porch she was beside the door, to open it at the first brush of a knuckle. She stepped out and closed the door behind her, looked up at the huge looming figure, stepped around him and down and then turned to face him again.

19

Oh, shit! thought Joe. This was going to be worse than he'd feared. She had those blue-gray eyes fixed on the cop like twin rifle barrels; you could probably get arrested just for *looking* at a cop like that. "Uh, Cat, this is Sergeant Mendenhall. He has, we have, a problem, and we thought you might be able to help. Sergeant, this is Cat Smith; she's been my tenant for more than six months."

Mendenhall was surveying the figure before him with disbelief. Couldn't be five feet tall, with a raggedy shock of black hair and a huge shapeless gray sweatshirt over Levi's and bare feet. And funny pale eyes in the dark face, eyes that said "Fuck you!" so plain he thought for a minute he'd heard the words. The name registered, and his outraged spine stiffened still further.

"Cat? What kind of name is that, Cat?"

"It's my name."

"Now you look here—"

"What do you want?" Her voice was direct but less challenging; she moved farther from the cottage as she spoke.

"I want to know what your name is," said Mendenhall, refusing to be mollified.

"My name is Cat Smith."

"I'll need to see some identification."

"My name is whatever I say it is. I say it's Cat Smith. The phone book is full of Smiths; are they all supposed to be liars?"

"Identification," he repeated, looking beyond her toward the cottage.

"I don't have to show you identification; I haven't done anything."

"Come on, little lady, let's go inside and find your driver's license or something." He reached for her arm, but she put both hands behind her and took two quick steps backward.

"Do you have a warrant? You can't search my home with-

20

out a warrant. And I don't have a driver's license; I don't drive."

Mendenhall planted his feet wide and stared at her: one more loony to make his life miserable. A big orange and white cat came around the side of the cottage and paced forward to sit down beside the girl's feet. Goddamn cat didn't even have a decent tail, just a stub.

"Sergeant Mendenhall." Mancuso had his heavy shoulders forward and his chin out, more like a bodyguard than a college professor. "I have to agree with Cat. You're pushing; she hasn't done anything. Why not ask her what we came to ask her?"

Mendenhall took a deep breath, waiting for the pounding in his temples to subside. As he pictured himself dragging this miniature warrior into the police station, he remembered that Chief Gutierrez's lady had a daughter of ten or eleven, a little girl who looked a lot like this one, and near the same size.

Another deep breath. "A young woman is missing," he intoned, "and her father is worried. She was at Mr. Mancuso's dinner party Saturday night and was apparently the last to leave. Tall, blond, driving a . . ." He looked at Joe, who filled in, "A little red sports car, an Alfa Romeo."

"Right, an Alfa. So, did you see her leave?"

Cat nodded. "I didn't notice the time, but it was late, and everybody else was gone. Except for Joe, of course."

"Was anyone with her? Did she stop to talk to anyone?"

A shake of the head. "I was on the porch calling Arthur— my cat," she added with a glance downward. "She came out in a hurry, got in the little car, drove off in a hurry all alone. Then Arthur finally came and I grabbed him and took him inside. I went right to bed. I don't remember hearing anything else."

CHAPTER 3

In times of confusion and stress, Joe Mancuso normally found refuge in physical labor . . . not pure exercise, like jogging, but a definable task that dirtied the hands and raised a sweat. Today, in the bean house, the raspberry patch, the potting shed, he found himself *listening*, head cocked and jaw loose. Every now and then he caught a glimpse of George, who was hanging around safely out of earshot, hands empty of trowel or hoe or anything even minimally useful. Finally Joe threw down his gloves, strode around the side of the house, and pounced on his brother as he blew a fleck of dust off his motorcycle's gleaming fender.

"If you've got nothing to do you can listen for the phone, so I don't have to drop what *I'm* doing and track dirt in."

Cat was at home, too; at least he thought she was. After the cop left, she'd borrowed Joe's ten-speed bike, returned it a short time later, and disappeared into the cottage. Usually she came out when she saw him working in the garden, either to earn her keep or to prevent his awkward mistakes. Cat had neat hands, tireless legs, and an unerring instinct for a plant's best interests. Joe caught his breath, suppressing a shudder as a small snake took alarm at his approach and made an undulating escape through the grass. Snakes, ladybugs, praying mantises, spiders, toads—all to be left to their proper pursuits, according to Cat.

He sank back onto his heels, wiped his forehead against a shirt-sleeve, and tried without success to imagine Ilona Berggren scooping muddy little holes for onion sets or picking worms from tomato plants. Easier to picture her whipping her open car along the coast highway, or defying gravity on a ski slope, or sailing; she and Ed had sailed his 38-foot Hans Christian to Hawaii last year. Did it bother her that her father used the boat to entertain a succession of dollies, young women her own age?

Probably not. He pushed himself to his feet, stretched, stamped to loosen cramped thigh muscles. Ten-year-old Ilona had chosen to remain with her father at the time of her parents' divorce. Sixteen-year-old Ilona had moved into her own apartment when she started at Cal. His daughter was a modern young woman, Ed would say, with a proud grin: bright, healthy, independent.

Joe squinted at the sun. Must be one o'clock or later; funny he wasn't hungry. Ilona had certainly radiated health Saturday night, standing in his kitchen with head thrown back and arms akimbo, man-tailored shirt buttoned so low it seemed only her erect nipples kept the garment from sliding off her shoulders. His cock gave a remorseful twitch at the memory. What if he hadn't been such a . . . a prude, what if he'd accepted her unspoken but obvious challenge and hustled that fine long body off to his bed? Maybe she'd be here still, and the air in his garden warmly peaceful, not charged with an unease that prickled his skin like sleet.

"No calls?" he asked George, who was slumped on the living room sofa punching the television's remote button from one soap opera to the next.

George merely shook his head, and shook it again when Joe asked whether he wanted lunch. "I had a beer, and some cheese and crackers."

Now there was a good idea. Joe cut himself a chunk of Cheddar and opened a bottle of beer. "What do you think?" he asked as he returned to the living room.

"About what?" George didn't lift his eyes.

"About Ilona," he said replied sharply. "After all, you knew her better than I did; didn't you take her out a couple of times?"

"No, I did not 'take her out'!" George sat up straight, the heels of his running shoes squeaking across the coffee table. "What it was, I ran into her now and then, I think we had coffee twice and a beer one time."

"My mistake," Joe said. "But maybe you noticed, when you were at work, whether she was particularly friendly with any of the others in the program?"

"Maybe you *haven't* noticed, Joey, but that is not a friendly bunch of people. Bunch of sharks is more like it, including Ilona." George twisted his mouth in a grimace of distaste. "Any of them banging each other, they probably do it in LISP right at the terminal."

Interesting images on the mind's screen: a row of monitors blinking and beeping and flashing "Beg your pardon?" while a row of Balans chairs rocked and rattled busily and probably, finally, went over backwards. Jesus, Mancuso! Joe chided himself.

"No, but what I really think, Joey"—George put his feet back on the table and squinted at them—"I'll bet Ilona got fed up with computers pretty quick that night, and went out in the parking lot to meet . . . oh, some no-neck jock or maybe a black guy, somebody she wouldn't want Daddy to know about. And she'll trail in any minute, all tired out."

Joe looked at his brother with distaste. Self-centered young tomcat. "Get your feet off the table," he snapped. And if George was a tomcat, he himself was turning into an old maid. "I'm going out for a while," he told his brother. "I need to take a sample down to the paint store and have some exterior enamel mixed."

The Fuller Paint store was just off Main Street downtown. Joe pulled his pickup into the lot behind the store and went inside to lose himself among a handful of slow-moving, serious-faced men in painty jeans or overalls and billed paper caps. Mixing machines thumped and shook, the smell of paint thinner bit at the nostrils. Mr. Henderson knit bushy gray brows over the old brown-painted board, said he'd do his best to match it, was not sanguine about a latex exterior enamel but maybe if an oil-based primer were well and extensively applied first . . .

Altogether, thought Joe, a very satisfying way to spend half an hour. He came out blinking into the sunlight, gave a moment's thought to the mesquite-grilled fish at the shiny new restaurant across the street, and decided Arminos' Bakery and Coffee Shop was more suited to his mood. He found an empty table by a gingham-curtained window, ordered roast beef on whole wheat, and was sipping coffee from a thick white cup and enjoying the smell of baking bread when he saw a familiar figure across the street.

Two familiar figures. The cop, Mendenhall, stood before an open doorway occupied by Malcolm Burns, Ed Berggren's old friend and one of the guests at the dinner party Joe heartily wished he'd never thought of. The policeman nodded abruptly and strode off, and Burns stepped back into the dark interior. His shop, of course. Burns had a Ph.D. in engineering from Cal, but he had dropped out of city life some years earlier to set up as an electrical contractor and sometime computer consultant here in Port Silva.

The bright-faced young waitress brought more coffee, and catsup, mustard, horseradish. Then the two-inch-thick sandwich, with a sheaf of green onions at one end of the oval plate and a giant dill pickle at the other. "Mancuso," said a low voice from behind him, and Joe took a larger-than-intended gulp of coffee and spent a moment sputtering.

Mal Burns moved around the table and settled into the opposite chair. His graying brown hair was gathered into a sparse ponytail; carpenter's overalls hung loosely from broad bony shoulders, and the sleeves of a chambray workshirt were rolled high on brown arms corded with muscle. "Cop came by the shop asking about Ilona," he said softly, "and I called Ed, but he said he had to keep the phone free. Then I looked across the street and saw you. Maybe you can tell me what's going down."

"Hello, Aaron," Joe said to the young man who stood beside the table. Mal's son ducked his head in a diffident nod; not quite so tall as his father, he had the same big frame with more meat on it, lightish hair cut close, eyes of a pale yellow-brown. Aaron and George Mancuso had become buddies this summer; the two shared an interest in motorcycles and, more significantly in Joe's view, a kind of aimlessness that made them seem boys rather than young men.

"Big dumb cop," Mal said, and turned at the approach of the waitress. "Just coffee for me, please. Well, maybe one of your famous sticky buns. Aaron, what about you? Pull up a chair and have a second lunch."

"No. Thanks. George at home?" he asked Joe.

"He was an hour ago." Aaron's face wore its habitually stolid expression; but Joe was surprised to note a mouse under the left eye, a scabbed scrape from the right temple down over the cheekbone. "Watching television," Joe added. "He'd probably be glad of company."

Aaron hesitated, looked at his father, then turned to leave. Mal said, "Hey, wait a minute, take the van. Just pick me up at the shop by five at the latest, okay?"

Aaron ducked his head again, took the proffered keys, and left. "Kid decided to visit the redwoods in the moonlight, with a six-pack in his saddlebag," Mal explained. "And he wound up in an argument with a tree. He was just banged up a little, but we had to order a new front wheel for his bike.

"Anyway, this cop was the kind of guy who talks without opening his mouth and has to hold his arms out like an ape because he's got so much gear on his belt. He said they'd had a report from a worried father, wanted to talk to all the people who'd seen Ilona Berggren Saturday night or later."

Joe hunched his shoulders, tossed a quick look around to make sure no one was close enough to overhear, then told Burns what he knew. "I don't think the cop is dumb, exactly," he added.

"All cops are dumb; it's in the job description. Sorry, that's my sixties warp showing." A faint grin faded away, leaving the long-jawed face somber. "You know, when we were grad students at Cal, Ed and I both lived in student housing, Albany Village. Evenings we'd take the kids out to play so Yvonne and Nancy could get supper. Just like all the other daddies." He took a sip of coffee. "Aaron was older by more than a year, and big for his age, but Ilona had the most nerve; three years old, and you couldn't swing her high enough to scare her."

This was the kind of reminiscence people exchanged at funerals. Suddenly chilly, Joe beckoned the waitress and asked for more coffee. When she had departed, he remarked, "Ed told me you and he go way back."

"Two brilliant young men with the world at their feet," drawled Mal. "Now he's a millionaire designer of computer security systems and I'm an aging ex-hippie. Actually, that's not quite true," he amended. "I re-upped this very morning; I'm filling in for a colleague of yours, man going on sabbatical."

27

"That would be Paul Dutra, he's off to Oxford for the year."

"Dutra, right. That's a lucky break for me. I didn't mention this the other night because he hates being talked about, but Aaron's been accepted at Santa Barbara and Cal Poly. I'm for Santa Barbara; be nice to have another UC man in the family. Anyway, I want him free to give all his energy to school and not worry about a job."

Joe hoped his face didn't reflect his surprise. Aaron Burns had spent his childhood with his footloose mother in various isolated northern California communities, receiving a spotty education: mostly goat-milking and pot-farming, according to George. A year of catch-up work at a community college some miles inland had apparently paid off. "Good for him. Maybe my baby brother will note the example and get his act together."

"You never know." Burns swallowed the last bite of his bun and then licked his fingers. "What does George have to say about Ilona's . . . absence, I guess is the best term?"

"George thinks Ilona went off for a long weekend with some new guy." Joe looked at his coffee cup, finding George's notion no more compelling now than he had an hour ago. "*I* think she might be angry at everybody and staying away to make a point."

"What I think," said Burns in measured tones, "is that the new and liberated woman is just as much of a cock-teaser as the old one was. Which could get her into just the same kind of trouble. In my next incarnation, Mancuso, I'm planning to be gay." Burns got to his feet, dropped two dollars on the table. "Let's keep in touch, okay? If this thing goes bad, Ed is going to need his friends."

Brisk of air and bright of sky, Port Silva was presenting its most charming face to summer visitors. Joe plodded unseeing along a crowded sidewalk, stopped to pick up his paint, and drove home with the slow caution his body had learned to employ when his mind was engaged elsewhere.

The ancient Volks van was parked before the cottage, which meant Cat was busy with company, the Bremen-town musicians. And a new van, smallish and shiny brown, sat very close to his driveway. Aaron Burns, no doubt. Joe edged past the van and wondered whether he could edge past Aaron and George, into his study.

". . . little and dark, nothing to look at," came George's voice from the deck. "She generally heads for cover when I'm around; I guess she can tell I'm not the soft touch my big brother is."

"Well, if he's not banging her himself . . ." Aaron's voice had an edge of doubt.

"Hard to believe, buddy, but he's not."

"Then he probably wouldn't care that she's got, what, five or six guys in there with her."

"Burns, what we ought to do is grab a look through a window, make sure there's nothing illegal or immoral going on."

Joe slammed the refrigerator door with a force that set bottles rattling. At George's "Hey, Joey?" he sighed, uncapped his beer, and walked to the open French door.

"Joey, we were just noticing that your little house-cat seems to have some fairly weird friends."

"One of whom is standing right here getting ready to kick ass," Joe said in flat tones. "Principally yours."

"Mea culpa, big brother, mea maxima culpa. Or however the hell it goes," George said to Aaron Burns with a grin. "See, we started out Catholic. No, but Joey, a whole bunch of guys came out of that van, and even you'd have to admit they were extremely unusual-looking."

"My tenant is a young woman named Cat Smith," Joe said to Aaron. "She's a gardener, a carpenter, and a musician.

The people you just saw are the other members of her rock band, a group called Animal Fare." He tipped his bottle up for a long swallow.

"Animal Fare? Hey, I saw them on campus last week," remarked George. "Playing for the animal rights demonstrators."

"Animal rights?" Aaron spoke the words as if they felt odd in his mouth.

"There are organizations worldwide trying to promote better treatment for animals used in scientific experiments," Joe told him.

"Right," added George, "and some of them don't think animals should be used at all."

"So what are they supposed to use, people?"

Maybe not the worst idea he'd ever heard. "I have work to do," said Joe. "You guys keep the noise level down out here."

"Big brother, we'll do even better than that." George got to his feet and turned a hopeful grin in Joe's direction. "We're going downtown; maybe you could let me borrow a few bucks? I thought I'd try to square things with my old landlady, then she'll probably give me my key back. Seeing as how you don't have room for me here."

A public request, oiled with a little guilt. Joe's spurt of anger fizzled quickly into near-pity. Mama Mancuso had spoiled her handsome younger son relentlessly for twenty-two years; it was unrealistic to expect him to grow up overnight. "Okay, George, tell me what you owe and I'll give you a check."

Inside the cottage, Cat flew at the four men and hugged each of them. "Oh, God, I thought you guys would never get here. I was afraid you hadn't come to town today, or somebody'd knocked my card off the message board, or. . . . Did anybody notice you?" She spoke in a near-whisper.

30

"Couple of guys on the deck saw us drive up, so we ran around some, like marching four soldiers back and forth to make an army." The one who called himself Squirrel squinted down at Cat from bright, nearly black eyes under a wild mop of red curls. "So they won't notice how many of us go out, you think?"

"I think. I mean, I don't think," she told him, grinning. Squirrel lived on society's edge mostly from choice; beneath his irreverent mind lay a peaceful spirit. "Actually, he's a lot better. Aren't you a lot better, Antelope?" she said in hearty tones.

Moose, tall and broad and heavy, moved across the room to the redwood lounge, where Antelope huddled with his chin resting on his drawn-up knees. "Hey, Antelope, how's it going, man?"

"Hi, Moose." A tentative smile creased the angular face, followed by a frown. "I don't know. All right, I think. I was just real loose, playing to the moon. Missed your drums, Moose, but the ocean lays a neat line, did you know that? Like whoosh whoosh whooosssssssh whoomp. You might try it with brushes."

"Another fuckin' pusher's got to him." Not much bigger than Cat, Possum had brass-colored spiky hair and ice-gray eyes. Now his lips curled back from teeth filed to points. "Let's go downtown and find the bastard."

"You up for another cell or a hospital room?" Badger propped a shoulder against the wall and put on a stern look. Two years earlier, at eighteen, he had lost much of his hair during treatment for Hodgkin's disease. When it grew back, the original black was heavily threaded with gray; Badger intensified the effect by bleaching a white streak down the center of his head. "What do you think, Cat? Anything weird on the street around here?"

She shook her head. "I don't go downtown much; I wouldn't know. He was here when I got home last night; he

31

dug the key out of the hanging fuchsia and let himself in." She glanced over her shoulder and lowered her voice. "His pants and shoes were wet and sandy, he had dirt and leaves all over the rest of him, and his hands were filthy. There was even sand in his flute case. He was half-frozen and acting scared to death, but he wouldn't talk. So I just got his clothes off and got him into the shower and then put him to bed."

"So why not just keep him here; what's the big fuss?" Possum shifted from foot to foot, twitching with frantic energy. "That's what frosts my butt about women. You fish in some guy to set you up like a goddamn queen"—he gestured at the room—"right away you forget when you were sleeping under bushes, gettin' peed on by dogs and drunks."

"Sure, and you're still spending your nights over the steam vents! Possum, I'm too tired to fight with you, so just *shut up!*"

Moose came across the room with surprising speed; he wrapped one long arm around the small man, pinning his arms to his sides and lifting him clear of the floor. "Possum, you got to quit that meanness; you know Cat thinks as much of Antelope as you do. Just stay still now!" he said, squeezing. "And you sink them little bitty teeth in any piece of me, I swear I'll take a pliers to the lot of them."

"Okay." Possum waited until his feet were on the floor. "Okay, I'm sorry. I didn't mean it, Cat. It just makes me mad, guys out there shoving shit at people who can't take care of themselves."

"I know. I'm sorry I can't keep him here, but there were cops around and they'll probably be back. They're looking for a missing woman, somebody Joe knows."

"Antelope says he had himself some wine, red wine," Moose told them. "No pills, no crank, none of that bad stuff."

32

"Flashback," said Badger, nodding sagely. He had experimented widely himself before illness demanded caution.

There was a creak of wood as Antelope pushed himself upright from the lounge. "Where's my pants, Cat?" he asked, and stood swaying for a moment. Below his buttoned-up khaki shirt were a pair of jockey shorts and then long, pale bony legs.

As all of them gaped at him, he braced himself wider and said, "I took along a jug of wine, for company like. I was having a fine time all by myself, then I guess I must have started thinking about people getting hurt. I even thought I saw my dad, helmet and gun and stick and everything." His teeth began to chatter and he clenched his jaw for a moment before saying again, plaintively, "Hey, my pants?"

Pants in hand, he sank to the edge of the lounge and looked around the room, into the corners. "And my mother. I thought I saw my mother again, and this time I got to bury her."

CHAPTER 4

"**G**oddamn it to hell." Chief of Police Vincent Gutierrez spoke the words softly as he shoved the telephone aside. The knot was there in his gut again like a clenched fist, bred of months of apprehension and frustration. "Svoboda!" he barked. "Mendenhall! Get in here.

"And close the door," he added as the men filed in. "Berggren hasn't heard anything. Nothing from the girl, no ransom call. He had a second phone line run in yesterday and spent the evening calling her friends, with zero results."

Lieutenant Hank Svoboda, a big rawboned man in his middle fifties, propped his shoulders against a filing cabinet and eyed the man who was both his boss and his good friend. Gutierrez's black brows were knit in a straight line, his black eyes hooded, his mouth so tight that the vertical creases in the lean cheeks might have been cut by a chisel.

"Vince, you better loosen up," Svoboda suggested. "I know what you're afraid of. But remember, somebody found the others inside of a couple hours, he didn't try to hide either one."

"I remember." Gutierrez stared bleakly at the coffee mug in his hands. He hated early mornings, he hated bad, cold coffee, and most of all he hated the fact that a young woman had been reported missing.

"And this is a whole different kind of girl, Chief," offered Duane Mendenhall. He turned a straight chair around and sat down astride it, resting his forearms on its back. "What I hear, she wasn't real nice, but she *was* smart, too smart to let herself get picked up by some crazy."

Maybe, thought Gutierrez. Maybe. The victim of the April attack, Lisa Haffner, was a fairly dim seventeen-year-old, a girl from a small inland town who'd come over with several more experienced friends to pick up "college boys." Drunk and sick, she was abandoned by the others outside a bar a few miles up-coast. The "nice man" who gave her a ride raped her, beat her severely enough to break her nose, her jaw, her collarbone and several ribs, and then dumped her beside the highway. Two months later twenty-four-year-old Annie Willis, who sold vegetables and perhaps a little home-grown marijuana from an old stake-bed truck, apparently met the same man. Annie had not survived.

34

"Maybe," he said aloud. "But this guy is a bad actor—you remember what those two looked like?" Svoboda's mouth made a grim line as he nodded, and Mendenhall clenched his dangling hands into fists. "So I don't think I'd pin a lot of hope on his patterns. Until we get him, any young woman who's not where she's supposed to be is automatically our top priority."

"Yessir, and we'd better corral our own women. Or try to," added Mendenhall, the harried father of three teen-age daughters.

Gutierrez nodded glumly. His women were safely out of town; Meg Halloran, the widowed schoolteacher who'd turned up in his life only a year ago, had taken her daughter Katy to Arizona to visit grandparents. Selfish bastard that he was, he wished them both right back here right now. "Svoboda," he said, pulling himself back to the matter at hand, "what did you find out at Ilona Berggren's apartment building?"

"It's a fair-sized place, fourteen units, and expensive. Has a pool, tennis courts, like that. Not many transients or students, mostly single professional people or youngish couples with both people working. One guy invited this good-looking blonde to a party and got turned down. Another one played tennis with her twice, she beat him both times and wouldn't play again. Couple below her says if she had friends in, they were quiet. That's it, except for three units didn't answer last evening. I'm going back today."

"And the ex-boyfriend?"

"Seems like an okay guy," the gray-haired man said with a shrug. "Couple of years older than the Berggren girl, went out with her for a while; they lived together for six months and drove each other nuts."

"Then why was she still upset?"

Svoboda grinned briefly. "He's the one who left. Says he's sorry about that; if he'd given it more thought he'd have let

35

Ilona do the dumping. Other thing he says," Svoboda went on, his face hardening, "is that Ilona would *never* have run out on the program, or on her daddy."

Gutierrez's mouth drew tight, and he gave a small nod. "Yeah. Did he, the Renfrew boy, have an alibi for the weekend?"

"His new girl, name of Randy, um, Miranda Franklin, insists she was with him the whole time. I'd say, from the way she kept looking at him, he hardly even gets to go to the can by himself."

"Hank, check back with him, will you, and find out whether he was in town April 12 or June 8." Gutierrez didn't need to look at his notebook to remember the dates.

Svoboda didn't need to look, either. "I did. He had a full schedule at Berkeley last semester, and a job nights and weekends. He came up here in February for an interview, says he never came back until he moved here in July. I got his boss's name and two of his professors'."

"Okay. Thanks," Gutierrez muttered. "Duane, you talked to the people at the computer science building. Let's hear about it."

Mendenhall sat straighter and pulled a notebook from his shirt pocket. "See, they lock up the building nights; there's a bell and a sign-in sheet, and a guard on the door from six P.M. until two A.M. No Ilona Berggren on the sheet Saturday night. I ran down the kid who worked guard, and he says he didn't let anybody in without they signed.

"So I talked to everybody who *did* sign in—total of, um, fourteen people," he said, flourishing his notebook. "Turns out they open the door for each other, if the guard's in the can or after he goes off duty, but none of them let Ilona in. And nobody remembers seeing her. They're *used* to seeing her around there, of course, and most of them ain't positive they didn't, but what they do, they sit in little separate

36

booths talking to the computer. I mean, it's weird, buzz-whirr and then rattle-rattle-rattle, and not a human sound anywhere. They probably wouldn't notice a six-five on the Richter unless it happened to cut the power off."

"They have anything to say about Ilona?" inquired Svoboda.

"Nothing real personal, just that she's there a lot and works hard." Mendenhall tipped his head to one side, then lifted his meaty shoulders in a shrug. "I'd say the whole bunch of them showed a plain lack of interest in Ilona Berggren's welfare."

Svoboda broke the brief silence. "Vince, did you get anything from Berggren's neighbors at River's End?"

Gutierrez shook his head. "A big part of what people pay for there is privacy. The cottages are set apart, in a kind of garden with lots of trees and bushes, and they're solidly built. One older woman said she'd occasionally heard raised voices from what she called 'Mr. Berggren's young women.' She didn't know he had a daughter. But a couple who have a boat in the next berth knew Ilona and said she and her dad got along just fine, never a cross word."

"Bullshit!" said Mendenhall. Gutierrez's dark face creased briefly in a sardonic smile; he pulled his notebook closer and flipped pages. "Berggren insists he has no personal enemies, only business competitors. But he was very reluctant to give me the name and address of his ex-wife, Ilona's mother. He said she and Ilona had no interest in each other and never corresponded. The lady is remarried now and living in Massachusetts."

The phone on the desk buzzed and Gutierrez picked it up, signaling the others to stay where they were. After several one-word responses, he said, "Okay. But let's keep it a while; tuck it in the corner of the garage and put a cover over it. Thanks.

"Absolutely nothing wrong with that Alfa," he told the other two. "Tuned up a week ago, plenty of gas; our mechanic couldn't make it fail. Hansen says there were lots of prints inside, nearly all from one person, and they matched the ones he got from the girl's apartment." He pushed back his chair and got to his feet.

"Mendenhall, you finish up for Svoboda at the apartment building, then go to the university and check with the campus police, the custodial staff, anybody who works at night and might have seen something. Hank, you set up a phone line for public information, and pick somebody soft-spoken to man it. Then nose around for background on the people at the party Saturday."

Gutierrez tucked his shirt in, then moved to use a glass-fronted bookcase for a mirror as he straightened his tie and ran his palms over his close-cropped grizzled hair. "I'm meeting with His Honor, Mayor Wirkkala, to discuss arrangements for the Art Festival, and I guess I'd better alert him. If Ilona Berggren doesn't turn up quick in good health, the papers are going to be full of 'Port Silva Rapist' headlines again."

CHAPTER 5

"Tomorrow!" Joe said firmly and closed the door on the offended faces of two students. He was irritated by the kids who were dithery with excitement and even more irritated by those who pressed on with their own concerns as if nothing were amiss. He was tired of coming upon a cop, the same cop, every time he turned a corner. Maybe it was time for him to abandon the machines, cut loose from the university, move to a mountaintop somewhere.

His office of five years had one window; light that managed to penetrate a scraggly bush and dirty glass gave little life to beige walls, gray metal surfaces, the faded cushions of an old fake-Danish couch. A dusty cactus plant squatted in a ceramic pot, surrounded by half a dozen prickly offspring. There was one picture on the wall, his father and his uncle grinning from the bow of the small fishing boat that had gone to the bottom of the Pacific with them twenty years ago. And one flash of color, a goldfish bumping his nose against the side of his bowl, delighted to have company.

Or maybe just hungry. "Hi, Herman," said Joe, tapping a finger against the glass as his other hand reached for the cardboard cylinder of food. "Poor little guy, I should put you up for adoption."

He collected a spiral notebook, put some floppy disks in a small plastic case. If he did any more work today, it would be at home, where things were quiet. Or he might just sit on the deck in the sun and drink beer.

Halfway down the hall leading to the back door stood Mendenhall, legs planted wide and arms akimbo as he talked with two men. Reporters, or at least one of them was; Joe recognized the chunky balding man who covered City Council meetings for the *Port Silva Sentinal*. Hartwell, that was his name, Clive Hartwell, and his had been the byline on most of the "Port Silva Rapist" stories some months ago. Joe swung around and set off for the front door, head down.

The noonday sun struck him with a glare that was almost audible. He paused at the top of the broad, shallow flight of steps, rotated his shoulders, and then pulled his elbows back in an attempt to ease the ache at the base of his neck. He had had few violent impulses in his life; even in the tussles of childhood he'd never wanted to hurt anyone. The notion of rape was one his mind couldn't come to grips with. What kind of man—? He squeezed his eyes shut for a moment, then moved down the steps into a loud wash of sound that was vaguely familiar.

A band was set up in the brick-surfaced plaza near the central fountain, sinewy black cords snaking toward the performing arts building. Two squat amps, two stacks of speakers, several mikes; a guitar, an electric bass, a set of drums. A keyboard on spindly-looking legs, and a tall figure curved over a flute. Joe listened for a moment and recognized a Creedence song, "Bad Moon Rising."

Lunch-eaters or mere sun-lovers sprawled on benches and steps or simply sat on the bricks, backs against buildings. Joe watched an elderly woman in a sun bonnet move along the benches before the library to distribute leaflets; a tall man with a baby in a backpack was performing the same task around the fountain. A small group, men and women of various ages, clustered near the band, moving their placards slightly with the music. "Buddhists Concerned for Animals," said one sign. "All Life is One," proclaimed another. "The Good Lord Made Them All," insisted a curve of words along a painted rainbow. "Fair Representation!" demanded the largest sign. "Put a Real Pig on the Animal Research Committee!"

As the band paused, scattered shouts at the south end of the plaza announced the arrival of a blue van with KNOR lettered across its nose. The van swung about, stopped, spat a television cameraman from its rear doors. As the man adjusted his gear and settled his camera on his shoulder, a small pickup truck backed cautiously into the plaza from the north. A figure jumped from the truck bed, dropped the tail-

40

gate, then climbed back in to help lift the door of a large wooden crate. In ear-splitting cacophony, a flood of baby pigs poured out and down, tumbled, scrambled, and ran squealing in all directions.

The plaza exploded into noisy motion; people chased pigs, people ran from pigs, people climbed onto benches and railings to watch the action. The placard carriers and band members held their ground . . . except for the one with the guitar. The small guitarist thrust the instrument at someone not much bigger, brushed past the red-haired keyboard player, and disappeared into the melee. It wasn't until he saw her move that Joe recognized Cat.

He followed her around the computer science building, delayed by pigs and people; by the time he reached the rear parking lot she was nowhere in sight. What had set her to flight? he wondered as he scanned the lot. Damn it, if there was a rapist loose she should be more careful; he'd have to keep an eye on her. If she hadn't been in such a hurry right now, he'd have offered to take her . . . well, no, he wouldn't, because it turned out his truck wasn't here. He'd walked in this morning, enjoying the exercise and intending to beg a ride home after lunch from . . .

Alice. Oh, Jesus. He snatched a look at his watch and groaned. He was already late for their regular Tuesday lunch, and the Main Street Bar and Grill was half an hour's walk from here. Jesus.

How the hell could he have forgotten Alice? He set off for town at a pace that made his shins ache. He had planned to arrive early and order a bottle of very good Chardonnay in apology for Saturday night. Instead she'd be finishing her first martini right about now, eyeing the clock as she ordered her second. You could just forget the whole thing and head for home, a small inner voice suggested. But he dismissed the idea as cowardly and strode on.

41

* * *

Cat ran Badger's Honda over the grass and close beside her cottage; she set it up on its kickstand and gave its silver fender a regretful pat. Like Moose's ancient Volks van, the bike was used by any one of them who had need; but there'd be no more of that for her, not after her stupid admission to the cop that she had no license. She shouldn't have risked it now, but the sight of the television cameras had sent her into near-panic.

Arthur came around the corner of the cottage with a questioning "Rrrowrr?" and she picked him up to let him tuck his head under her chin. Something was coming to an end; she could feel it. The group was loosening, each member responding to a slightly different pull. Antelope had always stood at their center, the truest musician and the frailest soul; if his ghosts finally claimed him for good, Animal Fare would fly apart.

"Squirrel will go back to school," she told Arthur, who purred and rubbed his jawbone against hers. "Badger will go home to his mother. Moose will go . . . I wonder if there are monasteries for born-again Baptists; a brown robe with a rope belt would just suit him. Possum will go to jail, unless he can find work that's hard enough to keep the edge off his temper."

And where would she go, after more than a year as mother-sister-mascot? Back to Berkeley, maybe, to wash dishes for meals and play her guitar on street corners for handouts. Trouble was, she now looked like a healthy adult female rather than a scrawny twelve-year-old boy; she'd be sure to attract the wrong kind of interest. "Never mind," she said to the cat. "We'll miss this place, your own private jungle, my own private house. But we'll be okay."

A rustle in a nearby bush caught Arthur's attention, and he twisted free and jumped down. Watching him lower his head

42

and begin his stalk, she was surprised to find a haze of tears obscuring her vision. Silly bitch, she thought and blinked hard as she dug out her door key.

In the cottage Cat made herself a cheese sandwich, ate it with a glass of milk, then changed into cut-off Levi's and a tank top. Joe's vegetable garden was running amok in this stretch of warm weather, with weeds intruding everywhere, carrots and lettuce in need of thinning. Working with her hands would set her mind free; it always did.

She had to fight ivy to get the door of the garden shed open. Her live-and-let-live view of nature stopped short of ivy, which crept and climbed and strangled and made a haven for snails. Joe couldn't bring himself to root it out; he liked the glossy green leaves and the sense of springing vitality. So okay, she wouldn't kill it, but she could give it one hell of a trim. She got the electric pruning shears and a pair of spring-grip snips and went to work.

Half an hour later, sweaty and dirt-streaked, she heard an engine approach, roar, and cut off abruptly; George had arrived, with a friend. They climbed off George's bike, dropped helmets to the grass, and stood talking in low voices. Cat turned back to her task, snipping off a small forest of light green shoots to clear a path to a grandfather of a vine nearly an inch thick. She severed it halfway up, reached high to pull the top part away from the shed, then bent to set the snips around its enormous base.

"Nice ass!" There was a lingering pat on the taut seat of her shorts.

Cat was up and around in a single motion. She swept the snips forward and caught the index finger of George's still-reaching hand.

"Hey, let go! Jesus, watch out, you'll take my finger off!"

"Keep your opinions and your hands to yourself," she told

him, tightening her grip slightly. "Or you might lose something more important than a finger." She let the blades
spring apart.

George snatched his hand to his mouth and stepped back
to glare at her. "You crazy little bitch! You need somebody
to teach you some manners!"

"Come on, George, cool it." George's companion
slouched forward, thumbs hooked in the belt loops of his
Levi's. His big hands bore the nicks and scars of hard work,
and his thick forearms were weathered brown. "I never
could see why anybody'd give space to ivy," he remarked,
fixing pale yellow-brown eyes on Cat briefly before looking
at his own feet and then at the shed. "Want some help digging it out?"

"Thanks, but no." He was looming over her; big people
always felt free to do that to small people and it infuriated
her every time. Silence stretched; she stood where she was,
and finally he stepped back. "Thanks," she said again, "but
Joe likes the ivy."

George had spied the Honda. "Hey. Did you ride this
thing? Tsk tsk, and I heard you tell that cop that you didn't
have a license."

"You really are a dickhead, aren't you?" she said softly
and watched him flush. "Run along and report me if you feel
like it. I have work to do."

The two of them moved off and spoke briefly together
before climbing on the bike to roar away. Cat walked into
the shed and recited Kipling's "Ballad of the East and West"
loudly until her pulse and breathing were normal. Then she
put the tools away and went to kneel in the warm, damp
earth and deal with the useful plants.

Before long she had a small mound of weeds and a plastic
bowl full of the extra carrots, baby things not as long as her
little finger. Joe would just wash them off and steam them.

She sat back on her heels, wiped her forehead with the back of one wrist, and acknowledged the decision her subconscious had made: it was time for papers, fake papers, and a real job, probably in a city. Possum could help her; he hated rules and made it his business to know how to get around them.

So—think about the rest of it later. The lettuce now, much too thick. No invasion by rabbits so far; Joe said that was unusual and probably Arthur's doing. And the cat *had* brought a baby rabbit to her once. . . . She put that memory aside quickly and tried to concentrate on the warm touch of the sun on her shoulders, the small ruffled leaves so delicately crisp in her fingers. She was not a vegetarian like the rest of Animal Fare, but she did wish cats were less predatory, or less inclined to show off about it.

Lettuces, and weeds, and evidence of snails. She'd ask Joe to find her some live oak leaves to spread around the plants; ash just kept washing away. Slightly dizzy from bending over in the sun, she rested on her heels again and was staring toward the street with unfocused eyes when a car pulled to a stop under a redwood tree.

For long silent moments the car was simply a lighter spot in the tree's shade. Then the passenger door opened, Joe stepped out, and Cat thought, Oh, yeah. Green Mercedes sedan, right, that would be Alice, Joe's Dr. Alice. Today was Tuesday; he had lunch with her on Tuesdays, and sometimes they came back here for the afternoon.

Joe paused at the edge of the street, hands in his pockets and shoulders hunched. Alice came briskly around the car with her head high and her chin out. Her voice pierced the afternoon silence, words floating clear and separate. "I just can't believe you would do that to me, would expect me to tell a lie, you know I don't—"

"I didn't, and I don't."

"I can't see why you had to bring my name into it at all."
She flipped her reddish, very curly hair over her shoulders
and moved past Joe toward the house, long arms and legs
flashing white in the sunlight. Alice was a tall woman, arrow-
slim except for enormous breasts that stuck straight out and
moved hardly at all.

Foundation garment, that was the term her grandmother
had used. Sounded exactly right. Blinking drowsily in the
sun, Cat speculated on what such a garment might look like.
And then on what Alice must look like without it; those
boobs would probably hang down about to . . .

"Cat, hello!" Joe spotted her and moved quickly across
the grass. "I'm glad to see you made it home. I saw you with
your band on campus today, but you got away so fast, I
thought maybe the pigs had frightened you." His face
creased in a grin; she gripped his outstretched hand and let
him pull her to her feet. "Alice," he said over his shoulder,
"I don't think you've met my tenant, Cat Smith. Cat, this is
Dr. Alice Magruder."

Cat brushed dirt off her knees, dusted her hands on her
shorts, and looked up to meet protuberant eyes of a chilly
pale green.

"On campus. Then you were part of the group playing for
those animal rights idiots. How would those people like it, I
wonder, if there were no doctors?"

"I'd like it just fine," said Cat, and cleared her throat,
darting an apologetic glance at Joe. "That is, I'm not sick
very often."

"Most people aren't so fortunate," said Alice crisply.
"The Magruders have been medical people for four generations, and I assure you we could not have been so well
trained without the use of laboratory animals."

Yes ma'am, thought Cat, keeping her face blank.

Alice inspected her more closely, then turned to Joe. "Is

this the girl George was telling me about, the one you picked up behind Silveiras'? You know, Joe, there are public agencies set up to help people who can't take care of themselves; and the county hospital runs a perfectly good clinic."

"Cat's just fine now," said Joe quickly. "Alice, you said you wanted a cup of tea."

Alice ignored him. "And in this day and age most places don't even require identification. I don't suppose Cat Smith is your real name?"

Cat let go of held-in breath. "No."

"Oh. Well, no, of course not."

"I come from a family of circus people," Cat said. "They've been famous aerialists for *five* generations. They gave me up for adoption when it turned out I was afraid of heights." She pressed her lips together and smiled a tight, three-cornered smile.

"Oh. Really. That's too bad." Alice glanced over her shoulder at Joe.

"In fact, you've probably heard of them, they called themselves the Flying—"

"Cat!" Joe's voice was sharp.

"Foxes," Cat drawled, and widened her smile to show her teeth. "Excuse me, I have work to do. Have a nice afternoon."

At six-thirty Cat heard a gentle knock at her front door. She stood very still, hardly breathing. After several moments the knock was repeated; she squared her shoulders and opened the door.

"Cat, I'm making chicken piccata. It's a new recipe and I need your opinion."

"I was planning to come over later to apologize."

"Just come now and forget the apology," he said with a grin. She slid her feet into moccasins and followed him across

47

the yard. The evening sun, filtered through a light haze of fog, made a misty halo around Joe's blocky body. That was why she'd trusted him, even when she was sick and scared in that alley and looked up to see him between her and the street. He reminded her of the Ortegas, the "uncles" of her childhood: solid and square and built for a day's work.

"But I am sorry," she said as she settled onto a stool beside the counter. It was understood between them that Cat would work in the garden, would help with carpentry or plumbing or general maintenance, but would have nothing to do with kitchen chores; she had, she'd told him, already washed her lifetime's share of dishes.

"What for?" He gave a covered pan a shake, set it off the burner, then dropped a pat of butter into a skillet and added a little olive oil.

"I was rude to Dr. Alice."

"True. But she was rude to you first."

Cat watched him pour white wine into two glasses; she picked hers up, took a sip. "Yes. But she's a friend of yours." Cat was the sole child of apparently ill-matched parents who had somehow managed to be happily married. She had determined early that sex and love, separately or together, were life's great mysteries, and personal experience with both had not altered her view by much. Now she remembered a sharp voice and cold green eyes and felt a pang for Joe; Alice Magruder seemed a poor match for his warm and generous spirit. "I didn't mean to spoil your day," she went on, "your Tuesday afternoon."

"My Tuesday . . . Jesus!" Joe set the skillet aside with a clatter, picked up his wineglass, and turned a round-eyed stare on her. "I hadn't thought of it quite like that. Not that there's anything wrong with friends going to bed, but every Tuesday afternoon gives it more importance than it deserves. Or maybe less. Anyway, you didn't spoil it; it was spoiled already."

"Then I take back the apology."

Joe grinned ruefully as he set the pan back on the flame. "I was forty-five minutes late for lunch today, and she'd had two martinis before I got there." He dipped two boned and flattened chicken breasts in seasoned flour, shook them off, and laid them gently in bubbling butter. "Then I had a Reuben sandwich and two dark beers. I think alcohol inhibits the sexual impulse."

"Or maybe sauerkraut does," she suggested.

"Could be." He turned the chicken pieces, whistled softly at them for a few moments, lifted them out to a warm pan, and replaced them with two others. "She was mad at me Saturday night, because I got to her house later than I'd planned. Then that cop apparently got it wrong; he made it sound as if I'd told him I'd spent the night there. So after she talked to him she was mad because I'd set her up as an alibi. And then by God I think she was mad when I told her I wouldn't do something like that."

Cat picked up her wineglass and held it in her lap. "Where *did* you go?"

"Drove around for a while, parked and watched the moon, then came home and went to bed." He turned the chicken pieces and added a little butter. Something in the quality of her silence caught at him and he swung around to face her. "Cat, don't look so frightened! I didn't have anything to do with Ilona's disappearance; no one could seriously think I did."

Oh boy. She swirled the wine in her glass, then stopped because the motion of the slightly oily liquid seemed to be making her seasick. It was her experience that cops, with a few exceptions, didn't believe there was any such thing as an honest citizen. "Joe," she said and then paused to clear her throat. "I think I probably heard you come home."

"No you didn't. Don't worry about it, Cat." He set the chicken aside, poured sherry and then lemon juice into the skillet, scooped something from a small jar. "Capers. I hope you like capers. How's your friend the flute player?"

"I beg your pardon?"

"The fellow you all spirited out of here yesterday. It's your cottage, you know. You don't have to ask permission to have an overnight guest."

There was a very long silence as Joe scraped a wooden spoon around and around in the pan and Cat tried to decide what to say. "Thank you, I know that," she murmured. "But that wasn't . . . that was Antelope; he gets these terrors and then he comes to me. And I had to get him away before that cop came back. Antelope's father was a cop and a . . . a very bad man."

"Oh." Joe poured the sauce over the chicken. "There. The pilaf is done, and there's a salad in the fridge. Let's eat; I'm starved."

CHAPTER 6

At the creak of the door, Officer Dunnegan laid his pen aside, looked up, then moved his gaze lower. "Hey, kid, you can't bring that dog in here; tie him outside."

A whip-thin boy of nine or ten, the policeman noted, with whitish brush-cut hair, a dust-streaked face, the big hands and heavy-boned wrists that said he was going to do a lot more growing. And a stubborn set to the wide mouth as he shook his head. "You hear me, kid?" Dunnegan hitched up his belt and lumbered around the high counter. "This ain't the license bureau."

The dog was a rangy, wolfish beast standing a good two and a half feet high at shoulder. He lifted his lip silently, exposing glistening fangs, and Dunnegan stopped where he was.

"My name is Petey . . . Peter Birdsong," the boy said quickly. He put an arm around the dog's neck. "This is Fenris. He found it . . . her. He found the dead lady."

The boy clapped his free hand over his mouth, and Dunnegan saw the dirty face go gray. "Take it easy, kid, Petey, just take it easy now. You and your dog come along back here; we got a Coke machine and a place you can sit down."

Dunnegan ushered boy and dog down a hall and into a large, dusty room with lockers along one wall; there were two old couches and several easy chairs, as well as a soft-drink machine and a scarred wooden table cluttered with coffee gear. "Here, you drink this real slow, and I'll go get the chief."

A moment later Vince Gutierrez paused in the doorway. The boy sat stiffly on the edge of a couch, both hands clasped around a red and white can. "Hello, Petey." Gutierrez spoke softly, keeping his arms loose at his sides as he moved into the room. "And this is . . . ?"

"Fen. Fenris. He's named after a wolf so strong only magic could hold him. But you don't have to worry; he minds me."

"I can see that." Gutierrez pushed a chair close to the couch and sat down. "I'm Vince Gutierrez, Chief Gutierrez. Officer Dunnegan tells me you have some information for me." Petey opened his mouth and closed it again, eyes so wide that white showed all around the blue. "You found

51

something?" Gutierrez prompted softly. "Petey, would you like me to call your mother? Would it make you feel better to have her here?"

Petey shook his head. "No. We found a dead lady. Fen was running ahead and he started to dig and then he . . . he howled." The boy shivered. "I never heard him do that before."

"She was buried?"

Petey nodded.

"Can you tell me where?"

"Sure I can!" He sat straighter. "Off Lupine Road, on the east side of the highway where it's not paved. There's a gully runs beside the road; sometimes there's water in it. I was on the road on my bike, and Fen went down into the gully and was digging under a bank, where the dirt was soft." He took a quick swallow of Coke, then wiped his mouth with the back of one hand. "When he howled, I went down, and there was this yellow hair, and something blue like a tarp; Fen was pulling at that till I made him stop. But I could see one side of a face. I think she was a pretty lady before somebody hurt her."

As the thin voice squeaked to silence, Gutierrez moved quickly, to sit beside the boy and wrap an arm around his shoulders. "Okay, Petey, you did fine." He waited a moment before adding, "It would be a help if you could take us there. Do you think you can do that?"

Petey leaned his forehead against Gutierrez's shoulder. "Sure I can." He sat up and pulled away. "I can ride my bike."

Gutierrez shook his head. "We'll take a van; that'll give us room for the bike and the dog. Now give me your phone number and I'll call your mother, to let her know you're helping us."

* * *

The Chevy van pulled to a stop at the very edge of the hard-packed dirt road, behind two police cars and a pickup truck. Hank Svoboda got out, slammed the door, and trudged up the road, placing his dusty black boots with care. Gutierrez flicked a glance at him, then resumed his study of the action in the gully, which was roped off with bright yellow tape. "Everybody okay?"

"Yup." Svoboda planted his feet wide and crossed his arms as his gaze followed Gutierrez's. "Nice smart lady, just like her kid. Told him she'd packed a lunch, she was gonna shut up the shop and they were going to the beach, even the dog." He watched as two men slid a long form into a plastic bag, laid the bag on a stretcher. "I see the doc's gone. He have anything to say?"

"She's been dead several days; she was beaten severely and was probably killed by blows to the head with something heavy, more than a fist. He couldn't tell immediately whether or not she'd been raped."

"Doesn't feel like the same guy, Vince."

"She took the same kind of brutal beating," Gutierrez snapped. He sighed, closing his eyes for a moment. "But why the burial treatment? He buttoned all her buttons, laid her out straight with her arms at her sides, wrapped her up tight in a blue nylon tarp that probably came from somebody's boat."

"And dug a trench," Svoboda said softly, "with just his hands and maybe a branch from the way it looked to me. Then he pulled that dirt bank down on top. It's like he knew her, maybe, and was sorry."

There was a shout from the gully, from a uniformed man bending low perhaps a dozen yards to the east of the burial spot. Gutierrez moved quickly along a marked path, Svoboda on his heels.

"Two footprints, Chief." Bob Englund's pale and boyish

53

face was flushed with satisfaction. "Or really one, second one's just a blur." In a damp depression near the edge of the gully was the deep print of a bare foot, toes splayed.

"Man, that's one big bastard!" Englund went on. "My size twelves would miss him by a good inch."

Gutierrez squatted to survey the print, then lifted his gaze slowly to scan the bank above. "Okay, Englund, cast this one, and measure the distance between the two. This far from the body, it might not mean anything, but keep looking." He rose, gave the officer a brief nod of approval, and turned to retrace his steps.

"Hank, you handle things here. I have to go tell Edward Berggren we've found his daughter."

It was a familiar sound, Moose's old van; they'd come for the bike. Cat upended the teapot in the dish drainer, dried her hands, and moved across the room. She opened the door to another burst of engine noise, that loose rattle which always reminded her of a giant sewing machine. The van was departing, and Antelope came across the grass toward her.

"Antelope, hi." She shaded her eyes with the flat of one hand and inspected him. Hi-toppers on the enormous feet, laced and tied; clean Levi's, plain white T-shirt, bushy hair tied back. "How are you?" In his bad times Antelope was frightened of the bike. But as he came closer she could see his eyes, gray-green and clear and direct.

"I'm good, Cat. Everybody else had something to do, so I said they could drop me off to get the Honda. How're *you*?"

"I'm good, too." She flung her arms around him and hugged him hard. "And I'm really glad to see you. Want a cup of tea, or a Coke?"

George and his friend Aaron, lounging on Joe's deck, had obviously noted Antelope's arrival. Ignoring them, Cat dragged two canvas chairs to the far side of her cottage, set-

54

tled Antelope there, brought him a big apple with red streaking its pale green and one for herself. "Gravensteins, from Joe's tree. The band isn't playing today?"

He shook his head, sinking further into the chair and stretching his legs out. "The demonstrators figure they made a big point yesterday; the television coverage went all over the state. Today they're out with petitions. Listen, Cat, I want to thank you. For helping me out the other night. I don't remember much but I remember you."

"So okay. We're a family." She held her hand out and they linked fingers for a moment. Intending to lighten the atmosphere, she remarked, "You know, that was a book I had when I was a kid, *Animal Family;* I haven't thought of it in years. I think it was my favorite of all, except for *The Secret Garden.*"

"I heard *The Secret Garden* when my mom read it to Rachel. Rachel wasn't really old enough, but Mom couldn't wait."

Rachel had been his sister's name. "Oh. Well, I'm glad you got to hear it; most boys don't."

He glanced at her and managed a painful smile. "Cat, how long since I was real bad? I mean, before this last time?"

She sat straighter and folded her hands in her lap. "I think more than two months . . . Memorial Day?"

He hunched his shoulders. "Yeah, and I got drunk that day, too, on beer. But you see how long that was? I'm getting better; at least I think I am." He crunched the last chunk off his apple and set the core in the grass beside his chair. "Moose says a Christian repays good by *doing* good, passing it on. I understand that; you help me, but you don't need help right now, so someday I help somebody else."

Cat kept silent, watching him.

"My problem is, what do you do about repaying the bad?

55

Moose says you turn the other cheek, but I have trouble with that."

Right, and with the trials of Job, and the meek who were supposed to wait meekly around until the next life. "I know. Me, I like to hit back," she told him.

"But there's nobody left for me to hit, is the problem." He took a long breath. "Except myself, and I'm getting tired of that."

"'You may rest content in the sure and certain knowledge of hell.'"

"Huh?"

"I'm quoting my grandfather, what he liked about Christianity. The bastards, the ones you can't reach or won't let yourself, you just have to remember that they're going to hell; they'll sizzle and spit there into everlasting eternity."

Antelope gave a great roar of laughter, a sound she'd never heard from him. He stood up, stretched, and grinned down at her. "That's great, I'm going to write 'Hell' on my hands or someplace, just to remember. Look, I'd better get on the bike and head out; it's my turn to chop wood."

"Wait." She dug into the pockets of her jeans, came up with some crumpled bills. "I got paid for a gardening job up the street, and I don't need the money. On the way home you can stop at McDonald's and stuff yourself and nobody will know." Cat had read half a dozen books explaining vegetarian principles, but some corner of her mind firmly believed that a big frame like Antelope's should have meat.

"No, I . . . yeah, I will; I think they've got tofu and lentils on for tonight." He took the money, put his hands on her shoulders, and bent to kiss the top of her head. "Thanks, Cat, and thanks and thanks again. See you."

George and his friend hung around into the evening; Joe would have someone to feed, guinea pigs if needed. Still

56

buoyed by Antelope's visit, Cat grinned as she prepared her own accidentally vegetarian meal: grated cheese melted on tortillas, refried beans from a can, sun-warm tomatoes from the garden.

Antelope had mentioned that Animal Fare might have a job over the weekend, a paying stint. With all the others present and healthy, Cat would probably roadie rather than play, but she tuned her cherry-red electric guitar anyway, and practiced dutifully for a while.

Boring without amplification, that kind of music. She closed her windows against the foggy evening and took up the acoustic guitar, a big old flattop that had hung on Joe's living room wall until last week, when she asked to borrow it. Mellow of tone, with an easy action, it was alive and friendly in her hands without being plugged into anything. She played folk song chords for a while, singing softly. And then, tentatively, using the work-hardened edges of her fingers in lieu of fingernails, she searched for the notes of a simple Sor piece.

The bike departed noisily at about ten, and Cat, wide awake, stretched and put the guitar away and looked for her shoes. Maybe Joe would like to play some gin.

Even though she had no desire to work there, Cat loved Joe's kitchen. He had designed it and done much of the work himself, and he'd gotten it just right in proportions and lighting and color. She settled at the round table and shuffled cards while he made two cups of filter coffee; a few moments later, watching him balance full mugs carefully, she sat straighter and frowned. His face wore a slack, pulled-down look, and his shoulders had a weary slump.

"What's the matter?"

"What?" Dark liquid sloshed over rims and dampened paper napkins set out as coasters. "Haven't you . . . no, of course you haven't; it was just on the ten o'clock news." He dropped into a chair and leaned his elbows on the table. "Ilona Berggren is dead. The police found her body today."

"I'm sorry," Cat said softly. "What happened?"

"Someone murdered her; that's all I know," he said, taking a slow sip of coffee. "I haven't talked with Ed, her father. I called, but there was someone there, a policeman I guess, taking messages."

"I'm sorry," she said again.

"Yeah. I wish you'd be a little more careful, Cat, not wander around by yourself all the time. Be sure to lock your doors."

Cat thought about life on the streets in Berkeley and other places, and the reflexes she had developed there. All she said was, "I do lock my doors."

"That's right, you do." He sighed and settled back into his chair. "Anyway, all of us—the people who were here for dinner Saturday night, not you—all of us are to go to the police station tomorrow, to amplify our statements."

"Dr. Alice will love that," said Cat, dealing the cards.

"Yeah, won't she?" Joe's face lifted into a close approximation of his usual grin as he inspected his cards, rearranged them to suit him, reached out to cut the deck. "Aha, I'll have that ace, thank you." He discarded the five of clubs. "George says your friend was here today, the tall one. How is he?"

"He's doing okay, a lot better in fact." Cat had intended to talk to Joe about Antelope, in general terms or even more specific ones, to sound him out on the likelihood of such a battered spirit healing itself. But tonight didn't seem the time. She scooped up the five, added it to four clubs she already held, discarded a queen.

"Ah. That's good." Joe ignored the queen, drawing instead from the pack. "I understand that you had some trou-

58

ble with my brother." When she merely looked across the table at him, he flushed. "George said he was teasing you and you took it too seriously. I guess that means he did something rank and you slapped him down. I'm sorry, and he is, too; I think he'll apologize when he gets up the nerve."

Nerve did not seem to Cat something George lacked. "You don't have to be sorry; it had nothing to do with you. And anyway, I can take care of myself." She lifted her eyes, met Joe's, and felt her face grow warm. "Most of the time I can. Really."

"I know you can. What I'm trying to say is, George is a spoiled kid, but he's not really a bad person." She concentrated on her cards, and he went on. "My father was killed when George was only two, and my mother—she comes from Virginia, a Scottish-English background, George looks just like her—my mother was left in the middle of this noisy Italian family she'd never really understood. So she just wrapped her life around George."

And what about you; who wrapped around you? Cat kept her eyes down and her mouth shut, wondering what Joe had looked like at, say, twelve. Fat, probably, and worried, stumbling all over himself in an effort to be helpful.

"Anyway, it's not really George's fault." Joe drew a card, slid it into his hand, and discarded his original ace, the ace of clubs.

"Okay," said Cat. She picked up the ace, tucked it into place, slapped another queen on the discard. "Gin."

CHAPTER 7

Midmorning Friday Cat locked her front door, put the key in her pocket, and swung her backpack around to slip her left arm through the other strap. She shrugged the pack into a comfortable position, reached for the helmet Badger was holding out to her, then turned instead to look over her shoulder. "Can you hang on just a minute, Badger?" Without waiting for an answer, she set off at a trot toward the main house.

This is ridiculous, she thought as she gave the doorbell a vicious twist. She wasn't a high school kid with a curfew; she hadn't reported to anyone in years and certainly didn't intend to make a habit of it now. When Joe finally opened the door, she said, "I'm leaving!" so sharply that his welcoming grin congealed. "What I mean is," she added in a rush, "I'm going out to see the Animals. Badger came to get me. You know, I told you they have a place out in the hills, an old farm."

"Oh. Right."

"And I probably won't be back until tomorrow; I just thought I'd tell you."

"Right. Thanks. I'll feed Arthur. Be careful, Cat."

"Oh, for . . . yes, okay, I will." Her irritation faded as she looked at him, at the dark patches beneath his eyes and the weary heaviness of his face. "You be careful, too." She stood on tiptoe to brush a kiss across his whiskery cheek; then she turned and fled.

As the bike moved from the relative smoothness of the secondary road to the rutted surface of something called Portagee Trail, she gave up trying to avoid Badger's whipping hair and spent her energy in holding onto him and keeping her feet on the posts. Stupid means of transportation anyway, particularly when you were on the back end; she'd much rather have a horse. Maybe, if the others decided to stay on out here, she could board a horse with them, something nice like a little Morgan. If she could find one, and the money to buy him, and then to buy feed. Dreamer.

Badger, actually a very careful biker, eased the machine around a curve and past a stand of scraggly redwoods to stop before a small unpainted house whose sagging porch roof gave it a sleepy look. Possum ignored their arrival and threw two more darts at a target hung in a tree; the darts hit the board with a dull, angry sound. Squirrel set down a chipped ceramic mug and rose from the porch steps.

"Hey, Cat," he greeted her. "Want some coffee?"

She shook her head, stamping her feet and flexing her knees to work out the kinks of the ride. "Thanks, but I'll make myself a cup of tea." She followed Squirrel across the porch, stepping carefully on ancient, uneven boards.

It was a simple structure dating from the turn of the century or even earlier. A long living room ran full width, making an L at the right end for a kitchen. The bedroom filled out the left rear corner of the basic rectangle, with the bathroom a lean-to tacked on behind the kitchen. A new stainless-steel teakettle sat oddly on a leggy old stove whose original green-and-cream colors were dim behind layers of smoke and grease. Cat lifted the kettle and found water still hot enough to send a breathy little squeak through the whistle. She cast a surreptitious glance around, wrinkling her nose at the general grubbiness. She'd been living easy too long; she was getting spoiled.

The kitchen window looked out on wooded hills that rolled gently up to meet the sky. Directly behind the house was a stretch of flat ground covered with patchy grass and the soft debris from redwoods. Beside a garden fenced with chicken wire, Moose bent to measure a plank set on sawhorses, then drew a line and picked up a handsaw.

"What's Moose doing?" Cat rapped on the window glass and waved to Moose when he looked up.

"He's going to start reflooring the porch," Squirrel told her. "We haven't gotten very far with Badger's mom's list of improvements, and Moose is feeling guilty."

Badger's mother, a big real estate person in the Bay Area, had acquired the house and shed and some forty acres more or less by accident. When her son and his friends followed Cat north, she'd offered to let them stay on the place, mainly to see that no wandering marijuana grower tried to make a crop there while the property was in her name.

"Goody, I'll help," said Cat. Working with Moose was her idea of therapy, guaranteed to slow the pulse and soothe the spirit. The screen door to the porch screeched open and slammed shut as Possum burst in, Moose's antithesis; suddenly the air was full of prickles.

"And greetings to you, too!" she snapped.

He glared at her, then grinned, lifting both hands in a shielding gesture. "Back off, mean mama, life is too hard on me already. Glad to see you, okay?" He clasped her in a gingerly hug, then stepped back and spread his palms in helplessness. "See, I been rejected by a woman, and the cops want to talk to me, and I'd like to split, but it looks like I'll have to walk 'cause nobody else wants to go."

"Cops?" Cat froze in place and stared at him.

"No big deal, Cat," said Squirrel. "See, Possum and I know these two women; they go to school here and they're in with the animal rights people. Wendy and Marybeth, they live in a co-op dorm close to campus."

She swished the teabag a time or two before lifting it from the mug. "So?"

"So the cops are all over the campus about this missing woman, the one turned up dead," said Possum. "And Wendy and Marybeth tell the cops sure, they were around the plaza late Saturday night, with these two guys, so now the cops want to talk to us. Which is fine for the redhead here; he spent the night in the dorm with Wendy. But I struck out and slept alone in the van, which doesn't stack up as the best alibi I ever had."

Cat shivered and tucked her elbows tight against her sides. "Ilona Berggren was her name. She was a friend of Joe's and her father is an important man. You guys better go see the police; there's going to be a lot of heavy action on this."

"Did she get shot, or what?" Possum asked, his face intent.

Cat shook her head. "All I know is, she's been dead the whole time they were looking for her; Joe told me that." She looked harder at Possum. "Why? Possum, do you still have that stupid gun?"

"It's a nice little gun, cost me a chunk of money. What I thought was, I could give it to you, and you—"

"Don't be ridiculous!"

"Would you listen for once?" he asked in plaintive tones. "I could give it to you, and you could hide it. That way, I won't have to tell any lies, and it'll still be around after this is over."

"No." In the interest of remaining legally invisible, Cat obeyed all laws; she didn't jaywalk, she didn't litter, and she had no intention of coming into possession of an unregistered weapon that was probably stolen as well.

"Well, we can talk about it later," said Possum with a shrug.

"No, we can't." Cat spoke absently and looked toward the door. "Where's Antelope? Is he still okay?"

"He's fine," Squirrel told her. "He's down by the creek, I think; he says he's going to write a concerto for flute and water."

"Good." Cat grinned and set down her empty mug. "Okay, I'm going to work now. I even brought my own hammer."

The house felt stuffy, cavelike. Joe opened curtains, found the day's brightness unnerving, compromised by pulling the curtains again but leaving doors open for air. When he heard the sound of feet on his front steps, he'd been staring at his monitor for perhaps two hours and had written less than a full paragraph of the textbook review he had promised.

"Joe." Mal Burns's face seemed even more gaunt than usual, with pale blue eyes peering from cavernous sockets and hollows showing in the angles of his jaw. "We came in to pick up Aaron's new wheel; I didn't want them trying to carry it on George's bike. I haven't been able to get through to Ed, and I wondered if you've heard from him, if you know how he's doing."

George, unsuccessful in mending fences with his former landlady, had been staying with Aaron at the Burns house, an ocean-view cottage below the south edge of Port Silva. His brother looked terrible, Joe observed. The expensively cut hair was lank and dull, and his passage left a whiff of rank sweat on the air. Aaron trudged along behind the others, hands jammed in his pockets. His eyes were roundly blank, his smile the merest lifting of his lip to expose gappy front teeth.

"He called me late yesterday afternoon," Joe said. The others followed him into the kitchen and made a half-circle before him, three looming, in-tilting figures. "He was crying. He said it wouldn't have happened if I hadn't . . . if I hadn't sent her away alone Saturday night." Joe paused to clear his throat. "He said he thought I should go look at her, so I'd have to remember her the way he will, the way she is now."

George drew in his breath with a hiss. "Christ," he muttered. Aaron narrowed his eyes in the sun-bright room and said, "*God* but she was pretty." His voice had a deep but impersonal sadness.

"Then he cried some more, and apologized." Joe's lips felt numb as he spoke. "He was going to climb on his boat and take a pill and sleep long enough to get himself back together. That was it; I haven't heard anything more."

With a collective sigh the trio eased, separated. Mal sat down beside the counter, and after a moment of foot-shuffling, George and Aaron took chairs at the table. "I expect the poor bastard's still up to his ass in cops," Mal remarked. "And probably reporters, too; the San Francisco and L.A. papers had the story this morning."

"Anything new?" Joe asked.

Burns shook his head. "Just a rehash of the *Sentinel* story, daughter of prominent et cetera found in shallow grave in woods near Port Silva, presumed murdered, investigation proceeding. Vince Gutierrez grew up in this town, so he gets a lot of cozy cooperation from the local news folks; but he's about to meet the big leagues."

"Nothing about how she was killed? I mean, whether it was like the other two," Joe added hastily. Lieutenant Svoboda, questioning him the previous day, would say of Ilona's death only that it was clearly murder.

"No, but I see a certain significance in the fact that we've all been asked where we were at the time of the earlier rapes." Burns's voice was grim. "I was here in town, so far as I can remember."

"Me, too. Wouldn't we all live different lives if we knew we were going to need alibis?" Joe's half-hearted attempt at a grin faded as he turned to glare at his brother, who had tipped his chair up on its back legs and was rocking it with a rhythmical squee-ech, squee-ech. "Goddamn it, George, knock that off! Go find yourself something to do, like watering the garden!"

The younger men sprang to their feet like a pair of chastised twelve-year-olds, George's face outraged and Aaron's a stolid mask. "Sorry," Joe muttered.

"Okay, okay," said George with a shrug. He started for the door, then turned to the refrigerator to collect two bottles of beer. "But I don't know anything about plants; where's your regular gardener?"

"She took the day off!" snapped Joe, and Aaron said quickly, "Never mind, I know what to do."

Joe looked at the beer and thought it would probably feel good on his dry and aching throat. "Cat went to spend the day with her musician friends. They're all camping out, I guess, at an old farm somewhere out in the hills. Beer, Mal?"

A few minutes later Joe propped his forearms on the deck rail and eyed the two younger men, who had already shed their shirts. George looked like someone who worked out regularly, Aaron like someone who worked. And there you go again, he chided himself.

"They're still kids; they don't believe in death," Mal offered in quiet tones. "If it happens to somebody they know, somebody their own age, they're caught between being sorry and being scared."

And feeling guilty, Joe thought, at their own pleasure in sun on the skin and breath deep in the lungs and the steady mindless pumping of the heart. At being alive. All he said was, "Right." After a moment, he asked idly, "Is Aaron your only kid?"

"One and only." Mal came to share the rail. "Nancy and I believed no one was entitled to produce more than that, so I had the appropriate surgery right after our one was born. Then she and I started having trouble, and one day, when he was about five, I came back to Berkeley from this seminar in Washington and they were gone, vamoosed, back to the land to be independent. New people living in the house, my clothes and books in boxes in the garage."

"Did you try to find them? Him?"

Mal pressed his lips tight, considering. "Not very hard, I guess. I mean, she was his mother; kids belong with their mothers. Then about a year ago, or more like a year and a half, he turned up looking for me, and I was glad to see him, damned glad to see him." Mal took a swig of beer and gazed out at his son's broad back; Aaron was squatting next to the bean house, adjusting some of the newest plants toward their climbing strings.

"But I think she did all right by him, Nancy did. Kid is strong as an ox, he can do anything: butcher a pig, build a barn, rewire a house. The way I see it, he's lived that kind of basic life, and now he's ready for the other part. I had him tested; his IQ's higher than mine. We're filling in a few gaps, and then he can probably do his B.S. in three years. That would put him in grad school at twenty-five. I don't think that's too old.

"Incidentally," Mal went on, "I told George that he's welcome to stay out at the house as long as he likes. There's an extra bed in Aaron's room, and a big couch in the living room. Half the time I sleep at my shop in town, anyway."

Joe straightened and took a long swallow of beer. "Up to

67

you. I get the feeling he's going to be between jobs before long; he doesn't like working nights."

"He seems to think your mother will help him out when school starts," Mal said. "And he says he wouldn't mind tutoring Aaron in math. It's turning out to be trickier than I thought, teaching my own kid."

Joe sometimes had to remind himself that his brother had gone to UCLA with advanced-placement credit for calculus and physics. He hadn't even flunked out; he'd just decided in the middle of his second year that he was tired of school. "George is capable, if he wants to bother," he told Mal and tipped the bottle for the last of the beer. "Speaking of jobs and work and all that, did the cop at the computer science building give you any idea when we could get to our offices?"

Mal shook his head. "Just said nobody but the police were allowed on the first floor."

"I'm going to call Vince Gutierrez to see if I can't go in under escort or something; there are things I need." The phone rang on his last word; he raised his eyebrows at Burns, and went to answer.

He returned almost at once, frowning. "That was an Officer Dunnegan. Stay and have another beer if you want; I have to go downtown. Chief Gutierrez wants to talk to me."

"Didn't you put in your half hour there yesterday, like the rest of us?"

"I sure did."

"Look, I can work at home, but there's some stuff in the office I need," Joe was saying to the man behind the counter when Chief Gutierrez appeared. "Oh, Vince. Hello."

Gutierrez nodded. "Joe. Come on back to my office."

The chief led the way down a dim hall, opened a door at the end, moved to one side. Joe walked into a drab room that smelled of dust and old smoke; Gutierrez closed the door and moved behind the scarred oak desk. Joe had known Port Silva's police chief for years, because they both coached in a city-sponsored basketball program. He judged Gutierrez to be in his late forties, with the trim body and fast reflexes of a man ten years younger. In uniform, in his own office, he seemed not larger exactly but more dense, someone you could bruise yourself against.

"Sit down," Gutierrez said, nodding to a big wooden chair with arms, a chair that reminded Joe of one he'd occupied a time or two in the principal's office at St. Ignatius. He sat, and was unable to think of anything to say.

"I have your statement here," Gutierrez told him, eyes on the folder that lay open on the desk. After a long moment of silence he looked up. "You told Sergeant Chang that you did not go to the computer science building Saturday night."

"That's true. I mean, that's what I told him, and it's the truth."

"But the system manager, Frank Lee, retrieved the computer records for us, and you're shown as logging on that night at 1:47, rolling off at 3:31."

"But it can't . . . that's impossible!"

Gutierrez raised his eyebrows. "Lee wouldn't give me your password, but he assures me it was used."

"The word is Garibaldi and it's encrypted, strictly between me and Vera. The computer," Joe added. "But passwords are never as secret as they're supposed to be; I'll bet half a dozen of the kids know mine. I was *not* there Saturday night. The guard is on until two A.M. and he'll tell you he didn't see me."

"How do you normally get into the building? In the daytime, I mean."

"The back door, the side door really; it opens from the

little north-end parking lot. But that's an emergency-only exit at night, with an alarm."

"But you have a key." As Joe merely looked at him, Gutierrez went on. "It turns out the kids like that exit; they can park closer there for carrying heavy stuff, and it's well lighted, which is nice for the women after the guard goes off. And they don't need a key from the inside."

"Yes, but the alarm—"

"They turn it off. And the last one leaving has to turn it back on and go out the front."

"Oh, Christ. Of course they would. But I didn't know about it," Joe added quickly. "And I wasn't there. I told Chang; I was at home until around two, and I went to Dr. Magruder's after that."

"Dr. Magruder isn't absolutely sure about the time. And the thing is," said Gutierrez, leaning back in his chair, "Garibaldi logged on from your terminal, in your office." Eyebrows high again, over eyes like cold black stones. "Do you lock your office?"

"Yes I lock my office!" Joe snapped. "But here's an interesting fact about computer people, the real hackers at least: it's a point of pride with them that nothing keeps them out of a place or a computer if they want in. Some have even been known to carry lock-picks on their key chains. Although I haven't actually seen one on any of the present group," he hastened to add. "Anyway, lots of people have master keys: guards, campus police, custodians."

Gutierrez's head moved in the faintest of nods, and he made a brief note before looking at Joe again. "Do you entertain women in your office?"

"Entertain?" Joe's mind conjured up stemmed glasses, an ice bucket with a leaning champagne bottle. Music.

"There's evidence that someone had sex there recently. On the couch."

70

"On the . . . are you out of your goddamned mind?" Joe shot to his feet, shoving the chair back so hard it tumbled over. "Not me, not on that couch, not in some backseat, not standing up in the custodian's closet." He picked up the chair, set it straight. "If I want to take a woman to bed, Chief Gutierrez, I take her to *bed*, mine or possibly hers. I'm not a horny sixteen-year-old. Now if you don't mind I'd like to call my attorney."

"Ever see these before?"

Joe stared at three, no, four silver circlets that Gutierrez spread across the desk blotter. One was perhaps half an inch wide, with the dull gleam of a sand-cast piece, several turquoises set as if at random. The others were twisted and polished, delicate, without stones. They belonged on a tanned wrist, clinking gently as the long tanned fingers reached across the table.

"Ilona's." Joe's voice sounded odd and distant in his own ears, and Gutierrez came around the desk quickly. "Never mind," Joe muttered, shaking the hand off his shoulder. "Why am I so sure you didn't find those on her body?"

"They were in a drawer in a table, in your office."

"She was wearing them Saturday night at dinner." Joe reached behind him for the chair and sat down carefully, like an old man. "Table. It's right next to the . . . she was the one who used the terminal!" Noting Gutierrez's frown, he said, "The keyboard shelf is low, twenty-six inches. Bracelets would be a nuisance; I always take my watch off."

CHAPTER 8

"**N**o problem, Mancuso." Rod Phillips—Dr.
Rodney A. Phillips, assistant professor of computer science—shook back a curly blond fore-
lock recently gilded by a month's sailing in the Caribbean.
"Be glad to take the group over; should be fun." He lowered
thick, straight lashes to mute a bright blue gleam of pleasure. "Just keeping things warm for you, so to speak."

"Right." Not under arrest, but not exactly a free man either ("Please let me know if you plan to leave town,"
Gutierrez had said to him with a straight, unsmiling look),
Joe had done the decent thing, offering to take a leave of
absence. He hadn't expected the dean to agree so speedily,
nor to replace him with golden boy here. Well, the department's reigning stud would find he'd met his match; Ilona
would . . . Joe took a very deep breath and shoved his hands
into his pockets. "So call me at home if you need anything."
Without looking at Phillips, he shouldered open the door of
the engineering building and stepped out into the sunlit
plaza.

The computer science building was directly across the
plaza. Still a cop on the front door, Joe observed. He'd miss
a few of the kids, and one or two—say, Epstein—would
miss *him* before long. Phillips was a lazy bastard. But the way
it looked right now, one of those kids had set up good old

Joe Mancuso, by accident or design. And killed Ilona? Hot rage gripped him, an emotion so unfamiliar that he read it first as fear.

He strode through the plaza, keeping his gaze ahead: thoughtful professor in a hurry. Through the parking lot, where his truck wasn't parked today, either. No surprise in that; he knew perfectly and painfully well where it was. Gutierrez had impounded it, although he'd made the whole business sound like a personal favor that he, Joe, was doing the police department.

He skirted the campus and then trudged east, eyes down. Good thing he'd worn his running shoes today, not that he ever ran. Complicated patterns of leather strips and shiny nylon, blue and silver and white twinkling along in the sun. A grown man shouldn't put such foolishness on his feet.

The third honk, very close, brought his head up. A big car glided to the curb just ahead, the passenger door swung open, and Alice leaned out.

"You're walking as if each foot weighed fifty pounds. Care for a lift?" As he hesitated, she said, "Please? I want to apologize for my behavior on Tuesday, Joseph. I should never drink gin in the middle of the day; it turns me into a shrew."

Now that he thought about it, he felt lonely. Cat had abandoned him for the day and probably the night; there was nobody at home. "Okay, sure. Thanks, Alice."

"Did your truck break down?" she inquired as she pulled smoothly away from the curb.

Oh, Christ. She'd probably put him out as soon as she heard. "The police have it; Chief Gutierrez. I gather he wants to make sure I haven't been using it to transport bodies."

"Bodies?" A honk from an oncoming car pulled her eyes back to the road.

"Well, one body anyway. Gutierrez found evidence that

Ilona was in my office Saturday night late, and he thinks I was there with her. It seems that I am"—he paused to clear his throat—"a murder suspect."

"You? But Joseph, that's ridiculous!"

"Damn right!" he said in fervent agreement.

"You're the least . . . the least *violent* man I know. Only an idiot would think you capable of beating a girl to death."

"Is that what happened? Somebody beat her to death?" Joe hastily rolled the window down to let air blow over his face.

"I am acquainted with every physician in town, including the one who works with the police." Alice glanced at him. "Joseph, do you want me to stop?"

"No, I don't think so."

"She was apparently beaten with fists and perhaps an object of some sort. And manually strangled, but it was the beating that killed her, Edgar thinks. She'd had intercourse and it was probably rape; he can't be absolutely sure."

What difference did that make now? thought Joe wearily. Well, except to the police, as part of a pattern. He leaned his head back, closed his eyes, and opened them again quickly as Alice asked, "Joseph, do you have an attorney?"

"Jack Montoya helps me out with contracts and such, but I can't see him playing F. Lee Bailey." He heard the smart-ass tone of his own words and felt his stomach roll again. Beaten to death. Jesus, Mary, and Joseph. "I'll call him and ask what he thinks."

"You do that right away," she instructed as she pulled up before his house. "And while you do it . . . have you had lunch?" He winced and shook his head. "Then I'll come in and scramble some eggs or something, while you call."

Joe came back into the kitchen to find Alice rattling through drawers. "I can't find an eggbeater; don't you have an ordi-

74

nary eggbeater?" She pulled another drawer open. "What did Jack say?"

"That he knows a good man in San Francisco, but that I should hang loose and save my money until Gutierrez actually charges me. Alice, why don't you just sit down?" Joe uncapped two bottles of beer and set them on the counter, with a glass for his guest. "I'll make grilled cheese sandwiches, okay?"

Alice poured beer, sipped, grimaced. "Well. Joseph, it appears to me that . . . I mean, I suppose the trouble is that you don't have an alibi. After leaving my house, that is."

"That's part of it." Joe buttered slices of rye bread, turned on the griddle of his old Wedgwood stove, took a chunk of red-wax Cheddar from the refrigerator.

"So if I hadn't been such a bitch that night, you wouldn't be in trouble."

The bread was a warm brown, the cheese a satisfying creamy yellow. Then thin strips of canned peppers, a dull and gentle green. A shame to blot it all out with another slice of bread. What this combination would do to his nervous stomach he couldn't imagine, and he didn't care. "That's hindsight, Alice, and a waste of time. Besides, I could have sneaked out of your house in the early morning and committed murder and then sneaked back."

He glanced over his shoulder. Eyes down, eyelids and the tip of her nose a flaming pink in her white face, she was the picture of misery. What did she think, that she'd turned him into a ravening fiend by denying him her bed? Was that what Gutierrez thought?

"I had my thirty-sixth birthday last week, Joseph. And no, you didn't forget; I simply didn't tell anyone. Then I came to dinner here, and found myself at table with a beautiful and brilliant twenty-year-old girl who obviously owned the world, including every man in the room. I might have been

75

invisible. So later," she went on, her bitter tone softening, "I gathered my wounded pride around me and sent you away, and I'm more sorry than you can possibly know."

Joe turned the sandwiches, pressed them lightly with his spatula. Cheese began to melt out around the edges, spitting and steaming as it made a shiny frame, a kind of golden ruffle.

"Joseph!"

"Oh. Sorry, Alice. If we all have some responsibility in this, I don't think your share is very large." Headed for the deck, he reconsidered and set plates down on the table beside the French doors. Alice wasn't fond of sitting in the sun.

Beyond the open doors lay his garden, green, and green, and another green, sunlit, shade-dappled. One day he'd counted eleven distinct shades of green there. He blinked, and the colors blurred. "Um, there's one more thing." He set his sandwich down and wiped greasy fingers on the leg of his Levi's. "I'm not precisely employed right now."

Alice's eyes looked like two pale grapes, yet another shade of green.

"There's some confusion at the computer science building; someone was in my office Saturday night. That is, Ilona and somebody were in my office. So under the circumstances," he added quickly, "I thought I should take a leave of absence. For the time being." Redundant, he noted with a frown. The mind is going. "So that's what I did," he finished lamely.

"Ah!" she said brightly. "Well, you'll have more time for your consulting work, then. In fact, Joseph," she went on, "a leave may prove useful, a blessing in disguise. You have enormous ability and excellent credentials, and I think you're wasting yourself in a university job. Perhaps it's time for you to make a move."

76

Like maybe to San Quentin. "Right now," he told her, "I have two consulting jobs going, and I've signed a contract for my book on Pascal; it's more than half finished. And there's a good six months' work to do around this place. I won't be bored, and I'm a long way from being broke." He turned his attention to his sandwich.

Alice was less fond of beer than of gin; she had half a bottle left when Joe got up to fetch himself another. As he returned, she propped her elbows on the table and folded her hands beneath her chin. "Do you have any idea what her plans are? That girl, I mean, the girl living in your cottage?"

Joe turned his glance on the cottage. Windows were closed, curtains drawn. Arthur lay on the back step, front paws tucked under and white chest gleaming.

"I don't know that she has any immediate plans," he told Alice. "She's just a kid."

"She's, what, eighteen or nineteen? Old enough to have goals, I should think. Do you suppose she's interested in school? College?"

"I don't . . . I suppose she might be, she's bright enough."

"Not UC, she probably didn't finish high school. But perhaps one of the state colleges. Joe, I have a friend who's an administrator at Humboldt State; she could help . . . Cat," she said carefully, "find a job, perhaps even get some financial aid."

"Humboldt State. In Eureka."

"Yes. The climate's not unlike this one, and Humboldt is a fine school for someone interested in forestry and, oh, outdoor things of that sort. I don't suppose you've noticed, Joseph, but the child is quite attractive in a big-eyed, waiflike fashion, and her deprived background could seem romantic. So having her here is just asking for trouble. If your mother knew, she'd worry."

"My mother?" Joe stared, then shook his head. "My mother doesn't care what I do; she hasn't worried about me in years. If ever."

"No, of course not, but what about George?"

This time he simply stared.

Alice sighed and spread her hands. "George is not much older than Cat, undoubtedly younger in actual experience. If a big handsome lusty boy and a cute little waif keep stumbling over each other, problems are inevitable."

"Alice, that's an absolute crock. George doesn't like Cat, and she can't stand him."

Her smile was sad. "How quickly we forget. At their age mutual antipathy makes things more exciting; it's just a kind of foreplay." Alice stood up, collected the plates and her glass. "I'm on at the clinic this afternoon, so I'd better run. But Joseph, promise you'll think about what I've said."

"Oh, I promise."

"And why don't I take you to dinner tonight? It's my turn."

He shook his head. "Thanks, but I've got some work to do, and I'm pretty tired."

"Well, take care. And don't worry." She patted his shoulder before departing in a smart click-click of high heels.

Arthur turned up at the open deck door about eight-thirty. He said, "Mmmrrrrpp?" politely and sat down. Joe put a lid on his skillet of corned-beef hash and poked about in the refrigerator without finding any suitable leftovers. There were cans of Friskies in the cottage; Cat had assumed he would use those, but he didn't feel like going in there just now. Finally he opened a can of tuna, people tuna, and set it out on the deck.

It was the rare fog-free summer night, balmy and still. Joe put ice in a plastic cooler and jammed in as many bottles of beer as would fit. He set the cooler on the deck within reach of his chair, returned to the kitchen to dump the hash onto a plate and turn out the light. He'd sit out here in the warm soft dark as long as he liked, probably as long as the dark lasted.

He opened a bottle of beer at random, found it creamy and almost thick, Anchor Steam. Suitable for a farewell toast to Ilona. My best to you, golden lady, and for once I wish the priests right about it all, and you on your way to heaven with only the briefest of stopovers in purgatory. He drank deeply, then rested the bottle on his belly. If she hadn't always made people comfortable, she'd at least reminded them they were alive. Joe took another pull at the bottle, decided that he would favor the death penalty from now on, then wondered at his logic.

There was a slight clatter from the small side table as Arthur set his front paws on its edge to inspect the untouched hash. He shook his head, sneezed, dropped gently back to all fours.

"Kitty kitty?" Joe tossed his empty bottle off the deck into the grass, stretched out in the long chair, patted his thigh. "Here, kitty." Arthur flattened his ears and paced to the edge of the deck, where he settled facing the cottage, paws tucked and head up. Whenever Cat sat down, Arthur would materialize within two minutes to claim lap privileges. Apparently foreign laps were unsatisfactory.

Probably no pets in jail, thought Joe. Except whatever wanders in, mice or spiders. Rats. Bats. He pried the top off another cool bottle, longer neck. Bohemia.

He contemplated the idea of jail as he had once, briefly, the seminary. A closed society, all male, where everybody else understood the patterns and communicated by the appropriate glances and signals. Joe's childhood had ended at twelve, with his father's death. He had dropped out of Pop

Warner football and the church softball league and even the Scouts, to give his time and energy to his mother and baby brother. He had lived at home through six, no, *seven* years of school, clear through his doctorate. He had never served in the army, couldn't recall even a kidding fistfight since about age eight. Had never been in physical danger, except maybe from electricity. Jail would certainly be a change.

Stars tonight, another unusual feature of a north-coast summer evening. He'd begun to learn about stars once, on the boat with his father. He looked now for Orion or the Big Dipper. Probably the wrong time of the night, or of the year. Or probably he was beginning to need glasses. As Alice had suggested, he wasn't all that young anymore. His bladder was full already, another sign of age. He pushed to his feet, turned to the house, then turned back and stepped to the edge of the deck, unbuttoning his Levi's. Some things were still satisfying.

He had polished off a Moosehead and was well into another Anchor Steam when headlights washed his street and a car pulled up out front and braked abruptly. Cat! he thought, and then knew the sounds were wrong for the band's old Volks. Alice? Eyes fogged with beer and profound weariness, he peered through the night at a smallish, open-topped car. Ilona, why not? Come to say goodbye before the next step in her journey, to tell him she forgave him.

The moon was newly risen, throwing a long silver light. In an eye's blink Joe lost ghostly Ilona and found instead a solid Ed Berggren, moving at full charge. Not forgiveness, but vengeance, and Joe couldn't move.

"Goddamn it, Mancuso, can't you afford lights out here?"

"I was enjoying the dark," Joe said, and found he was speaking in a whisper. "There's beer in the cooler."

Berggren dropped into a chair with a force that shook the deck. "Hand me one. Please."

Joe watched the older man tilt his head back, watched the Adam's apple rise and fall. Berggren drained the entire bottle and let it drop beside him. "Jesus," he said, and the word had a bitter finality. "Well, I'm through crying. Never could cry for long." He rose, pulled two more bottles from the cooler, peered at those remaining, and put the lid back. "Looks like you're supplied for the night."

"What I had in mind," Joe told him. "But there's enough for two."

"I wouldn't count on it." Berggren thrust a bottle at Joe and sat down again with a gusty sigh. "You watch the evening news tonight?" he asked abruptly.

"Nope."

"Shame. You missed a real treat." Berggren stretched his feet out and fixed narrowed eyes on them. "It was a segment out of San Francisco . . . my dear ex-wife, chin up and bravely blinking back tears."

"Ilona's mother."

"Pure accident, some genetic miracle. Woman's got a cunt like a dollar slot machine, liquid nitrogen for blood. She's flown out from Boston, come to bury the daughter I took from her. I kept them apart all these years, she said, wouldn't let the poor child correspond with her own mother." He gave a snort of disgust, then tipped his beer bottle high. "Let's go in and catch the late run; you've gotta see this."

Joe was reluctant to leave the soft night air for the stuffy house. "Stay there; I'll bring the portable from the kitchen."

He pulled a low table before their chairs, set the little Sony there, turned it on, and adjusted the sound to reach their ears without assaulting the night around them. Berggren leaned forward and played the dial from channel to channel, back again. Baseball scores, summer storms in the Sierras. A bombing in Belfast, and bodies. Joe closed his eyes, tuned his ears away; frogs made a rhythmical serenade from a pond nearby.

"There!" Berggren's venomous tone drowned out the frogs. "There she is, damn her soul!"

The woman was slim and straight, probably tall. Black hair in longish, stiff-looking wisps framed a narrow face in which Joe caught, just for a moment, a glimpse of Ilona. Then he thought not; this face was harsh long lines and gaunt cheekbones, a dark smear under each eye . . . a bruise, or smudged makeup. The woman sat erect on a couch, feet neatly together and knees to one side. A hotel room?

". . . Mrs. Willis Farrington, mother of Ilona Berggren, who was found dead near Port Silva, California, on Wednesday. Ilona, a brilliant student, appeared in January on the CBS Sunday feature 'America's Future.'" Fade-out to a group picture, perhaps a dozen young people sitting around a table. Ilona was there, and Joe recognized Jason Epstein and maybe a kid named Paul. The camera shifted focus and other faces faded into background blurs to leave just Ilona, head tilted and lips opening to speak.

As Joe caught his breath and Berggren groaned, the glowing face dissolved, grew younger, became a photograph in the hand of the dark-haired woman. "This is what she looked like the last time I saw her, my beautiful little girl." A child of nine or ten, with stubby pigtails and a gap-toothed grin.

"My former husband kept her when our marriage ended." Mrs. Farrington set the photo down on a nearby low table. "But recently she began to reply to my letters. We were making arrangements to meet after all these years." Thin lips pressed tight, a trembling hand lifted a lacy square to dab at glistening eyes. "All I can do for my daughter now is bury her." More business with the handkerchief, and a visible effort at swallowing. "And pray to God that her father receives the punishment he deserves."

The image faded and a meadow appeared, with mares and foals. Berggren reached out to snap the set off; he and Joe stared at each other in the moonlight.

"What was that all about?"

"That woman has been trying to cut my balls off for twenty-five years. Goddamn her soul! Mancuso, can I bunk on your couch, just for the one night? Tomorrow I'll have the boat moved and anchored out."

Joe pulled himself straight in his chair and set his feet on the deck. "You're welcome to stay. But you might not want to when you know that I'm on Chief Gutierrez's list of murder suspects."

"And so are we all, my friend; so are we all."

CHAPTER 9

"**M**rs. Farrington, I can't help you." The dark head bent forward, the slim shoulders drooped.

"If you want to claim your daughter's body," Gutierrez went on, "you'll have to take it up with the county officials, you and your attorney. But Ilona is known to have maintained close ties with her father. I understand that they owned property together, that each was the other's heir." Gutierrez sat squarely behind his desk, hands flat on the blotter.

"But you're in charge of the murder investigation; I

thought you could speak to the officials for me." She flung her head up, presenting a pale face behind a pair of very dark glasses. "A man can't inherit from his victim, can he?"

"No, ma'am, not if he's convicted. Mrs. Farrington, have you any evidence that Edward Berggren killed his daughter?"

"Well, no, not evidence exactly, but I *believe*—"

Gutierrez glanced at his watch as he interrupted her. "And if you suspected your husband of molesting your daughter, why didn't you bring charges against him at the time? Mr. Berggren says that you separated by mutual agreement, that he had sole custody of Ilona, while you had your son, Christopher."

"I am ashamed to admit that that is true." Yvonne Farrington took her dark glasses off, revealing bloodshot eyes under dark, swollen lids. "Chief Gutierrez, I was desperate to escape my husband. Edward Berggren is sexually insatiable; throughout our marriage I was treated like a whore, expected to perform disgusting, unnatural acts. I had begged and begged for a divorce with reasonable maintenance, and when he finally agreed, I fled." She closed her eyes briefly.

"I made a successful second marriage and raised my son, and almost daily I would think of my daughter and tell myself that even Edward Berggren would not despoil a child. But when Ilona and I began to correspond, I sensed an undertone in her letters, a deep pain she wanted to reveal to me."

"Do you have letters from your daughter accusing her father of sexual abuse?"

"I wouldn't say that exactly. And of course I'm reluctant to make public my daughter's private thoughts."

"Of course." Gutierrez rose, moved around the desk and toward the door. "I intend to find and convict your daughter's killer, Mrs. Farrington, and I'll certainly keep in mind what you've just told me."

"Hah!" On the one bitter syllable, she gathered her handbag close and stood up. "May I at least see where Ilona was found?"

"I'll have someone drive you there."

"Thing is, she could be right." Duane Mendenhall took his usual position astride a chair and waited for the others to file in, Svoboda to close the office door. "I mean, wrapping the body up that way, that's the kind of thing a father might do."

"Or a lover, or someone who was sorry or maybe just squeamish." Gutierrez looked down at the papers spread across his desk, looked up to nod at his troops. Hank Svoboda propped his rump on the edge of the desk and yawned so widely that his jaw produced an audible crack. Mort Hansen stood pink-cheeked and square-shouldered, looking more like a ship's captain than a police lieutenant. Val Kuisma perched on the edge of a chair, a whippet in quivering wait for the rabbit.

Gutierrez himself had risen after four hours' sleep to face a hard-eyed, snarling bandit in his bathroom mirror. Shower and shave had improved his appearance, breakfast had quieted his stomach, but he knew his temper was balanced on a knife edge. Port Silva was by God his town; his mother lived here still, his brother, and two of his sisters and their kids. And this raping, murdering bastard. . . . He drew a deep breath, exhaled slowly. "Mrs. Farrington has revenge in mind, among other things. But when we're through here, we'll see if we can locate the letters Ilona *received*. Now," he said, "the medical report."

Four pairs of eyes fixed on him, and he picked up a sheet of paper. "The victim was killed sometime Sunday morning," Gutierrez said. "Her stomach was empty, although she'd had a large meal between eight and nine P.M., and rigor had almost gone off by the time she was found." He paused. "Victim died as a result of blows to the face and head, with fists and with what was apparently a small log; shreds of bark were found in some of the wounds."

Hansen, Mendenhall, and Kuisma scribbled in notebooks. Svoboda merely listened, pale eyes unblinking.

"She'd had intercourse; there was semen in her vagina and on her underpants. Some bruising of the genitals and inner thighs, so *probably* rape, but that's as far as the doctor would commit himself." Gutierrez put the paper down. "Another possible, although I'd make it a probable, is that she was killed somewhere else. There was beach sand on her body and on the inside and the outside of her clothes, which incidentally were the same clothes she had on at the party. And the tarp she was wrapped in was stained by saltwater."

"There's a long stretch of beach just the other side of the highway from where she was buried, below that row of houses." Kuisma leaned forward as he spoke.

"And no vehicle tracks near the body," said Svoboda softly.

"Shit, the highway's not that far," said Mendenhall. "He might've parked on the shoulder to walk in from there."

"He could have," agreed Gutierrez, "although there's no sign that he did. But if he was a big man, big enough to have killed that strong young woman—"

"He could just have carried her over from the beach," Kuisma finished for him.

"He could have. Val, when we're through here, I want you to take Englund and, let's see, Costello. Work that stretch of beach, inch by inch, and check out all the houses." Kuisma nodded smartly.

Gutierrez pushed his chair back, looking at his watch. "Okay. I was about to read the reports when Mrs. Farrington arrived. So, let's have two days' work in capsule form. Mendenhall, anything solid on the computer people?"

Mendenhall grimaced and shook his head. "First of all, the kids in that program were checked clear back to kindergarten before they were accepted; the dean has files an inch thick on every one. Nothing showing meaner than a parking ticket. Second, all of them have been in Mancuso's office lots of times, hands all over the place. Prints on everything but the ceiling.

"Then there's what Ilona allegedly told Mancuso, somebody interfering with her program. Now there are eighteen kids in that program, fifteen of 'em male. Of those, looks to me like six are what you'd call hackers, what my girls would call nerds. But none of them ever laid a bug on Ilona Berggren or anybody at all, no way; absolutely wouldn't do a thing like that. How 'bout I go out and lean on Mancuso some? He's got to know who and how, or be able to find out."

Gutierrez shook his head. "Better to lean on the kids themselves, in your dumb-cop way, and take Chang along. He speaks their language."

"Yeah, but not mine." Mendenhall sighed and pulled his aviator's glasses down.

"Hank?"

"Nothing much, Vince. Of the six men at that party, there's only one solid alibi: Renfrew's."

"Just his girl?"

"Nope, a neighbor. Guy in the next apartment went over at three-thirty A.M. Sunday to tell Renfrew to turn down his music."

"Ah."

"But that leaves five who couldn't prove where they spent the rest of the night. The three older guys say they went home and went to bed alone, Joe Mancuso after paying a two-A.M. call on his doctor friend. The boys helled around on their bikes, separately and alone.

"For what it's worth," Svoboda went on, "all five were in town when the earlier attacks took place. None of them is living what I'd call a normal life, no wife or regular girlfriend. Joe Mancuso has never been married; spends time with Dr. Magruder now and then and they have what she calls a 'relationship.' He has no police record; he's well liked at the university. Couple of people even said he couldn't possibly have killed anyone; he's too nice a guy."

"But his report on his whereabouts is vague," offered Gutierrez grimly, "and the girl was definitely in his office that night. And he was both friend and authority figure to her; she'd have trusted him."

Svoboda nodded and went on. "Malcolm Burns was married twice, divorced twice, lives alone except for his son. No local lady friends so far as anyone has noticed. I'd say he's bitter about both wives, but so are lots of other men in his position, and I'm still trying to find either wife. Has no record except for two protest arrests in Berkeley, Vietnam stuff. Good enough reputation so far as his work is concerned."

He held up a third finger. "Edward Berggren was married only once, got rich after that, and is known for a steady string of young lady companions. No record. Doesn't bother to own a house, just rents or lives on his boat, so neighbors are hard to find. John Freund is in Santa Cruz now, trying to talk to Berggren's employees."

Another finger. "Georgy Porgy says he has girls when he wants 'em. But never Ilona. He used to room at Grace Boyle's, and *she* says he got physical, her words, when she kicked him out late Sunday for not paying his rent. With Grace, there's physical and physical. George has no record. George does have a mama, and Mama will get me if I'm nasty to George. George works at the computer science building, but he swears he turned in his keys after his last shift, Friday morning, just like usual, and I can't find anyone

88

to say he didn't. Whole operation there looks kinda loose to me." A bristle-browed frown gave a hard edge to Svoboda's broad face.

"That leaves the Burns kid. No girlfriend; he says he's been too busy working and going to school. I talked with people he worked for. Pete Conyers of Conyers Construction here in town says he's strong and dependable but not friendly. Small timber company out of Eureka says he was a good worker, but they weren't sorry to see him go; he had a real short fuse. As for a record, the kid says he and his mama lived all over northern California and he does recall trouble with the law now and then, because his mama used to grow marijuana some before she got born again. But he doesn't remember that they were ever charged, just chased off. Makes checking hard; it'll take some time."

Gutierrez nodded, then leaned back in his chair and bit down on a yawn. "Okay. Hansen."

The sea captain shook his close-clipped head. "Nothing over the information line, nothing from campus personnel. I'm still tracking down several people. A night janitor went on vacation that Monday, a campus cop had a bad car smash and is in the hospital in San Francisco. Couple of musicians who played for the animal rights demonstrations were around that night; I'm looking for them."

"Okay, then here's this," Gutierrez picked up a pen and pointed it at Hansen. "Get to the Haffner family in Willits and find out where Lisa is living now." Lisa Haffner, the first victim, had been able to describe her assailant only as white and enormous; he had assaulted her in a high-off-the-ground vehicle she remembered only as some kind of van. When the Port Silva police attempted to question Lisa after Annie Willis's death, the girl dissolved into hysteria and her father threatened lawsuits as well as bodily injury.

"She's no longer a minor; she was eighteen in July,"

Gutierrez added. "So her father can't keep us from talking to her."

Hansen nodded, but Svoboda rubbed his forehead thoughtfully. "That's one mean old bastard, Vince. Approach him head on, he'll go to jail before telling you where she is. Or fill you full of buckshot."

Gutierrez glared at Svoboda for a long moment, then sighed. "Right; you're right. Hansen, check DMV for a current address, talk to the chief of police in Willits, do whatever makes sense. But find her. If this is the same guy, and I think it is, she has by God *seen* him."

Mendenhall, Hansen, and Kuisma stood up and moved toward the door. Gutierrez called Kuisma back, to give him a copy of the medical report. Then he locked his hands behind his head and sighed.

"Well, I guess I'll get back to work," Svoboda said.

"Right. And I'll go out front to deal with the media people before poor old Dunnegan snaps. Christ."

Svoboda stopped at the door. "Meg still out of town?"

Gutierrez nodded glumly. "In Tucson, at her parents' home. I talked to her Wednesday night."

"You ought to marry that lady, Vince."

"I don't know. I sometimes think she still feels married to Dan Halloran even though he's been dead four years. Anyway, it took all my natural charm and then some to convince her she should move in with me, so I guess I won't push it. And you're not my grandmother, Svoboda," Gutierrez added. "Just get your ass out of here and get some work done."

The door closed gently. A moment later it opened, and Gutierrez refused to look up.

"Vince?"

He shot to his feet. A tall woman closed the door and turned to face him, a woman with greenish eyes and a heavy

90

mane of graying dark hair. "It was very hot in Tucson, and lonely," she said. "I came to take you to lunch and tell you about it. But with all the action around here, I guess we'd better make it dinner. I'll see you later at home."

CHAPTER 10

"Christ, Mancuso, I feel really bad about this."

Not nearly as bad as I feel, thought Joe as he unplugged plugs, disconnected cables. He'd all but forgotten that the AT belonged not to him but to the university.

"Like I said on the phone, the storeroom is out of these babies right now, and I don't own a micro, so the dean suggested . . . he said he was sure you'd understand." Rod Phillips's face showed pink under its tan, and his glance slid away as Joe approached him. "Oof. Heavy bastard."

"Right," Joe replied. He set the keyboard atop the system unit, draped several cables over Phillips's shoulder, and went to open the front door.

Phillips stowed the unit in a sleek little Datsun sports model, then came back to the house in his long, unhurried stride. "Peripherals," he said in reply to Joe's questioning look. "Maybe you could carry the printer while I—"

"No."

"No?"

"The monitor and printer belong to me."

"Ah, you wouldn't consider loaning . . ." Phillips let his voice trail away. "No."

"No."

"Well, I'll be on my way then. See you."

Joe closed the door and trudged back to his denuded workroom. At the back of his closet was an old IBM PC, one he'd bought as a vegetable and built up himself by means of loans, swaps, and computer-fair purchases. For the tasks he had presently at hand, its two disk drives would suffice.

Saturday's *Port Silva Sentinel* lay on the kitchen table. The three-column picture on the bottom half of page one was innocuously sylvan, until one looked more closely to see the police tapes enclosing a section of the wooded site. Joe picked the paper up, then folded it and set it aside. Ed had left early to take his boat out, before daylight and before newspaper delivery. He'd be interested in the story on page four, which featured an interview with Yvonne Farrington.

Joe opened his refrigerator and looked at its interior blankly for several moments before remembering his purpose. Groceries, milk and butter and, um, cheese. Celery, and perhaps cabbage; he tried to grow cabbage but worms kept outsmarting him. Maybe veal? He picked up the pad he kept on the counter and dropped it. He had no car, no means of transporting himself or groceries. Shit. Could you rent a car by phone and have it delivered?

The raspy doorbell sent a jolt along his spine. Phillips, after a missing cable? Joe pulled the door open and found himself facing a smiling young woman who swept a card past his eyes and back into her shoulder bag.

"Joseph Mancuso? Dr. Mancuso? I'm Deborah Adams; please call me Debbie." She had masses of shiny dark hair, a dress of soft blue with a neckline scooped just low enough to expose the creamy tops of her breasts. No belt, Joe noted, but a piece of print fabric, like a scarf, wrapped and tied well below her hipbones. On a better day, a package to make his palms tingle. Perhaps he could ask her to come back tomorrow.

"Dr. Mancuso, I understand that you knew Ilona, Ilona Berggren, quite well."

A classmate or friend of Ilona's then; she was the same type, forceful California female, maybe a few years older. "I'd known her for some time, but I wouldn't say I knew her well."

"But you were a family friend, and her professor?" Debbie Adams kept her eyes on his face as she moved past him.

Was that what he had been? Joe thought for a moment and decided he could find no fault with either term. "I guess I was. And where did you—?"

"And that pigtailed little girl had certainly grown up, hadn't she?"

"I beg your pardon?"

"I understand that the police have questioned you several times, Dr. Mancuso, and that you're presently on leave of absence from your job. Suppose you're charged? Wouldn't you like to have someone tell *your* side of the story, right from the beginning? Someone to hold your hand through the whole ordeal?"

"Get out of here." Joe reached for the door, but she slid past him once again and propped her back against it.

"No, please, just listen to me. I'm a free-lance writer. I'll show you clips of my published stuff. I *know* I can get national coverage on this; it's a good story with unusual characters. Lots of people will be interested and what that will do for *you* is keep the police honest. At least," she added. "Also it would be a terrific break for me." She tipped her head to one side and widened her deep blue eyes.

"But suppose I'm guilty." Joe folded his arms on his chest.

"That doesn't matter," she said impatiently. "It'll still be a good story, maybe even better."

"Lady, you're suffering from a serious case of stupidity."

She glared at him. "Listen, you, I almost have my master's from San Francisco State, and my work has appeared in—" He moved a step closer, and she closed her mouth.

"And you're so hot for a story that you walk alone into the private house of a possible murderer and close the door behind you? Christ, woman, have you read about what happened to Ilona?"

"Yes," she whispered.

"And to the other two?"

She merely nodded.

Feeling very weary, Joe dropped his arms to his sides and moved back. "Just get out of here, will you?"

She put a hand behind her, found the doorknob, pulled the door open, and scuttled around it. Once in the doorway, she straightened and glared at him. "In this country you can't dodge the press."

"I can try," he told her. "Go away, Deborah Adams, and think about how lucky you were not to run into a murderer." It was with a sadly detached appreciation that he watched the movement of her hips under the print wrap as she fled down the sidewalk. When she had climbed into her small, dusty sedan, he touched the switch panel just inside his front door to turn his lawn sprinklers on, high. The next inquiring reporter would have to get wet.

He'd drunk too much beer the previous night, and besides, the last thing he needed right now was a depressant. In the kitchen Joe got out the teapot he kept for Cat and brewed a pot of her favorite Earl Grey.

"One, you have no job." He sipped the dark liquid, grimaced, and stared out at his garden. "Two, you may get hauled off to jail any moment." In fact, if he were Vince Gutierrez, he would probably arrest Joe Mancuso right now. "Three, somebody, at the police station or at the university, is talking, and pretty Deborah won't be the only one listening; the media will get to you eventually." He sighed. "Which means four, you'd better call Mama and warn her."

Better clue George in, too, he thought as he refilled his cup. Because it was George Mama would be worried about. He looked up Mal Burns's number, punched the buttons, listened to ten rings before hanging up. Burns's downtown shop next, and no answer there, either. Mal Burns was a man who would view machines as his servants, not his keepers; probably he had unplugged his phones.

So lock up the place and go out to Burns's house, which as he recalled was south of town on Lupine Road. Yes, indeed, friend, and that's a hell of a walk and you have no wheels.

Depends on what you call wheels, he told himself some minutes later. His old but little-used Univega had two of them, and ten gears, and rat-catchers on the pedals that had twice caused him to pitch headlong. His fellow grad students had zipped all over Berkeley on ten-speeds, but Joe never felt easy on his. Such bikes were for slim, fast people who were comfortable in a forty-five-degree lean at thirty miles an hour on a machine weighing twenty-five pounds. With little skinny tires making for a coefficient of friction of about. . . .

Shut up and get moving, Mancuso. And wear the helmet; it'll serve as a disguise and you might even want to save your head.

The derailleur moved smoothly, the brakes no longer squealed; apparently Cat had worked the bike over. Joe rode through town keeping his mind on his machine and the road, seeing no one he knew well and causing no public outcry. Beyond the city park he swung off onto Frontage Road; perhaps a mile of that, and then Lupine Road, presenting ruts and potholes and sneaky patches of sand in low spots.

95

The left side of the road was open to a rough kind of meadow, bunch grass and scrub brush and patches of tall lupine, even a few late-blooming poppies. Young redwoods made a scraggly screen on the right, and behind them widely spaced cottages clung to the headland, most of them gray-shingled and quite a few occupied; he saw vehicles in driveways, an occasional putterer among rock gardens.

The sound of the Pacific came only faintly to his ears now, buildings and trees muffling its roar. Much louder were songbirds in the meadow. Hearing a cascade of notes, Joe looked up to catch a flash of brilliant red, the shoulder patches of a red-winged blackbird. A pothole caught the front wheel and nearly threw him over the handlebars.

A bridge arched over a small creek. He fought his way through the sand trap on the other side, looked at smoke rising from the chimney of a gray cottage, and recognized the place he had rented years earlier. It seemed lower than he remembered and had developed a southward tilt; he had been correct in mistrusting its foundation. Several more houses of much the same type and then Burns's brown van standing in a driveway, beside another chimney drifting thin smoke.

Mal Burns had indeed unplugged his phone. "I've already had my call from our chief of police," he said, "who would like to see me this afternoon with 'a few more questions about my statement.' And Yvonne Berggren—oops, Farrington—has called three times, same miserable bitch she always was. She's looking for Nancy, my old wife; *that* should be interesting."

"Hey, Joey, there are cops crawling all over the beach," said George as he came in from the deck. Joe looked past his brother to see a broad blue-shirted back; Aaron, elbows propped on the deck rail, was intent on the action below.

"Turned up about eight-thirty, with rakes and bags, and I think one of them has a metal detector."

Joe raised his eyebrows at Mal, who shrugged. "Connected with the murder investigation, that's all they'd say. Cops are cops, even when you know their names; they've got about as much respect for a civilian as a sheepdog has for a sheep."

"Speaking of the police . . ." Joe looked at George, considered taking him aside, and decided not to bother. "When I saw Gutierrez yesterday," he said, embarrassment tightening his throat, "he told me he'd found some evidence that appears to incriminate me. So he has his men looking my truck over. And I've, uh, taken a leave of absence from work; an associate is filling in for me."

"Evidence?" George's voice squeaked.

Joe shrugged and pushed his hands into his hip pockets. "Somebody used my office Saturday night, logged in from my terminal. And made love on my couch. To Ilona, as the cops figure it, since they found her bracelets there in a drawer. Logically enough, Vince Gutierrez sees me as the most likely somebody."

"Jesus, Joey," George whispered, his face suddenly gray.

"Eventually they'll find the guy who *was* there," Joe said quickly. "But in case that takes a while, I thought we should call Mama. I've already had a reporter, a free-lancer, at the house, so somebody's talking. I'd hate to have Mama turn on her television set and see me being hauled off in cuffs."

Mal ushered the two of them to his study, pointed out the phone, and left, closing the door softly. George sat down and stared at his feet; Joe took a deep breath and plugged in the phone and punched buttons. His mother answered on the third ring.

". . . So that's the way things stand right now," he finished a few moments later. "It'll work out, don't worry, but

97

I just thought you should know." He hunched his shoulders and listened. "Yes, I've talked to a lawyer." A crackle from the receiver. "No, I can't do that; I haven't been arrested, but they told me not to leave town." Another longer crackle. "I'm sorry, Mama. I said I'm sorry," he repeated, louder. "Yes, he's here, just a minute."

"Hi, Mama." George balanced the receiver on his shoulder and listened. "I don't think that would be . . . Mama, it would look lousy for me to leave here while Joey's in trouble."

Go, go, Joe signaled with hands and eyebrows, but George shook his head. "Take it easy, Mama, or you'll work yourself up to one of your migraines. Just sit down now, and close your eyes, and listen to me." He paused, grimacing in Joe's direction.

"I am just fine. And Joey will be okay, too; everybody knows Joey wouldn't hurt anyone. You be a good girl, and don't worry, and we'll call again soon, okay? Love you."

Joe trudged back into the living room, feeling the way he always felt after an encounter with his mother: awkward and generally unnecessary. "Thanks," he muttered to Mal, who was standing by the open deck door. Aaron was still leaning on the rail watching activity on the beach.

"Anytime. How about a beer? You look like a man who needs a drink."

Joe shook his head. "It's a long bike ride back to town, and I think the car rental place closes at one."

"Car rental? That's right, you said the cops have your truck." Mal crinkled his brow in a frown. "Look, let me help you out here. I've got a small motorcycle down at the shop I don't use much."

"Thanks, but I don't think so," said Joe.

"Then take my old van. The guy I sold it to is out of town until September, and I know he won't mind. You wouldn't want to head for San Francisco in it, but it'll get you around town. Aaron?" he called.

"Yeah?" Aaron didn't turn around.

"Joe needs transportation. If you don't have any plans for it, I'm going to loan him the Volks."

Aaron straightened, turned. "Sure, no problem." He gave Joe a broad grin. "Good idea. I'll go get the keys."

George Mancuso took a quick swipe at the stove-top, tossed the dishcloth in the sink, and left the kitchen at a near trot, closing the heavy swinging door behind him. Spaghetti sauce out of a jar, for Christ's sake, and now Joey had the stereo turned so high it could probably cause brain damage.

He sat down on the front porch, stretched his legs out; Beethoven inhabited the boards beneath him, traveling from the deck through the very bones of the house. With a sigh he levered himself to his feet, strolled aimlessly down the walk, turned to watch his brother. Joe was splitting wood, placing a wedge in a huge log and settling it with a sledge and then driving it through. The music was so loud that these vigorous actions were weirdly silent.

The bike stood there gleaming at him, an eager steed ready for a run. George turned his back on it and went to sit on the front steps of the cottage. Temperamental display was *his* kind of thing, not Joe's; Joe didn't have moods. Christ, you'd think Joe was the only person suspected, the only one called back for "a few more questions." Goddamned unfair, George thought, and tried without success to work up a little anger of his own. Could they actually, incredibly, hang this whole mess on his big brother?

He shivered and drew his knees up under his chin, wrapping his arms around. Must be after six; he'd more or less told the Burnses he'd be back there tonight, but the thought of leaving Joe alone made him jumpy. Suppose the police came, and this new and unpredictable Joey was still angry, with the sledge in his hands? Damn Ilona Berggren anyway.

He was only mildly embarrassed to feel his balls tingle at the thought of Ilona. Aaron probably wouldn't be interested, he was a real country boy around women, but by God what George wanted to do tonight was go hunting. Saturday night, he was nothing but horny; there had to be action someplace. He frowned, trying to remember the name of the place four or five miles north of town on the coast road. Miss Molly's, that was it, and they had live music on weekends. Sometimes country-western, but what the hell.

Maybe Joey would come along, be good for him. George turned the idea around in his mind, looking at it from different angles. Joe liked all kinds of music. Probably he could dance; he liked to sing. But if he, George, connected, he couldn't very well say, Hey, babe, gotta bring my big brother along. Be instant chill for sure. And to simply take off and leave Joe there . . . George had never seen his brother drunk or out of control, but the way he was acting right now, who could tell? No, better settle for a boring night at home.

"And then as if by magic!" he crowed softly as a van pulled up in the street. Luck was back on his side, where it belonged. Joey would have company he preferred anyway, and baby brother could go about his own pursuits. George came slowly to his feet as Cat slid out the passenger door, reached back in for her pack, came around the van, and stood talking to the driver.

She wore Levi's cut off short and rolled high, and her tanned skin had a satiny sheen. George eyed the slim, muscular legs, the tight little ass; got a nice jolt from the roll of her breasts against her tank top as she swung the backpack to one shoulder. If Joe thought she weighed ninety pounds, he hadn't looked lately. Tasty, very tasty.

And you'd better cool it right there, he admonished himself as she turned and started across the grass. She plain doesn't like you, tiger, and she's a mean-tempered little piece anyway. He arranged his face in an open, boyish smile. But she does like Joe, and he likes her. "Hi, Cat. I already fed Arthur; he was hungry and I didn't know what time you might turn up."

Cat was physically weary, emotionally easy, willing for the moment to let old antagonisms slide. If George's sleek handsomeness was not to her taste, he did have a nice smile. "Thanks, I appreciate it," she told him.

"Glad to help," he said with a deprecatory duck of his head. "You have a good time out in the country?"

"I worked," she said in tart tones, and then sighed inwardly. Bitchy bitchy. "We all worked, and yes, it was a good time. But I'm glad to be home."

His smile widened into a grin so obviously heartfelt that she couldn't help grinning back. "That's good," he told her, "because I know Joe missed you. He's out there by the deck splitting hell out of a pile of logs."

As Cat turned to look, the "Ode to Joy" ended and a stunning silence settled around them like a frame. Joe wore ancient Levi's hacked off just above the knee. Slanting rays of late-day sun glinted off his damp hair and limned heavy muscles as they bunched and slid under sweaty skin. He lifted the long-handled sledge easily, tapped the wedge. He widened his stance, swiveled his hips slightly as a golfer does, brought the sledge back and over and down, and the log shrieked and fell in halves. Follow-through brought him around to face her, and Cat locked knees gone suddenly weak as she drew a shaky breath.

Mortal remains of an ancient Monterey pine, these logs had made an untidy pile beside the deck for two years, a resource he hadn't known he would ever need. Each piece was twisty and full of knots, proof against anything but brute strength. Leaving the kitchen to George, Joe had trundled his misery outside to drown it in sweat.

And in Beethoven, with the small but powerful stereo cranked just below speaker blowout. Anyone who objected could come past him to shut it off. He tapped the wedge, took a big swing, hit not wedge but log, and stumbled forward.

Watch it, shithead; self-destruction is not the object here. Brace and aim and swing and there! He shoved the halves aside, bent to pick up his wedge, muscled another log into place. Seven years of education and five years of serious, peaceful, goddamned dedication to his job, and then some goddamned *sailor* oozes up to take his place. Wham! and the log fell apart.

And all those acts of responsible small-town citizenship, hundreds of hours spent manning a voting booth and coaching potentially wayward youth and supplying vegetables to the senior center, and one day oops, citizen, you're screwed and maybe even in jail. Tap, and blam! Another.

He scythed sweat off his chest, shook his head and sent drops flying. Didn't own a fancy sports car, not even a big shiny motorcycle, just a nice solid Ford pickup he loved or anyway liked a lot, and now he was driving a cast-off fucking Volkswagen with sprung seats and a mismatched door. Tap and whap! The wedge said "spoingg" and leapt from its groove.

Joe's mind touched on the conversation with his mother and slid away. If a man in his thirties still needed his mother's approval, something was wrong with him, that was all. And she wasn't to blame; you couldn't help where you loved. As the music thundered to a close, he tapped again, came set, swung. Good one, he told himself, and lifted his head.

Cat was there, perhaps fifty feet away, the low sun outlining her in gold. And George close behind her, tall head bent attentively as if to hear what she was saying. Just what Alice had predicted, big lusty kid and cute little waif. Oh no, he thought, and he flung the sledge aside and said it aloud. "Oh no. No, you don't."

He meant to run; he must be running because patterns of light and shadow were breaking against his eyes and moving air chilled his damp skin. But it was a long long way and she wasn't running, she stood rooted in place, wide pale eyes fixed on his face. That's fine, you stay right there, he thought, and then wondered if he'd spoken, someone had spoken. Not Cat, but the out-of-focus figure behind her, saying something. . . . "Go away, George," Joe said mildly.

Cat blinked. Joe caught sight of his own muscled arms swinging to enclose her and reined himself in, took a deep breath, set his hands carefully around her waist. Muscle there, too, flexing beneath silky skin, a delicate arch of rib, hipbone solid against his palm. His fingers traced the curving valley of her spine and fanned out under the low waistband of her Levi's.

When Cat pulled away to breathe, his "No!" sounded even to him like a groan of pain, and she moved quickly close again, rubbing her forehead against his jaw. "I'm really glad to see you, too," she whispered. "Do you think maybe we should go inside?"

CHAPTER 11

Curled in the curve of Joe's arm, her head on his shoulder, Cat watched light from the window change slowly from tawny to gray. Have to move before long; she'd promised Squirrel she'd be ready by nine.

Joe's breathing was deep and even. She lifted her head to inspect his profile: high straight forehead, fan of thick black lashes, thrusting Roman nose. Mouth easy, with an upward curl at the corner. Friend become lover, one more change in her life; even in the drowsy aftermath of pleasure she had a twinge of sorrow for some inevitable loss.

The eyelid twitched and there was a gleam beneath the lowered lashes. Cat twisted her fingers in curly chest hair and yanked.

"Hey!" With a sweep of his arm he scooped her up. "Must be past suppertime; are you getting hungry?"

"No." She brushed her mouth across his and slid from his grasp. "I have to shower and dress and get my gear together by nine." Her shorts and tank top were a dusty tangle on the floor; feeling particularly naked, she plucked a white T-shirt from a stack on Joe's dresser and pulled it quickly over her head.

Joe had rolled up on one elbow and was staring at her, open-mouthed. "Animal Fare has a gig tonight in a club. They go on at ten and I promised I'd roadie for them. Well,

104

look," she went on defensively, "it wasn't some kind of plan, like, 'Guess I'll go to bed with Joe today; two hours should be about right.' I didn't see this coming."

"I didn't either." He sat up and swung his legs over the edge of the bed. "Do you know you look about twelve years old?" His voice was aggrieved.

"It's this sexy underwear," she told him, holding the hem of the T-shirt out as she bobbed a little curtsy. "Actually I am your senior, sir. My mother always said I was born thirty-five years old."

"Smart lady, your mother." Joe lifted a terrycloth robe from the bedpost and stood up to shrug it on. "Was she Mary Frances?"

With the gray rectangle of the window behind him, Joe's face was little more than a dark blur. Cat took several steps back and wrapped her arms across her chest. "How did you know that?"

"When I brought you home and you were so sick, I looked in your pack for someone to notify. There was this old book of children's poems. Mary Frances Connolley was written inside the cover, the ink pretty faded, and below that, Catherine Eulalia Morrison. Cat for Catherine?"

"And for Cat Stevens; we had all his records at home. At home I was Lally, for Eulalia."

"You got better, and I didn't pursue it. No one else saw it, Cat, and I didn't tell anyone."

"Okay." Catherine Eulalia Morrison: her mother had laughed and told her she'd grow into it. Lally was gone for good, soft sounds for a happy child. And Morrison, too; she'd never willingly call herself that again. Maybe, when she was finished with Cat Smith, she'd become Catherine Connolley. She sighed. "My mother is dead. I'll tell you the rest, if you want, but not right now." At the doorway she turned.

"We're playing at a club called Miss Molly's; maybe you'll feel like coming out later? You could give me a ride home."

There was a sign on the right side of the highway and a short graveled driveway to the flattened top of a hill. Miss Molly's was long and low, white-painted cinderblock with a shingled porch roof across its front. A string of colored lights outlined the roof edge, and candles gleamed from tables on the deck at the right end of the building, candles behind red or blue or green glass. Cat thought the effect charming and was sorry when Moose pulled the van through the crowded parking lot into a kind of alley between the main building and a much smaller structure.

"Door back here lets right in beside the stage," he announced. "Rest rooms in that storage building there, at the front."

Cat jumped out, slid the van's side door open, pulled out a coil of black electric cord, and draped it over her shoulder. "This place looks popular; how'd you guys connect?"

Squirrel was in the back, pushing his Korg keyboard toward the door. "The owner saw us on TV; that little shot they did on the demonstration the other day. The guy's an old hippie; he runs country-western bands Friday nights, soft rock Saturdays."

This was a big step up from parks and tiny halls in university dorms. Holding tight to the heavy cord, Cat edged through the door into a long room where wooden ceiling fans revolved slowly and an old Linda Ronstadt song wailed from a jukebox. There was a bar in the corner at the far end, under a high bank of fluorescent lights. Next to the bar a double door gaped wide, and pale smoke eddied out into blackness sparked by the multicolored gleams of the deck candles.

High-backed booths, all occupied, ran the length of the

back wall. Long tables in the center of the room might have come right out of a school cafeteria, except for the pitchers of beer and the ashtrays. Metal folding chairs, lots of them. And people, a great many people. Don't freak, just do your job, she told herself as she shrugged the cord off and set it down.

"Hey," said a voice near her, and she looked up to meet a stern dark gaze from a face that was mostly beard, curly gray beard. "You don't look old enough to drink."

"I'm not drinking."

"No, but you didn't get stamped." He gripped her right hand and pressed something cool against its back; the ink-blue outline of a quail appeared. "Quail for minors, roadrunners if you're over twenty-one," he told her. "Now don't you smoke in here, either."

"Everybody else is," she pointed out, wrinkling her nose.

"Just tobacco. Nicotine and tar and all that carcinogenic shit, go right ahead. Anything else has to be outside." He nodded solemnly and moved off.

Seemed to be a certain amount of weirdness around tonight. Cat glanced at the smallish dance floor, then ran up three steps to the black-painted stage, which had a wooden rail around it. Maybe country-western patrons got rowdy. She located electrical outlets, mentally set instruments and microphones in place, and repositioned the wedge-shaped monitor speakers.

Moose brought in two Roland amps and Cat set about hooking up. When Possum came in with his guitar case and a mike, she remembered her unasked question and beckoned him close. "Possum, did you and Squirrel go to the police?"

He drew his lips back in a sharp-toothed grimace. "Didn't get a chance yet, maybe tomorrow. And don't you give me shitty looks, either; it's nothing to do with you."

"Actually, Possum, it's the rest of us I'm worried about. If the cops haul you off, what will we do for sweetness and light?"

"Baby, *you'll* just have to fill in." He grinned a wide, mean grin. "Anyway, Squirrel's friend Wendy says she saw something on TV made it sound like that girl's *daddy* killed her, which wouldn't surprise me a whole lot." A childhood in a series of foster homes had left Possum with a sour view of families.

"No! Joe said—" Cat closed her mouth on the rest of that remark. Joe had said Ed Berggren was devastated by his daughter's death. Joe, however, probably knew more about computers than he did about people.

"If the cops decide they really gotta talk to us, they'll find us." Possum glanced toward the door. "But Antelope's cool right now; I don't think even a cop could upset him. He says that old sax is so fine it must have a soul."

"His, by now, as much work as he's put in on it. And maybe some of mine. Did he get it finished?"

"Yeah, so set his mike low."

By ten the tables as well as the booths were full, and a waitress hurried back and forth through the deck door bearing glasses and pitchers. Most of the crowd was from the university, Cat decided as she surveyed the room. Guys in Levi's or summer slacks, women in sleeveless dresses or shorts. Western boots now and then, and she noticed a few longhairs; was that country or hippie or what? Several little kids were running around, and a sedate golden retriever lay under one of the tables. All of this in an atmosphere made surreal by drifting smoke and glimmering candles.

They were ready to go. The owner, who was his own sound man, bent over his mixing console; Moose was settling behind his drums and the others were all in place. Cat skirted the dance floor, unplugged the jukebox, then turned to watch and listen as Animal Fare strode into the hard-driving beat of "Good Golly Miss Molly." Everything electrical seemed to be working, and Antelope's pawnshop sax was indeed fine, gleaming golden even in its dents, formerly sticky keys responding instantly to his long fingers. Would Joe come, she wondered as she hurried to her spot beside the stage?

The first set went smoothly; the dance floor stayed full and Cat had her guitar ready for Possum when he lost a string on his. During the first break, while the Animals went outside to cool off, she shifted the monitors slightly, checked connections, tuned instruments. If they were going to play clubs, they really should get a backup bass; she'd mention it to Badger.

Another set, and another break. When Moose came back in, he grinned at Cat and produced a rumbling beery belch. "You look about worn down, girl," he told her. "If you don't want to play . . ." She shook her head. "So watch the last set from out front, why don't you, and we'll holler if anything goes out."

Most of the dancers had rushed outside into the cool dark. Cat blew damp hair away from her face and headed for the busy bar. She'd ask the bartender for a Calistoga, and maybe he'd lose track in the rush and hand her a beer instead, just one nice beer to toast a satisfying performance and Antelope's saxophone.

Nope, plain old water, bubbly water. She raised it in salute anyway, to Antelope, who was standing at the end of the bar watching the big color television set and couldn't see her: mellow and true, you *and* the sax. She jumped and nearly dropped the bottle when a hand took her elbow.

"Sorry." Aaron Burns's smile was diffident. "I wasn't sure you could hear me; I wasn't even sure it was you. We've got a booth, and a pitcher. Can you sit down?"

109

It was a moment before she realized that he was asking her to join him. She glanced at the front door once more, then smiled and shrugged. "Why not? I'm off but on call, sort of, so I'll need to keep an eye on the band."

"We" turned out to include George Mancuso and a young woman whose long light brown hair had apparently been braided and then combed out, like a horse's tail before a show. George had one arm around the girl and was occupied in trailing a lock of the frizzy hair back and forth along the upper edge of her red tube top, watching her breasts bounce as she giggled.

"George, here's Cat." George looked up at Aaron's voice, blinked at Cat, frowned.

"I thought you were with my brother. Where's Joey?"

"He was at home at nine o'clock," she said crisply. "Where he might be now, I have no idea."

"Wow, you must be with the band!" The girl pointed a wobbly finger at Cat, who wore narrow black jeans and a black T-shirt with ANIMAL FARE across the chest, in crooked red letters edged here and there with white. "How come they spelled 'fair' wrong?"

There was a pitcher, as Aaron had promised, and it was nearly full. To hell with it, the booth was dark, and what could the owner do beyond asking her leave? "They didn't," she told the girl as she slid along the padded seat into the corner.

"But that means . . . that means food, that's silly. Animal food? Like you're walking around asking some animal to eat you?" She giggled and George grinned. "Are those shirts for sale? Where can I get one?"

"We had them specially done," Cat said, and watched Aaron pour beer into a glass. "The only way you could get one right now would be to peel it off somebody. Badger's might fit; he's the bass player."

110

"Oh. He is?" She stood up to peer over the back of the booth. "Come on, let's go dance," she said to George, who glared at Cat as he got to his feet.

Cat thought she might giggle, too, until she noted Aaron's somber face as he eyed the red letters. "Is it supposed to be a joke?" he asked.

"More of a play on words; there's a poem, a children's song, called 'Animal Fair,' and some of us already had animal names." Aaron's expression didn't change. "And a group needs a catchy title. And we're vegetarians," she added lamely.

"Why?"

"Because . . . The idea is that it's better to live without killing other creatures." She picked up the glass of beer and took a long swallow. "Actually I'm a failed vegetarian. I have this cat, a real cat." His flat stare changed not at all, and she found herself teetering between giddiness and irritation. "Arthur *has* to have meat, so I was eating tofu myself and opening cans for him, and then one day I looked at Friskies beef and liver and actually picked up a fork."

Aaron grinned slowly and shook his head. "I figure there's a whole lot of cows out there chewing grass all day just so *I* don't have to. Want some more beer?"

Cat glanced around the room before nudging her glass toward him. "Yes, please, but quietly." She showed him her quail-stamped hand.

"Oh, for Christ's sake," he muttered as he filled her glass. "I've been on my own since I was sixteen."

Cat looked at him in surprise, but her "Me, too," was lost in his next words.

"And I've always figured I should be able to do what I want, including drink."

"Mm," said Cat. A sixteen-year-old *female* who wanted to

survive avoided all mind-benders and stayed seriously sober and alert.

Aaron had done farm work, he told her, all kinds. He had been a logger; he'd been a hand on a fishing boat. Cat sipped beer and listened politely. It sounded much more satisfying, and rewarding, then standing on cold corners to hand out flyers for pizza joints or sloshing around up to your elbows in greasy dishwater.

Finally Aaron sighed, refilled his glass, and downed half of it in one draft. From the stage came the sound of drums, Moose having a good noisy time with a piece Antelope had written. "Hey, are those guys any good? Seems kind of a dumb thing for a bunch of grown men to do, dress up in silly clothes and make a lot of noise."

"They support themselves!" she snapped. Pompous jerk. "They give people pleasure. And they're not destroying any natural resources."

"Okay, okay. But I don't know anything about music; are they any *good?* Like, the big guy on the drums?"

"Moose grew up in Tennessee playing bluegrass fiddle. Yes, I think he's pretty good."

"And, um, the guy with the flute, what about him?"

Cat leaned across Aaron to look toward the stage. Antelope's saxophone was gone; he'd raised the mike and had the flute in his hands. Such a fragile little stick it looked with his six-foot-six frame curved over it. She hoped nothing had gone wrong with the sax.

"That's Antelope, and he's wonderful, the best. He can play any instrument and he writes, too."

"Writes?"

"Music. Well, stories, too, but mostly for songs. That's 'Strawberry Slide' they're just finishing. He wrote it after the cops did a sweep along Strawberry Creek to clear out people sleeping there."

112

"And you, George says you play guitar. Are you good?" He half-turned to look down at her, and his heavy shoulders made the booth small.

She gave the question some attention; it was something she'd been thinking about recently. "I have good hands and a good ear. No theory. No big talent. What I do for the band, besides roadie, is add a rhythm guitar when they want bigger sound."

"I thought guitar players had to have long fingernails," he remarked, as he tucked his right arm inside her left and picked up her hand.

She pulled free. "I don't like to be touched," she said firmly, "except by people I know very well. An electric guitar is played with a pick. Thanks for the beer, Aaron. I'd better get back to work."

He regarded her stolidly from eyes the color of weak tea; then he got to his feet and stood aside to let her out. He and George were a peculiar pair, she thought, one a boulder and the other a stream. What did they find to say to each other?

As she slid out and stood up, hands gripped her shoulders from behind; she spun around and fell against Joe, who looked startled and then pleased. "I got bored sulking at home," he said, settling an arm around her. "Hello, Aaron, what do you think of Animal Fare?"

Aaron shrugged. "They're okay. I just came along with George."

"Who disappeared some time ago with a girl," Cat remembered.

"He probably just went out to her car. For a while."

"Oh." Cat looked up at Joe and felt her face grow warm. "I'm glad to see you."

"I said I'd come to bring you home."

No, you didn't, she thought; *I* said it. "I'm glad to see you," she repeated. As she leaned her head against him, the

113

sound she'd heard and ignored finally pierced her absorption: Antelope's flute, low and hollow and throbbing. She pulled free of Joe's arm and turned to look.

". . . 'Tis I, my love, sits on your grave, and will not let you sleep," mourned the flute. "For I crave one kiss of your clay-cold lips, And that is all I seek." Antelope stood slightly away from the others, the guitar and keyboard and bass and drums, although they were making soft background for his flute. His long arms were bent and lifted, like sad bony wings; his face was turned aside.

"You crave one kiss of my clay-cold lips, But my breath smells earthy strong," Cat whispered with the spare, sad melody. "If you have one kiss of my clay-cold lips, Your time will not be long."

"Cat, what's wrong?"

"Antelope's wrong. That's 'Unquiet Grave'; he only plays that when his head's . . . Oh, shit, just shit, that's all. He seemed so much better!"

CHAPTER 12

From the deck of the hillside house the anchored fishing boats looked like toys dipping and bobbing in a child's bathtub. Beyond North Harbor, beyond Vince Gutierrez's propped feet, the Pacific winked and glistened, deeper and deeper blue until it met the sunlit, cloudless sky. The watch on his left wrist was a compelling weight; he ignored it and rolled his head sideways against the back of the canvas chair, to meet the greenish gaze of his companion.

"I think there's enough coffee left for one more cup," she told him. She lifted a gleaming Thermos pot from the deck; he held out his mug, watching her as she poured. Meg Halloran was long-limbed and energetic, sharp of wit and tongue, and somehow able to make him feel about twenty-five years old instead of almost fifty. After a single dumb early marriage, Gutierrez had remained more or less happily single, if not celibate. He certainly hadn't expected to fall in love in middle age; it was a little embarrassing. Also scary, more scary than he remembered.

"Seems funny without Katy here," he said, and took a cautious sip of the steaming coffee. Meg's eleven-year-old daughter had stayed in Tucson to spend another week or two with her grandparents. "She'll probably be taller when she comes back," he added glumly.

"You just shut up, Gutierrez!" Meg snapped, and then sighed, sinking lower in her chair. "Yes, of course she'll be taller. She'll be *older*, the little wretch."

"You look younger, I think." Gutierrez studied her. "And now and then your face is different, like an expression you wear for somebody you know well and I don't know at all."

"That's interesting, leftover expressions . . . daughter, little sister, big sister. I hope my relatives were less perceptive. I must have a whole range of fascinating expressions when I'm thinking about you."

His face grew warm around what was probably a silly grin. "I hope so. I missed you, Meg. So did Grendel." The enormous gray-white dog sprawled close to Meg's chair cocked an ear briefly at the sound of his name. "He and I were buddies while you were away," Gutierrez went on, "but when I came in last night, you'd have thought I was a burglar come to heist the family silver."

"Gutierrez, when a male animal thumps his chest and says 'Mine!' the sound travels right across species lines." A flash of evil grin, which softened into a smile. "I missed you, too, but I suspect I'd have missed you even if I'd been here. Your cop's persona is settling back into place, love; I can see the edges hardening."

"Um." He glanced at his watch, then took a gulp of coffee. "I'd better get it in gear. I promised to be in by noon."

"On a Sunday?" It was a rhetorical question, and she didn't wait for an answer. "Are you getting close?"

"Ha," he said bitterly. "Suspects unlimited, evidence zilch. And the one bit of evidence we've found points to the guy I'd have thought of as least likely ever to kill anybody. Which is why policemen have no business having opinions."

"Is there anything I can do to help?" she asked.

"Maybe stay in town for a while." He reached a hand out and they linked fingers. "But you know," he said after a moment, "there might be something." Her eyebrows lifted in silent inquiry, and he went on. "I need to find Lisa Haffner."

"The girl who was raped in April."

"Right, the first victim."

"You're putting a lot of energy behind your idea that there's one rapist-killer."

Gutierrez dropped her hand, rose, and moved to the deck rail to stare across the blue water. A light haze was developing on the horizon; there might be fog tonight. "Meg, these three women, some guy . . . it had to be some big strong guy . . . knocked each one down and probably sat on her and tried hard to break all her bones, from her face right down her ribs. All three had the worst damage on the left side, so the beatings were right-handed. Mostly he used his fists; there was *perhaps* a weapon involved in the second, definitely in the third." He took a long breath. "It looks to me as if the rape was incidental; what he really got off on was beating a woman to a pulp."

"Oh." Meg pulled her feet back and sat tight in her chair, gripping her coffee mug with both hands.

"So I am, we all are, following up what evidence we can find regarding Ilona Berggren's death, which as I've mentioned is damned little. But I want to talk to the Haffner girl, and I can't find her. DMV has her still in Willits, but the chief of police there says he thinks she moved away, was sent away. I know for damn sure that her parents will tell me nothing; her mother might, except she's afraid her old man would beat *her* to death. And any official inquiries, her parents will just alert the girl and send her scurrying."

Meg sat straighter, blinked, turned her narrowed gaze on him. "Willits. Vince, I know the head of the English department at Willits High School. I met her at the National Council of Teachers of English convention last year. She struck me as a bright, sensible lady; I'll call her."

"I don't think Lisa attended the public high school."

"Margaret Godshaw has lived in Willits for something like thirty years. She's sure to know Lisa's family, or know about them."

"Very likely. Okay, why don't you call her? But once we know where the girl is, the inquiry becomes mine, official, to avoid corrupting any evidence. Besides, you do not want to run across Mr. Haffner." He set his empty coffee mug on the deck rail, stamped his booted feet lightly to shake his trouser legs into place, tucked his shirt smooth.

"What time will you be back this evening?"

"Not for supper, but I'll try not to be too late."

"I'll wait up," Meg said, and he nodded, but absently. Putting on a cop's persona, she had called it. He thought of it as going from one real world to another equally real, through the kind of vacuum-locked sterile passageway labo-

117

ratories employed to prevent contamination. He was already through the first door.

Gutierrez approached the station from the rear, parked his red Porsche in the basement garage, and had just reached his office when what sounded like a riot began out front. He hurried through the hall and found Svoboda standing behind the high desk, leaning on his elbows and watching with solemn interest.

Edward Berggren had one hand on the front door; with the other he was fending off his ex-wife, who seemed intent on punching or clawing or both. Fascinated lookers-on made a circle at the bottom of the steps, and a television van was parked at the curb.

"Well, hell, Vince, I hate this domestic shit, sooner try to take two drunk loggers." Svoboda spread his hands and shrugged, then followed Gutierrez to the door.

"Mrs. Farrington, knock it off or you'll find yourself under arrest!"

The woman stepped back shakily on very high heels, lifting both hands to brush her hair away from her face. "That man, my daughter's father, has been hiding out on his boat avoiding me."

Gutierrez looked at Berggren, who said quietly, "Right. Her among others."

"And I can't get permission to see my daughter. I *demand* to see my daughter."

"Yvonne, believe me, that wouldn't be a good idea."

"That's not your decision to make." Gripping a big shoulder bag with both hands, she widened her stance and thrust her head forward. "If you won't let me take her home to bury her, surely I have the right at least to see her."

"Jesus Christ, woman, you haven't made the least effort to see her since she was nine years old." Berggren shook his head wearily. "Do what you want; you always have."

"I was *going* to see her; we were planning to get to know each other all over again." When Berggren grimaced and turned away, Yvonne Farrington reached into her bag and pulled out a slim packet of envelopes bound together with pink ribbon. "I have Ilona's letters here, letters she wrote to me."

Berggren gaped at her for a moment, then reached for the packet, but she shoved it back into the bag. "You can read it in the newspaper, Edward—how Ilona was coming to realize what she'd missed, what you'd robbed her of. How you'd used her."

Gutierrez held the wide door ajar; his face was expressionless but his body was collected, ready to move. He watched Berggren's shoulders as they hunched, Berggren's feet as they shifted. Then the fair-haired man shrugged. "Enjoy yourself, Yvonne," he said and turned his back on her. "Got a minute, Chief Gutierrez?"

"Hank, will you see that these people clear the sidewalk?"

Svoboda moved out the door, Berggren stepped in, and Gutierrez led the way down the hall to his office. "What can I do for you, Mr. Berggren? I'm afraid there's nothing new at this end."

Berggren sat down heavily, then leaned forward to brace his forearms on his thighs and stare at the floor. "I thought Ilona and I were just fine; I had no idea she was . . . needing something from Yvonne."

"Mm," said Gutierrez as he settled behind his desk.

"They hated each other when Ilona was little, or Yvonne hated and Ilona always fought back. It was a goddamn permanent battlefield around the house." He shook his head. "I honestly thought it was better for Ilona to be with me. We had a fine time. I thought I was a good father."

"A mother who walked out on you when you were nine would be a loose end in anybody's life. And Mrs. Farrington's letters were persuasive." A search of Ilona's apartment had turned up the letters, eight of them.

"Ah, well." Berggren sighed deeply and sat straighter. "I've done some checking; I don't like loose ends either, or mysteries. Farrington, Yvonne's husband, is in a drying-out clinic right now, and he's been eased out of his position in the family law firm. He was a partner, so he'll probably still have some income, but nothing like what Yvonne prefers." He drew his mouth down in a grimace of distaste.

"Obviously," he went on, "Yvonne had learned that Ilona was a wealthy young woman; my daughter owned a quarter of my company and had other money as well, investments. I've made a lot of money. I don't care about money for itself, but it gave me pleasure to be able to provide for my daughter, to make her independent and secure."

The last word seemed to hang in the air; Gutierrez watched the other man swallow and stretch his neck, as if his shirt collar were too tight.

"Well, it's been my experience, Chief Gutierrez, that Yvonne will do anything, anything in the world, for money." Berggren stood up. "Now, what I came about. I have a business that needs attention, and I'd like to go to my main office, in Santa Cruz, for a day or two. If it's all right with you."

"That's a reasonable request. Please leave a number where you can be reached. And let me know if you plan to go on from there."

Berggren stopped at the door and turned. "Joe Mancuso tells me he was not in his office with Ilona Saturday night. I've known him since he was eighteen; he can't manage even a social lie. I'd say he's the least likely suspect you have, except for me. Now, is there a back way out of this place?"

* * *

120

Gutierrez leaned back in his chair and watched Svoboda, Mendenhall, and Kuisma settle themselves. "Hansen called me this morning," said Mendenhall, and he pulled his small notebook out and flipped pages. "Nothing so far, he says. None of the campus people saw anything, nothing useful from the other tenants at the apartments. The two musicians never turned up. Hansen's at a horse show this afternoon, with his kid."

"Fair enough. In fact"—Gutierrez reached across his desk for a big looseleaf notebook—"I'm going to pull him back to regular duty. The Art Festival starts Thursday and Labor Day's the following weekend. Okay, Duane, how did you and Chang make out with the computer kids?"

"Just fine." Mendenhall's face reddened. "A little . . . kid named Jason Epstein was tired of having cops bother him, so he got on his machine and proved none of the group members could have murdered Ilona."

The others gaped, and Mendenhall shrugged. "Let me lay this on you. Eighteen in the program, three of them women; Epstein eliminated the other two women, even though one of them claimed that was sexist. So, fifteen kids, men, and twelve of them there Saturday night; the three who weren't all had solid alibis. What Epstein did, he plotted each person's night. Sign-in, log on, trips to the can, trips to the candy machine and to the fridge they've got there stuffed with Diet Pepsi and fruit juice, if you can believe it. Rest stops when they played something called Go."

"Plotted."

"Yessir, Chief. Points, you see. And intersections—times when one guy happened to run across another guy. Longest anybody in that building went without being seen by somebody else, up to five-thirty in the morning, worked out to twenty-seven minutes. And some seconds. Long enough to take Ilona into the office and fuck her, for sure. Not long enough to beat the crap out of her, take her out and bury her, and get back."

Mendenhall pulled his dark glasses down and sighed. "Now I hate to admit it, but it was goddamned convincing. Any one of those guys is guilty, he had to have at least three others covering for him."

"Which one of them had messed with her program?" Kuisma asked.

"Kid named Bill Armstrong, but he says that's a friendly thing, something hackers do to other hackers. Nobody mad. In fact, she . . . Berggren . . . caught on, and she played a little trick with *his* program. She did this probably Saturday night; he hit it Monday."

"Saturday night," Gutierrez repeated.

"Right. And chances are somebody helped her, like maybe Mancuso."

"Maybe." Gutierrez made a brief note. "Svoboda?"

Svoboda shook his head. "Not time enough yet, Vince. I did find Malcolm Burns's second wife, in Oakland. She never met the first wife, and says Burns would never talk about her. She, MaryJane Hughes it is now, says she left Burns because she wanted to stay in the city and she wanted to have a baby; he'd had a vasectomy and turned out it was permanent. She's got a kid now, seemed sort of irritated at being asked about her old life. Oh, she never met Aaron Burns. His father mentioned him now and then, even went looking for him a time or two, but never found him."

"Has John Freund turned up anything from Berggren's employees in Santa Cruz?"

Svoboda shook his head again.

"Okay, call John when we finish here. Berggren says Ilona owned a quarter of his company, and we know now that the girl had recently reestablished contact with her mother. So we need to find out more about Berggren's financial situa-

122

tion, whether he'd have been in trouble if his daughter had decided to pull her money out.

"Okay. Val? What about the beach?"

Kuisma had his notebook ready. "We combed the beach, but all we found was a lot of junk; I've got it in the back room. There are nineteen houses on the headland there, beach access from half a dozen points. Every house has a deck. The beach gets a lot of use, and people scramble up and down the cliff, which is just dirt and rocks and ice plants.

"So, we talked to the people who live there. Nobody remembers hearing any kind of fuss Saturday night. Several people think *maybe* there was a car or two late that night, or a motorcycle. One woman toward the north end says there's been music recently, like a person playing some kind of horn, and she *thinks* she heard it that night. And one old guy and his wife went for their regular beach walk Sunday about seven A.M. and everything was just like usual.

"And we got a quick look at houses, when we talked to people, and didn't see anything out of line. I didn't think we could get warrants."

"Probably not," murmured Gutierrez.

"Yeah, okay. But did you know that one of those houses, fourth from the south end, belongs to Malcolm Burns? He lives there with his son."

"I knew."

"Oh. Well, what about this? A little north of Burns's place, five houses up, is one Joseph Mancuso rented when he first came to town five years ago. I followed a hunch and had the rental agents let me look over their books. The place Mancuso had is vacant right now."

"Did you notice anything out of line *there?*" Gutierrez's voice was dry.

"Uh, no, but I didn't go inside; I just looked through the windows and around the deck."

123

"Good. We'll get a warrant tomorrow."

Mendenhall set his feet flat and crossed his arms. "Chief, we could pull him in."

"We could, but it's thin. His truck came up clean, and it's the only vehicle he owns. And he's not going anywhere. Okay, Val, let's go down and look at your beach exhibits."

"Exhibits is too fancy a word, Chief. Junk is more like it." Val led the way to the big room at the back of the building, where boxes and plastic bags were spread out over two tables.

"Condoms, about two dozen. We picked them up, for whatever good." He shrugged. "A diaphragm; some lady is asking for trouble. Bathing suit bottoms"—he pointed—"and tops, one matched set. A pair of jockey shorts. Toy shovels. One real shovel, short-handled. A little hatchet, old and rusty."

He moved around to the second table. "Money. A little tiny radio, buried. A dead cat; that's in the other room. Garbage from picnics. Three tennis balls, a Frisbee, a soccer ball. A tape cassette, too sandy to play. Four sheets of the kind of paper you write music on; some guy lost his songs." He separated the pages with the eraser end of a pencil. "They were folded fairly small and half-buried in the sand, so they're not too wet. And then this weird thing; it's some funny kind of brush."

The others gathered around to stare down at a narrow cylindrical brush perhaps four inches long with a skinny handle of twisted wire looped at the very end. The head was multicolored in streaks of blue, green, and pink on white; damp and sandy, it still looked soft. "A bottle brush?" guessed Svoboda. "For real narrow bottles?"

"Hell, that's a brush for cleaning out your flute," said Mendenhall. "My middle girl has one of those."

124

CHAPTER 13

"Joseph, there's a nasty burned smell here; have you had a fire?"

Joe jerked straight to look over his shoulder, and the leaning ladder shifted and rocked. He swung his weight forward, the quivering wooden frame stilled, and he backed down.

"I'm sorry." Alice Magruder wore a pale green linen dress; a broad-brimmed hat of white straw made lacy patterns of shade on her face and shoulders.

Joe shook his head and gave her a weary grin. "It's a stupid way to be working; I should rig a scaffolding. No, nobody's tried to burn us out yet; I'm just using a propane torch to take paint off the window frames." He looked down at himself: at arms streaked with dirt and sweat, at flecks of old paint caught in matted chest hair, at filthy Levi's riding below his belly. "I'm overdue for a beer break, Alice, but let me go clean up a bit first. Okay?"

"Don't be silly; you're obviously not finished. Besides, you look fine." Alice smiled at him, her eyes intensely green above the green dress.

"Well . . ." There was a faucet at the corner of the house. Joe turned it on and bent to splash his chest and shoulders, finally stuck his head under the cold stream. Christ, was it Tuesday? If Alice was set up for an afternoon's fucking, she'd have to get it somewhere else. No, today was Monday; she'd be on duty this afternoon. He ran his fingers through his hair, pulled his T-shirt from the deck rail, and toweled off with it.

He climbed wearily up the stairs to the deck, found his old blue workshirt on one of the lounges, quickly shrugged it on, and buttoned a couple of buttons. Casual, in fact gamy, but better than nothing. Alice came from the kitchen with a beer bottle in one hand, a tall glass of pale brown liquid in the other. "Ah, you found the tea, good. Better not sit downwind of me," he told her, and dropped into a canvas director's chair.

"What a very busy place this is today," she remarked, looking around the yard. "Are those gates new?"

"No, they've been stored under the house since I bought it. Well, the entrance and driveway gates were. The cottage path gate *is* new; Aaron and Cat built that."

"To repel invaders."

"Yes, ma'am." He tipped his beer bottle. "I've had visits from a free-lance writer, and two reporters, and a fellow who wanted to pray with me, and several people who just wanted to come in and look around. For a while I left the sprinklers on, but my lawn was turning into a lake. So, gates. And gatekeepers; Aaron Burns can look like a brick wall when he wants to. A *mean* brick wall."

"I noticed," Alice said tartly. "I also noticed that George looks absolutely awful; I think he's lost ten pounds in the past week."

"Ol' George sees his lifeline fraying away," Joe said, and then sighed. Mean-spirited, unkind, maybe even unfair. "George is worried about me, I guess. Besides, I've been careless about meals lately, and George isn't good at foraging."

"Well, try to feed him better, and don't work him to

126

death." Alice surveyed the yard's perimeter. A rail fence perhaps two and a half feet high marked the front of the wide lot and meandered along each side to meet the higher board fence that enclosed the backyard. Climbing roses gripped the rails with thick, snaky branches, blooming in clusters of deep scarlet. "I shouldn't think that little fence would stop anyone."

"Depends on how much blood he's willing to lose. Those are very old roses with very big thorns." Joe shifted his butt against uncompromising canvas. "Actually, Aaron and George wanted to get fancy, with an electrified wire along the top of the fence all around. But I pointed out that the last thing I needed to do was electrocute somebody's dog."

"Then what's that?" She pointed at a narrow plastic-coated wire running from the edge of the deck across the yard to the cottage.

"Phone wire." He took another drink of beer. "Cat's worried about one of her friends, so I put a long line on my work phone and took it out to her."

"Oh. Joseph . . ."

He drained the bottle and was on his feet as she spoke. "Thirsty out today; I think I'll have another beer. Can I bring you more tea?"

Joe stood before the open refrigerator for a long moment, absorbing the chill. He had always thought of himself as placid, even stolid. Now a persistent irritability encased him like a bad sunburn, and he couldn't think how to act through it. He certainly couldn't think how to deal with Alice.

"And what are you all dressed up for?" he asked as he returned to the deck. He directed what he hoped was an appreciative look at her; she was a friend, after all, and he didn't have so many friends that he could afford to be careless with them.

"I just came from DeTomasi's. . . . City lunch," she added with some sharpness when he didn't react.

"Oh. Yeah." Today must be the fourth Monday of the month, the day the mayor and the city council and the local service clubs met for lunch at the largest of the local seafood restaurants. Any citizen who wished to join them was welcome, so long as he paid for his own meal.

"We—my medical group—we want to buy the old municipal hospital and renovate it, to run it as a private hospital. It will require some local approval, so we're out taking pulses, you might say."

"Oh. Good." He stared at his outstretched legs and willed them to relax; he thought he detected the onset of a charley horse. Alice, dear Alice, my good friend, please go home, Alice, goddamn it. Could he manage another beer? Not and get back on the ladder he couldn't.

"But nobody was talking about hospitals today. Most of the talk was devoted to complaining about the police department."

He sat straighter and stared at her.

"It seems Mayor Wirkkala disagrees with his chief of police, at least as regards the present murder investigation. The mayor, along with three other council members and several officers of the chamber of commerce, does not believe Port Silva is being victimized by a serial rapist."

"Not by a . . ." Joe paused to sort this out. "'Serial' being the operative word."

"That's right." Alice finished her iced tea, set the glass down; she folded her hands in her lap and met Joe's eyes. "The two earlier victims were young women of questionable morals who lived dangerously; he didn't exactly say they got what they deserved, but that was the implication."

"And Ilona?"

"I believe he used the term 'copycat'; it's something of a

buzzword these days among crime journalists. Ilona was probably killed by someone who knew her, who then treated her like the others to confuse things."

"Someone who knew her. Like someone who was with her that evening, at a party." Joe's voice was bitter.

"I'm afraid so. Joseph," Alice said softly, leaning toward him, "it's not personal, I'm sure. But Mayor Wikkala's wife owns Whale Watch Inn; and I think he has money in that resort, River's End. We're coming up on Art Festival weekend, and then Labor Day weekend, and then six to eight very lucrative weeks of Indian summer, in a town that makes half its living off tourists. The chamber of commerce does not wish to hear about a lurking rapist."

"Vince Gutierrez is sure it's the same person."

"Vince Gutierrez is just a local boy who promoted himself a cushy job here because he'd spent a few years with the Los Angeles Police Department," said Alice smartly. "Have you arranged yet for an attorney?"

He stared at his feet and shook his head. "I'll do that when I'm arrested. Vince asks me questions, I tell him the truth, that ought to be enough." The back door of the cottage opened, Arthur bounded out, and Cat followed. She glanced in their direction, sketched a wave, and moved toward the sidewalk, where George and Aaron were still tinkering with the new gate.

"That should perk George up."

Alice's words caught only the edge of Joe's attention. Cat had stuck close to home since Saturday night, had worked with the boys over the gates, with him in his paint stripping project. Whenever he spoke to her, her glance met his and then slid past. She was his small quiet helper, just what she'd been three or four months ago. As he followed her movements now, his jaw ached from clenching and muscles twanged from his shoulders up the back of his neck.

129

"Oh," breathed Alice, a long descending note. "Oh my, I really blew that one, didn't I?"

Joe blinked and turned to frown at her, then swung to face the street again at the sound of an approaching car. It was pale gray-brown with a blue emblem on the door, a Port Silva police car. "Shit, maybe it *is* lawyer time," he muttered. As George and Aaron stiffened like a pair of sentries, Cat disappeared into her cottage.

There were two cops, one a big rawboned guy with brush-cut gray hair, the other a dark slim youngster. They exchanged remarks with the boys, and Joe stood up to button another button of his shirt. Two must mean business; would they give him time for a shower?

The big cop nodded and moved, not in the direction of the house but toward Cat's cottage, and up the two steps to its small porch. As his knock sounded, Joe vaulted over the deck rail and hit the ground running.

The green-gold summer day had moved past Cat like a jerky, out-of-focus film. She'd reached for a T-square and missed; she'd needed to blink and then blink again to read the bubbles on the carpenter's level. Driven by terrors none of his friends could name, Antelope had fled Miss Molly's Saturday night on the Honda, abandoning even his instruments. Cat had slept only sketchily since.

Joe looked almost as bad as she felt, and she didn't know what to do about it. She couldn't have him hovering protectively about her, or Antelope would never come in. In Joe's own troubles, she had nothing to offer him but her presence, big deal. Who is this no-name street person, Dr. Mancuso, and why is a respectable citizen like you harboring her?

George was morosely silent today, Aaron almost chatty. Cat meekly played gofer and took orders and dreamed. Antelope had talked to her often of the High Sierra, country where the earth's gray granite bones showed, where snows past and yet to come whispered in the summer air. Maybe that was where he'd gone.

When the police car pulled up, Cat ducked into her cottage from pure reflex. Nothing to do with you, dummy, she told herself as soon as the door was safely shut. Probably they'd come to tell Joe he could have his truck back.

She dropped into the room's single small armchair, pulled her knees up, and wrapped her arms tight around them. Joe's guitar lay on her bed; during sleepless hours, it had begun to give her back the classical repertory she'd studied at home. She stared at the instrument and remembered that time, when she was a wild little kid with two loving parents and a whole ranch to run on.

The knock at her door was four heavy, slow beats; she was on her feet before it finished. Two cops; she'd seen that from the corner of her eye as she fled. So, no back-door escape. She looked with helpless fury at her blue nylon backpack where it rested in the corner. She'd reached in yesterday for her hammer, and found instead Possum's revolver.

Another knock, slightly more rapid. She swept up the backpack and hurried with it to the back of her closet, where she crammed it between a loose floorboard and the subflooring beneath. Possum, you are a miserable prick and I'll get you. She called, "Coming," closed the closet tight, and went to the front door.

He was large, and fairly old, and had a face so calmly ordinary that she had to call herself back to caution. There was a younger face peering around his shoulder, bright-eyed. And Joe behind his other shoulder, *his* eyes wide and wild. "What do you want?" she asked the old cop, and she moved past him to wrap both her hands around Joe's right arm. Hard as iron, and throbbing with tension; she gripped it harder.

"Sorry to bother you, Miss; I'm Lieutenant Svoboda, Hank Svoboda, and this here is Officer Val Kuisma. If you're Cat Smith, I'd surely like to talk to you for a bit."

"It's small inside, stuffy. Can we talk out here?"

"Cat, you don't have to talk to anyone if you don't want to. And she should have a lawyer; I'll get her a lawyer," Joe snapped.

Svoboda merely looked thoughtful at this, but the young cop took offense at Joe's tone and came forward all abristle. What we really need now, thought Cat with a distant amusement, is for Aaron and George to join in; we can have our own riot. Aaron, in fact, was watching from beside the new gate, hands in his hip pockets and head cocked to listen. Where was George? "It's all right," she said loudly, and dug her fingers into Joe's arm.

Svoboda gave her a fatherly look, as if he might pat her head. "Now, Miss . . . Cat, if that's all right? Cat, I believe you play with a band calls itself Animal Fare?"

Antelope, she thought, and stepped close against Joe. "Yes, I do. Why?"

"We've been trying to reach a couple of your friends, talk to them because we heard they were on campus last Saturday night."

Possum again, he deserved boiling in oil. Squirrel, too, to be fair. "I heard them mention it, and both of them said they hadn't seen anything."

"Ah. Well, I'd kind of like to hear that from them. And I understand there's a flute player in your band?"

"Yes." The word came out small and high. She cleared her throat and tried again. "Yes. Antelope plays the flute."

"Antelope?" The young cop stared at her.

"Mind your manners, Val," said Svoboda mildly. "Miss Cat, I'd surely like to talk to this Antelope. Could you maybe tell me where I might find him?"

132

"I can't," she whispered. "I don't know where he is; nobody has seen him since Saturday night."

"Ah," he said again. "Jake Johnson, he runs Miss Molly's, he said this great big fella who played flute and sax started acting real funny, Saturday night it was, and then took off in a rush. Jake had noticed you, ma'am," he added with a dip of his head. "And he knew who Dr. Mancuso was, which is how we got this far."

"Oh."

"Yeah. Now this Antelope. He somebody who runs away, is he?"

"Sometimes. He gets . . . upset."

"What upset him this time?"

"I don't know." She stepped away from Joe, set her back against one of the posts supporting the porch roof, folded her arms.

"What's his real name?" demanded the other one, Val.

She simply shook her head.

"And what's *your* real name?" Val went on.

Joe started toward the questioner, but Svoboda's big frame moved between them. "Cat, I'll tell you the truth; we got reason to think your friend Antelope might know something about the dead young woman, Miss Berggren. Only a small reason, might be all wrong, and if that's the case, no harm done." He gazed at her for a moment from calm gray eyes. "Care to tell me why you're so scared about him?"

"I know he didn't hurt anyone, if that's what you're thinking."

"Why don't you tell me about him, let me judge for myself?" he suggested softly.

"I can't." When the younger cop stiffened and expelled his breath in a snort, Cat glared at him and then pointedly turned her gaze to Svoboda. "We've been together a long time, Animal Fare, looking after each other; some of us

133

don't have anybody else. I won't talk to you about Antelope until I talk to the others."

"Well, by God you will," the young cop began, but Svoboda put a big hand on his shoulder.

"No need yet to push anybody around. Miss Cat, would you tell me where to find the others? To see if they'll agree?"

She set her teeth in her lower lip and looked at the ground, very far away. They would all be at the farm now, a tidy package and no way for any one of them to elude the police if she brought them. Squirrel would be surprised and then interested; Moose would assume she'd done what she thought she had to. Badger—he needed always to be prepared, to be one step ahead; Badger would be frightened and then angry. And Possum would spark and snap with fury; what might he say to her, or more importantly about her?

She mentally dusted her hands and squared her shoulders: no matter. Their unity had already failed. Antelope had gone beyond the reach of loving friends, needed more help than she or any of them could give. "I can't *tell* you where they're staying," she said, "because I don't know the names of the roads. But I've been there several times; I can show you."

CHAPTER 14

Aaron took the bike to the coast highway and turned south, as Cat had instructed. She glanced over her shoulder, to make sure the police car was following, then settled to watch for the turnoff; should be a ways yet but better watch. Road name started with a B, odd name that she'd recognize when she saw it. Besides, there was a nursery on the corner with a blooming jacaranda tree, the only one she'd come across in Port Silva.

Aaron stayed carefully within the speed limit, carefully within the proper lane. No long hair to whip around her face this time, the way Badger's had. She adjusted her feet on the posts and sat back a little; she had matter-of-factly held tight to Badger, but Aaron's broad back was less welcoming. In fact, he seemed to lean forward, as if to avoid contact. Could have been worse, though; could have been old groper George.

Or it could have been the police car. Cat's unwillingness to go anywhere in a police car, and Svoboda's announcement that the chief needed to see Joe right away, had produced a silly impasse, a lot of angry foot-shuffling. And her own tentative suggestion that she might borrow Aaron's bike had led to this, another ride in the backseat, where women belonged. Tended to and looked after and ordered around by men, and fuck 'em all anyway. She drew a long, slow breath and savored the sea-tang on the light coastal breeze.

Intersection before long, she thought, and then she saw the tree, feathery green and luminous purple against a clear blue sky. She gripped Aaron's left shoulder and put her lips close to his helmet. "There. Turn left there." Bacheller Road, that was the name on the sign. Maybe Antelope had come home, sane and clear-eyed, and no one had yet had a chance to get to a phone to let her know.

Rougher tarmac now, with an occasional stretch of gravel giving the bike a skittish feel. There would be another turn in a mile or so, and then a third; she tried to watch without leaning too close or holding on too tight. Where had George disappeared to, and why? The notion of George as rapist-killer had crossed her mind earlier and been set promptly aside: Joe's *brother*? Besides, George was far too self-absorbed and indolent to be capable of murderous frenzy. And men who looked like George could always get women; why would he put himself at such hazard?

What did the police chief want with Joe this time? The question had been hanging just below her consciousness; she bit her lip hard and concentrated on the resulting pain and on her surroundings. She remembered that glossy modern farm on the right; the horses in the paddock were Arabians. The rutted dirt road surface; she remembered that, too. Abandoning politeness in the interest of safety, she wrapped her arms tightly around Aaron.

A short time later she signaled him and slid off the bike as soon as he'd brought it to a stop. The police car pulled up just behind them, in a cloud of dust that made her eyes sting. She yanked off her helmet and hurried to the car's passenger side, where Svoboda was rolling down the window. "They're here, the van's here," she told him, gesturing toward the small farmhouse. "I'd like to go talk to them first, please."

Svoboda took only a moment to survey the scene, the winding rutted driveway and the single vehicle beside the house. "Fine, you do that. We'll be right here."

"They found *me*," Cat repeated to the group clustered around her in the kitchen. "Possum, keep quiet and let me finish. They know what Antelope looks like and that he plays a flute and that there's something wrong with him. They say they have something to connect him with that murdered girl."

"But Cat, you didn't have to bring them out *here*," moaned Badger.

Possum swung around to face a new target. "Christ's sake,

you afraid all these neighbors might tell your mama and she'll spank your bottom?"

"Ever'body just get calm now, you all hear me?" Moose's heavy head swung slowly as he stared them to silence one by one. "You boys, you figure we should all just hunker down out here and let one little bitty girl—? Sorry, Cat," he added with an apologetic grin. "Why don't you say what *you* think we ought to do?"

The narrow, wavery line coming over the doorsill was ants, tiny ants trailing across the floor and up the table leg and over dishes and cups and a cube of butter melting to a puddle on its paper wrapper. Cat blinked and shoved her hands into her jeans pockets. "They're going to find out who he is. I think we should tell them, and tell them we know he wouldn't hurt anyone."

She looked from face to face and found no eyes that would meet hers. "But he wouldn't!"

No words or movements, hardly any breathing. Cat thought she could hear the ants marching, thousands of tiny feet. Moose drowned them out with a deep sigh and laid a hand on her shoulder. "Can't know that about anybody, Cat, not for sure."

"Well, *I* don't think he would. But he might hurt himself."

"Yes, ma'am, he surely might."

"So. So I'll bring the police in and we'll tell them what we know?" She stopped just short of saying that Lieutenant Svoboda was a good man, just another thing you couldn't know for sure.

"If the cops aren't just blowing smoke, if they do have evidence, then we don't have a whole lot of choice." Squirrel spread his hands wide and shrugged. He had once described his family to Cat as four generations of lawyers and rabbis. Although he was strenuously avoiding either profes-

137

sion, he seemed to possess an instinctive understanding of legal and ethical patterns.

"Well, shit." Possum sighed. "Okay, Cat, bring on the pigs. I got nothing to hide."

Remembering the cold, oily object now secreted beneath her closet floor, Cat snapped, "Not now you haven't!"

He stared at her blankly for a moment, and then red swept his face from chin to hairline. "I forgot. I'm sorry." His eyes slid away, pale stubby lashes blinking fast to conceal a glitter that might have been tears.

Cat moved close and put her arms around his stiff shoulders, spoke softly in his ear. "Just remember, I won't lie if they find it. And I want my hammer back."

The four of them followed Cat out the door and down the steps and formed a line there, just behind her. She watched the big policeman lumber across the dusty ground toward the house, his younger companion several steps behind. Which movie was this; was she the company commander greeting the reviewing general, or the warden turning over prisoners? "Lieutenant Svoboda," she said, stepping back and to one side, "this is the rest of Animal Fare. Moose, Badger, Squirrel, and Possum."

"Walt Chaffee," said Moose, stepping forward to offer his hand. "Bruce Graham," from Badger, and "Dan Goodman," from Squirrel. Possum kept his head down and his hands at his sides as he muttered, "Eddie Riley." Watching, Cat thought that the ordinary names had erased some magical quality, had stripped the wizards of their animal-skin cloaks to leave them blinking and ordinary in the dusty sunlight.

Svoboda stood with arms crossed, shoulders easy. "I've been looking for two of you fellows some days now, whichever two was on the university campus Saturday night with a couple of young ladies." Eddie Riley and Dan Goodman, primed for questions about Antelope, were startled into apologies and hasty explanations. Svoboda listened without changing expression, let silence lengthen, and then said, "Okay. Next thing is, we need you to help us find this big friend of yours, guy who calls himself Antelope."

"Why?" asked Bruce Graham. He shook back his streaked hair and settled his rear against the edge of the porch.

Svoboda sighed, shrugged. "Okay. Looking over an area where we think Miss Ilona Berggren *might* have been killed, Officer Kuisma here found a flute brush . . ."

"Come on, Lieutenant, a million of those things are sold every day." Danny Goodman shook his red curly head in disdain.

". . . and this. What I got here is a Xerox copy." Svoboda fished a wad of folded paper from his shirt pocket, opened it, passed the sheets around. "Also," he added, "it turns out that some of the people who live out there on the headland been hearing this odd music now and then, at night, probably a flute."

"Antelope loved . . . loves"—Danny, white-faced, corrected himself—"he loves the sound of the ocean. He likes to make music with it."

"And this is his music, all right, appears to be something he was still working on." Walt Chaffee's big shoulders slumped tiredly as he scanned the sheet of music paper.

With a nod Svoboda collected the pages. "Now, we got this stuff, so naturally we're checking on bands, and one of the guys we talked to was Jake Johnson at Miss Molly's. Jake says yeah, group last Saturday had a flute player, great big guy. Bartender particularly remembered, seems the guy comes to get a beer, watches the TV for a bit, then all of a sudden goes white and upsets his beer all over the bar. And the guy took off like a big bat not long after, *before* the band was supposed to quit.

"Now, nobody remembered just what was on right that minute, so I checked with the station. Turns out it was a repeat of a piece from the evening news, about the murder. A little interview, actually, with the girl's mother, and pictures of the girl, out at the site where the body was found. Where *we'd* found, pretty close to the body, a print from a great big bare foot, size foot you'd see on somebody about six-six." Svoboda looked slowly from face to face. "So I'm gonna have to insist on hearing about this missing friend of yours."

All the others looked at Cat, leaving the ultimate betrayal to her. She sat down on the porch step and knotted her hands together in her lap. "His name used to be Laurence Grodnik, Larry Grodnik."

Notebook and pen appeared in Kuisma's hands as Svoboda, frowning, said, "Never heard of him."

"Six or seven years ago, when he was fifteen, he shot his father. It was somewhere south?" She looked at her friends, and Eddie Riley pulled his lips back from his sharp teeth. "Central Valley. Modesto."

"But the father was only wounded," she went on. Svoboda said nothing, his eyes on Cat; she sighed, sat straighter. "Antelope's father was a marine, and then a cop; he had his uniforms tailored and his boots shined every day and he owned a houseful of guns. If his family didn't do whatever he ordered right away, he beat them; he beat Antelope and he beat Antelope's mother. Sometimes he threatened them with guns. Then he started in on the little sister, Rachel; she was seven or eight. That's when Antelope took one of his guns and shot him."

Cat paused to swallow and wet her lips. "After the trial Antelope's mother promised him she would take Rachel and leave the father, and she did. Antelope went to jail. About a month later the father went to where his wife and daughter were living and he shot both of them and set fire to the house and shot himself. Antelope couldn't get over thinking that their deaths, his mother's and his sister's, were his fault."

Svoboda, who had listened with an expressionless face, now turned his head away and spat in the dust.

"He's terrified of policemen, of *lots* of things," Cat went on. "But I never saw him do harm to anyone but himself."

"You happen to know where he was when Ilona Berggren was murdered? A week ago Saturday?"

Dry-mouthed, Cat looked at her friends, none of whom looked back. "Moose?" she said finally. "Squirrel?"

Walt sighed, and Danny said, "Tell him, Cat."

Svoboda listened to the tale of Antelope's earlier disappearance and return, while Kuisma scribbled furiously. "He didn't really remember what happened," Cat said helplessly. "He said he thought he saw his father. And he said he got to bury his mother. We didn't know then that anybody had been killed. And I still don't believe he killed her!"

Kuisma trotted to the car, to radio in a description of the Honda and its rider. Then more questions, the low-voiced Svoboda sweating in the sun, one foot propped on the lowest porch step. Where had they met Larry Grodnik; how long had they known him? Where were they and where was *he* at the time of the earlier attacks? What did they *know* happened to Larry when he took drugs, took liquor, when he was reminded of his past? Did he have girlfriends? Boyfriends? When Svoboda finally straightened and wiped his face, the others were sprawled along the steps like an exhausted relay team.

"Okay. Now if I could look over his stuff."

Cat stood up and stretched. "Lieutenant, may I go home now?"

Svoboda tucked his big white handkerchief into a hip

141

pocket and looked hard at her. "Well, let's think about that. You done fine so far. I'd sure hate to see you backslide."

"Backslide?"

"Maybe the best thing would be for me to put a man in the cottage with you. Might even be a good idea from your point of view. For your protection."

"*Please* don't do that! Antelope won't hurt me, but he'll know right away if someone else is there, and he'll just run again. Lieutenant Svoboda, I will call you if he comes; I promise."

His hand engulfed hers in a firm clasp. "Done. No reason you shouldn't go home, if you want. Wonder where that fellow with the bike got to?"

As he spoke, Aaron appeared from around the corner of the house.

CHAPTER 15

Trees throbbed and shimmered in dusty sunlight; her own hands and feet seemed half a beat slow. Probably shouldn't ask Aaron to let her drive. Cat settled the helmet over her damp hair and climbed onto the back of the already rumbling bike. She put her feet on the posts, placed her hands decorously to each side of the muscular torso before her, and then Aaron threw the machine forward in a leap that had her clutching for a better hold. "Hey!"

"Sorry." She caught the edge of a grin as he turned to the road again.

Cat tossed a glance over her shoulder. For a moment she could see Kuisma standing behind his police car and staring after them; then a cloud of dust billowed up to hide him. Maybe he'd follow.

They made a wide swoop around the first turn, and she could see that the road behind was clear, no dust but their own. Aaron sat easily now, moving the machine only slightly more rapidly than she'd have preferred. At the horse farm Cat caught a glimpse of several elegant Arabian heads gazing curiously over the fence, and then Aaron made another leaning swoop, this one around a pothole.

"Aaron!" she yelled, but a burst of engine noise drowned her out as he gunned the bike. She set her teeth and held tight. They slowed as a pickup went by in the other direction, leaped forward to flee the dust, slowed again as a small car appeared. Cat squeezed her eyes shut and tried to breathe shallowly.

Bacheller Road now, a better surface, at least intermittently. As Cat bent her head to wipe her face against her sleeve, Aaron settled further back in his seat, shoulders low and legs well forward. "Aaron!" she said again, and he turned his head.

"Hang on."

Great bursts of blinding speed along the tarmac, then slower on the gravel patches, back and forth like a ten-year-old on a new two-wheeler. He was playing with his control and his strength and his machine's center of gravity. Cat forced herself to keep her eyes open now, in the hope that she might be able to leap free when he pushed his skill that one step too far. Highway soon, please soon.

Then she could see it ahead: a distant wall of unmoving cars. Afternoon traffic time, she thought, and apparently a tie-up somewhere north beyond their view. Aaron slowed almost to a stop, then made an abrupt right turn onto a street that presented a paved surface and a scatter of small houses.

"No!" She dug her hands into his shoulders and pulled back hard. "Where are you going?"

"Hey, take it easy." The bike kept moving, but slowly, as he half-turned his head to speak. "Didn't you see the traffic jam on the highway?" A siren sounded, and both of them glanced to the west. "This street goes the same way," he added.

Obviously it did, with houses and yards and even people. "All right, but not so fast." She moved her hands from his shoulders to his waist, breathing carefully against a threatened catch in her throat. Show-off bastard and his fucking motorcycle. She wanted to be at home; she wanted to see Joe.

He did drive slowly, either from remorse or because there were people and cars around now, or simply because he felt like it. As they finally turned onto Shasta Road, she was leaning forward to watch for the truck, Joe's truck that was to be returned to him today, but it wasn't there. No vehicle in the street, and only the van in the driveway, the battered Volks he had borrowed from Aaron's father. Joe was still at the police station; they had arrested him.

Aaron pulled to a stop, kicked the stand down, dismounted at a bound, and dropped his helmet on the grass. "Sorry," he said again with a shrug; his head was high, pale eyes narrowed over a wide, tight-lipped smile.

She slid off the bike and steadied herself against it for a moment. "What have you been smoking? Did you find a stash out there?"

"Nothing, not a damned thing, but that's a great idea. Doesn't look like there's anybody around; how about we go someplace for a beer? And we don't have to go on the bike," he added quickly. "We can use the van there. Come on; I owe you one, for scaring you."

Cat was staring at him and shaking her head when George

144

appeared from the far side of the house. "Burns!" he called. "Burns, we need to talk."

"Where's Joe?" demanded Cat before Aaron could reply.

George flicked a glance over her. "The cops kept him for a couple of hours, something about that place out on the headlands where he used to live. They didn't charge him, not yet anyway. He got the truck back and then he had an appointment on campus."

"No sweat, George; your brother will be back to the chips and cards anytime now." Aaron spread his hands wide and grinned. "The cops have a better idea, they figure the band did it . . . or the flute player, anyway. Ask her," he added, nodding at Cat.

Joe, or Antelope? That was silly, made no sense at all. If you could line up the entire male population of this dumb town, or just all the men she'd known or come across in her life. . . .

"That big guy we saw at Miss Molly's?" George was staring at Cat. "Jesus Christ, I told Joey he was out of his mind, picking up derelicts."

Antelope or Joe. "Oh, shut up. Maybe the cops will get smart and take a good look at you or your show-off friend. Or the two of you together."

"Don't lose it there, ol' buddy," cautioned Aaron, laying a big hand on George's shoulder. "Get your bike and let's go down to the Hungry Wheels. I never had any lunch."

Inside the cottage Cat locked the doors, pulled all the curtains tight, listened to the bike engines until she could no longer hear them. Besides being tired and furious and worried, she was . . . she looked down at herself and wrinkled her nose . . . she was absolutely disgustingly filthy.

She stood in her shower until the hot water went cool, then cold. She wrapped a towel around her body and another around her wet hair and trailed damply through her living quarters. Clothes. Clean clothes, panties and a shirt anyway. Levi's, have to settle for almost clean, laundry time. A mournful wail pierced her brain and held her motionless for several long moments; then Arthur hissed and began to bang on the back door.

"If I stay in here, I'll be asleep in three minutes," she told the cat as she scooped food from a can. "And in five minutes I'll be dreaming about guns and flutes and motorcycles and blood." She propped the door open for him, picked up the acoustic guitar, and set off across the yard. There was a hint of cool dampness in the late-afternoon air, fog coming; but sun still shone on the deck, and Joe wouldn't mind if she took one little glass of wine from his refrigerator.

Car after car, some slowing, none stopping. She hadn't realized there was so much through traffic on this street. She probably hadn't paid attention before. A siren in the distance; she set the guitar down and listened, heard another and another and then fading, nothing.

Two cars, then a third, and a fourth, a van that stopped. She watched the driver alight and for just a minute she saw Antelope, but the wide spare shoulders and the ponytailed hair belonged to a smaller man, Aaron Burns's father. She sat still and kept her face still and watched him come toward her in quick long strides.

"Aaron around, Aaron Burns?" She simply shook her head, and he grimaced. "Shit. What about Mancuso?" He moved past her without waiting for an answer, to push the sliding door wider and step into the kitchen. "Mancuso?"

"Well?" he said to her a moment later. "What's the matter, don't you speak English? Where is everybody?"

She gave a moment's thought to answering him in her Tex-Mex Spanish. Which would make it a fight for sure, he looked ready to blow; and she was too tired for a fight.

"Aaron and George left here about an hour ago," she said. "I don't know where Joe is."

"Shit," he said again. He planted his feet, shoved his hands into the pockets of his overalls. "You're Mancuso's, Joe's, boarder, friend, whatever. Right?"

"I'm Cat Smith."

"And you live here."

"I live in the cottage."

He made a growling noise through his teeth. "But you will *be here*? I can leave a message with you?"

"A message for Joe?"

"A message for my son," he snapped.

"No." The word was out before she could stop it, hanging in the air. One of these days, Lally . . .

Burns dropped his jaw and drew a deep breath; and a car passed in the street. Another deep breath. "Would you *please*, Miss Smith, would you please *consider* telling my son, should he turn up here, that I'd like to see him at home? Sightseers have followed the police to our beach, and I could use Aaron *and* George to keep them at bay."

"Oh." The beach where they'd found Antelope's music, probably. "Yes. If I see him, I'll tell him."

"Thank you." He dropped the words like two rocks as he turned to stalk back to his van.

Cat watched shadows grow longer and played scales until her fingertips were bruised and finally the truck appeared. She set the guitar aside and watched Joe swing down from the cab, stumble, then straighten and set off toward the front door of the house. He saw her and corrected his course, placing each foot with the awkward caution of someone who isn't sure just where the ground is.

"Joe, what happened? Did they beat you up?"

"Beat . . . no." He put a hand on her shoulder and climbed the steps with solemn concentration. "I don't think

147

so." He pushed a canvas chair aside and sat down abruptly on a padded lounge. "Cat, would you get me a beer, please?"

Cat, who'd been hovering solicitously, caught his ripe breath and stepped back. "You're drunk!"

"Not yet I'm not." He swung his legs up and leaned back with a sigh. "What I decided was, I'd stop in at the Pine Cone and lay down a two-martini base . . . maybe three, I forget. And then I would drive home very carefully, and settle down to . . . isn't there any beer?"

"And it's almost dark and I have been sitting here for *hours* worrying about you, that you'd been arrested."

"Cat, I called George. Didn't he tell you I was okay?"

"For all I knew the police were trying to beat a confession out of you or had you locked in a cell with drunks and crazies."

"Cat, Vince Gutierrez isn't that kind of cop."

"And all the time you were in some *bar* drinking *gin*!"

"Okay, never mind," he said loudly. "Never mind, I'll get my own beer."

"Oh, for heaven's sake!" She whirled around and disappeared into the kitchen, to return in a moment with a bottle in one hand, the other covering her mouth. Joe looked at her wide eyes and her shaking shoulders and sat up quickly.

"Cat, don't cry."

"Shut up; I'm not crying." She sniffed and handed him the beer.

"I'm sorry."

She shook her head, wiped her eyes. "All of a sudden I was about eight years old again and lined up along the kitchen wall with the Ortega kids, and Aunt Soccorro is yelling at Uncle Rosario, how he's been drinking again down at La Posada, while his poor wife and his hungry children . . ." Cat sniffed again, and giggled. "And he's pounding on his

148

chest and yelling, a man works in the dirt and stink all day, he's goddamn it entitled to some peace and quiet and a beer."

"Peace and quiet and a beer. Three cheers for Uncle Rosario." Joe raised his bottle in salute.

"So what kind of dirt and stink did you run into today?"

"Oh, just a little more evidence; it's piling up slowly but steadily. Vincent Gutierrez, chief of police, does not appear to believe that I killed anybody. But if he doesn't soon find out who did, he may have to readjust his thinking. And good old kindly old Dean Schwartz thought he should remind me of the recent *guidelines* about professional—professoral? is that a word?—behavior. As regards sex with students. When the full faculty is back in September, the ethics committee might want to talk to me."

He pushed himself higher against the back of the lounge and looked at her. "Cat, if you cry I'll cry, too; you don't want to see a big dumb wop cry. It'll all work out. Come on, let's go inside and I'll fix supper. I brought home some veal, except I guess I left it in the truck."

He swung his legs around, got to his feet, and looked at her again. "*Now* what's the matter?"

"I can't eat veal." Her voice caught somewhere between a sob and a giggle. "I'm sorry, Joe, I really can't. You go ahead."

He sat back and stared at her. "Can't eat veal. Why is that, may I ask?"

"No. I mean, you don't want to know."

"Never mind what I want, tell me."

Cat cleared her throat. "What veal producers want is a great big calf with baby flesh." His eyes were fixed on her, unblinking. "Moving around makes muscle, so the calf lives in a stall too narrow to even turn in. They'd normally start eating grass at five or six weeks, but that would change the

149

flavor, so they get a concentrated milk substitute, vitamins and minerals but not much iron so they'll be anemic and their flesh will stay white. They stand and lie on slatted wood floors, because they would try to eat straw bedding. They're kept in the dark so they won't fuss, and kept very warm so they'll sweat and drink more liquid food; they don't get water. In about four months they're big enough to be very profitable."

"Oh." He stood up again. "How would you feel about giving it to Arthur?"

"Arthur doesn't have ethics; he'd be delighted."

"And I'll cook us some pasta and, let's see, I'll make a cream sauce with pancetta. If you know anything terrible about that, don't tell me tonight."

"I don't even know what it is."

"Ah. Come along, you'll love it; it is *not* veal."

Cat reached out and lifted the nine-inch chef's knife from Joe's uncertain grip. "If it's a matter of life and death," she told him, "as it certainly appears to be, I can cook. You drink, and I'll cook." She sliced tomatoes and red onions and red bell pepper for a salad and told Antelope's story for what she hoped was the last time.

"So that's that." She scattered small chunks of butter over a bowl of steaming fettuccine noodles, added a squeeze of juice from a garlic press, tossed in several handfuls of grated cheese. She got another beer for Joe and poured a glass of wine for herself. "I've just turned one of my dearest friends in to the police. How come I don't feel like a rat?"

"If he's not a murderer . . . Okay, okay! I'll take your word for it," Joe said quickly.

"What I'm really worried about," she said, poking at the noodles with her fork, "is that he's out on the highway somewhere. And some highway patrolman or something will see him, and know he's wanted, and . . . hurt him."

"Cat . . ."

"But there's nothing I can do about that now. Except keep my fingers crossed."

They ate in silence, until Joe pushed his plate away and sat back with a sigh. "Good, Cat. So now what? I mean, what will the other guys do now? Will you all still make a band?"

Cat shook her head as she picked up her wineglass. "I don't think so. Antelope is the musician; the rest of us are kids who like music."

"Where did you all get together?"

"Let's see. I knew Squirrel in L.A., and we headed north together. We met Moose, I don't remember just where, some highway town; we were in trouble and he was big enough to get us out."

"What kind of trouble?"

"I don't feel like horror stories tonight, okay? Just trouble. Anyway, we kept moving, and we met Possum and Antelope in Santa Cruz. We stayed there awhile, and then Antelope wandered off the way he does, and some kids beat him up; they call it troll-bashing in Santa Cruz. So we headed for Berkeley, which is where we collected Badger."

"Was it better there?" he asked. "I went to school in Berkeley, to Cal, but I lived at home in San Francisco."

"It was okay," she said with a shrug. "Druggies and weirdos might bother you in Berkeley, but ordinary people don't, and the cops generally don't, unless you make trouble. You can find shit jobs for eating money, like leafleting or collecting for the Free Clinic. There are lots of restaurants; some restaurants will give away leftover stuff at night. Or you can play music on the busy streets; Antelope made good money at that and so did I. On weekends groups play, in a place they call Provo Park downtown by the high school."

"And why were you all . . . just loose out there in the world?"

"Different reasons. Moose is Walter Chaffee from some little town in Tennessee. His father and his brothers are farmers and hunters and general rednecks; he says not quite Klan but almost. He loves them, but he doesn't want to be like them."

"The guy with the striped hair? Badger?"

"He's Bruce Graham from Mill Valley. Bruce has had, let's see, two stepmothers and three stepfathers and I think five half-brothers and sisters. And he's been sick, he had Hodgkin's."

"The redhead?"

Cat smiled. "Danny Goodman, a nice Jewish boy from Chicago. He was going to music school in L.A. and having a fine time. Then his older brother was killed in an accident, and Danny was supposed to come right home and be *the* son, finish college and head for law school. He couldn't, not right away."

"And the punk?" Joe asked, baring his teeth in imitation of Possum's grin.

"Eddie Riley, from Oakland. He had alcoholic parents who couldn't deal with a kid but wouldn't release him for adoption until he was about eight. By then he was skinny and ugly and mean. Eddie remembers every pair of potential adoptive parents who took one look at him and left in a hurry; he remembers their names and what they looked like and what they said."

"And what about you?"

"Me?" Cat got up and began carrying dishes to the sink for rinsing. "I grew up on a ranch in Arizona. My mother died, my father married somebody I didn't like, and I left. That was a long time ago." She turned the water on, hard.

"Oh. Cat? Cat!"

She shut the water off but didn't turn around.

"Look, I should at least wash the pans."

"You just sit there and watch; it's not a sight you're likely to see again soon. Maybe not ever."

The beer bottle was empty. Joe gave it a gloomy look, then reached for the wine bottle. "Too late to stop now," he remarked, and appropriated Cat's empty glass. He stretched his legs out under the table and watched her move about the room. "You know what I'd really like to do? I'd like to toss a sleeping bag and the Coleman chest in the truck and head for the hills. And maybe a lantern, and an axe, and . . . Cat, would you come with me?"

"Not tonight." She closed the door of the dishwasher and turned to face him. "But maybe tomorrow, or whenever things get settled down. Let's go into the real mountains, the High Sierra."

"Okay. I'll make a list. Fuel. Mink oil. Moleskin. Cutter's." He drank off the last of his wine, got to his feet. He put a hand on the table to steady himself and looked at Cat. "Are you coming to bed with me?"

"Not tonight." She crossed the room quickly, to wrap her arms around him. "I'm too tired, and you're too drunk. Besides, there's still a chance Antelope might turn up, so I'd better be in the cottage." She stepped back and regarded him with some concern. "Are you okay? Do you want me to help you to bed?"

"No, indeed. Thank you very much." He drew himself straight. "I am a grown man; I can get to bed all on my own. Alone. My lonely bed."

"Poor thing," she said solemnly. "Have a nice long sleep, and I'll see you in the morning."

CHAPTER 16

Ants covered the road in a thick red carpet. Cat felt them crunch under the tires, felt the bike slip and slide. She pounded on Badger's shoulders to make him stop, tried to shriek at him but his blowing hair was sharp across her face, in her mouth. Her hand brushed at the hair and it was softer, a thick frizzy clump, wet. She pulled hard, the head turned, and Antelope's face peered sadly at her from under the helmet, tears in his eyes, sand clinging to his unshaven cheeks. He grinned, and it was Aaron's face, and then no face at all.

She was trying to run, but thick soft sand trapped her feet, making each step a separate effort. The flute was heavy in her outstretched hand; she held it out to Antelope but he was running, skimming over the lapping waves. He slowed, stopped, turned, and when she had nearly reached him he turned away, pale bony knees lifting high as he ran. She tried to call him as she bent to pick up the saxophone he had dropped, great shiny thing weighted with sand. He was running faster; he and Joe were running together and leaving her behind; she couldn't pull her feet from the sand.

Total darkness, thick and black; no line of light now from under the wedged-shut door. And it was growing cold; the tin-roofed feed shed had been an oven all day, but when the sun was gone the desert air chilled at once. She shivered and

154

huddled into a tight ball on the dirt floor and tried not to whimper. Please let me out.

Cat opened her eyelids to blackness, closed them again, and waited for the dreams to fade. She was on her back in her own narrow bed, one leg bent and the foot trailing over the edge. Sheet and blanket trailing, too, and the air cool on her bare skin; was that why she had wakened?

Eyes wide again, she still saw blackness. She didn't like the dark, but she no longer left a light on because . . . because Joe did; he always left one deck bulb burning, a friendly glimmer through her kitchen curtains. She must have unthinkingly closed the pocket door to the kitchen; she'd get up and open it and then everything would be . . .

A tiny sound pinned her in place: Arthur, not his plaintive "mrowp," but the soft angry growl that meant stranger, invader. Cat took breath in shallow, silent drafts, listened hard, and thought perhaps someone mimicked her. Clammy sheet beneath her shoulders, smooth floorboard under her reaching foot, a chill across sweaty ribs, as if the air had moved. She tightened her muscles, drew a deeper breath, and inhaled an odor that clogged her throat and sent time spinning backwards: lemony musk of some macho-named cologne over the acrid sting of sweat, a hint of sweetish smoke . . . and surely hay, and sunburned dust?

She flung herself over and off the far edge of the bed. A blow grazed her shoulder, numbing it, and something heavy clattered to the floor. Hands grabbed at her, nails raking her back as she wriggled and lunged and jerked her leg free and hit the floor on knees and elbows. "Noooooo," she heard herself begging, in her voice of years ago, "no, please!"

A shriek of springs and casters, and he was on her like a tackler; her forehead banged the floor and bright lights exploded behind her eyes. She twisted and kicked and elbowed her way forward, banged against something, the

155

director's chair, heard it hit the wall. Her assailant swarmed up and over her. One hand clutched at her neck and shoulder, pulling back, while the other groped around, over her face.

Hooked fingers scraped down past her eyes, dug into her cheeks, plastered a sweaty palm over her mouth. She clawed at his wrist, tried to bite. He slammed her head to the floor again, and her teeth met through her own tongue.

Jagged surges of nausea and an odd wavering of sound. He was whispering to her now, his voice only a rumble from outside the shed, and she tried to speak through warm salty blood, beg him to open the door. Pain jolted time again as he twisted a hand in her hair and hauled her back from the corner, flipping her over with the aid of a ramming knee that emptied her lungs and left her gasping.

She had come to rest against something hard, a table leg, and she curled herself around it. He snaked an arm across her belly and yanked her free. She rolled and was coming to hands and knees when a swinging foot caught her just below the ribs. Another kick and then she was flat on her back, gagging and trying not to vomit, needing to pull her legs up but she couldn't because he was sitting astride her.

Rolling and twisting but he was too heavy, her clawed hands finding only slippery fabric over hard flesh, and her own voice deep in her head saying, Stop the fuss you silly bitch; you knew he'd get you, always knew it. A blow glanced off her right cheekbone, drawing a yelp of pain. She sensed the next one coming, a full-armed swing and an enormous fist, but there was nowhere for her to go.

Joe turned the water on to run cold, found the aspirin but couldn't locate a glass, finally fumbled two tablets into his mouth and simply put his mouth under the faucet. Things were loose inside his head, rolling around like unsecured cargo in a ship's hold; and a cloud of beer fumes had moved with him from the bedroom, a kind of personal fogbank. And there was something funny about his kitchen, some hungover oddity.

He waited by the sink for a moment, in case his stomach should decide to register a protest. No cure but time, time and sleep. How much night was left to him? He glanced out the deck door into blackness and frowned. No deck light; that's what was wrong. Practically new bulb, too; lousy quality control everywhere these days.

He padded to the door, slid it open, reached around to jiggle the switch, and found it down. Down? He flipped it up and blinked in the glare. That bulb was his city boy's response to a neighborhood without streetlights; had he been too drunk last night to remember to turn it on?

A sound caught his ear, a faint cry or moan. He flipped the light out again, squeezed his eyes shut for a moment, and then looked toward the cottage. No light there either, but where else could the sound have come from? Maybe she was having nightmares; he could wake her and comfort her. Or suppose Antelope had come back. Cat had insisted that he wasn't dangerous, but still . . .

He stepped out the door, realized he was naked, hesitated just a moment, and then picked up a beach towel from one of the lounges, to knot it around his waist. As he moved quickly down the steps and across the yard, it occurred to him that Antelope might indeed be inside, in Cat's bed with her. Joe swallowed sourness and plodded on. Her business, he still wanted to check; he could always apologize and back out. Closer now, he heard sounds of movement and then a sharp cry and a thud.

"Hey! Cat!" he yelled as he flung himself into a headlong dash. "Cat, I'm coming!" He yanked the back door open and was knocked flying by the lowered shoulder of a black-

157

clad figure. He scrambled to his feet, shook his head, heard thudding footsteps fading. "Cat?" he called again, and lurched through the door.

His fingers found the switch and the room leaped to life. Cat was on the floor half under the big table, small and white and blood-drenched, curled tight. "Oh, Christ. Cat?" He knelt beside her, touched her hair gently and then her shoulder. She wouldn't answer him, nor open her eyes; she wouldn't let him straighten her out. She simply huddled, clenched tight and barely breathing, her skin damp and chilly to the touch. She was naked except for panties twisted around her thighs, and her face and upper body were streaked and smeared with blood. No bleeding wounds that he could find; maybe the blood was from her nose. Or from her mouth. God! What would that mean? He brought the blanket from the bed and tucked it around her. He fetched the telephone, sat down on the floor beside her, dialed information, and asked for Dr. Brodhaus's number.

"Shock." Dr. Brodhaus shook his bearded head and sank back on his heels. He had turned Cat over gently, had explored her body with careful hands and crooned to her, and had tried only once, briefly, to make her stretch out. "The blood's from her tongue; she bit right through it. Looks as if she was kicked as well as punched; I'll have to watch her for signs of internal hemorrhage." He got to his feet and stood looking down at her. "Some bastard deserves to have his balls cut off for this."

Joe had his eyes on Cat, and it was a moment before he noticed the lengthening silence. When he lifted his head, he met a direct and level gaze, somewhere between questioning and accusing. "Oh no, not me!" He looked down at his own blood-smeared hands. "I looked her over for bleeding wounds, before I called you. The guy took off as I arrived; he knocked me down at the door."

158

"Well." The word was a long sigh, as Brodhaus looked down at Cat. "Such a little girl to have had so much trouble. I need to do a vaginal swab, for evidence in the event she was raped, but I think it would be better at the hospital. The ambulance should be here any minute," he added with a glance at his watch, "and the police. You know, Mancuso, it would probably be a good idea for you to put some pants on."

There was a squeal of tires as a police car pulled up, and a second right behind it. Sergeant Mendenhall reached the door first, Val Kuisma on his heels. "I made my last drive-by twenty-five minutes ago," Kuisma was saying, "and there was nothing, everything just the same."

"Yeah," said Mendenhall. He gave Joe a curt nod and turned his attention to Cat and to Dr. Brodhaus. "What happened to her?"

"She was beaten with fists, almost certainly kicked, possibly raped."

Mendenhall moved closer to look down at the figure huddled beneath the blanket. She lay on her right side, knees up, head tucked behind her upstretched arms. The visible eye was closed, dark lashes fanned against a rapidly darkening bruise. "I'll need to talk to her," the policeman said.

"Not tonight. She's in shock; I've given her a sedative and called for an ambulance. Come to the hospital tomorrow."

Mendenhall cast another look downwards and then moved away, beckoning the doctor to follow. "You her regular doctor?"

Brodhaus shrugged and looked at Joe. "I saw her once before, six months ago. Mancuso called me."

"What was wrong with her *then*?"

"She'd been beaten up," Brodhaus replied in even tones. "Bad things keep happening to women who know you,

159

Mancuso." Mendenhall planted his feet, rocked back on his heels, and stared at Joe.

"She, the girl, was perfectly lucid the last time," Brodhaus offered, "and she made no accusations. And she's obviously chosen to stay here."

"Women do all sorts of crazy things," Mendenhall replied. "Okay, Mancuso, what do *you* say happened here tonight?"

"I got up to take an aspirin, heard a noise from the cottage, and came out. I thought perhaps Cat's missing friend had turned up." Joe spoke evenly, determined not to let the policeman provoke him. "Then I heard a scream, and *I* yelled, and then this guy knocked me down as he came out the back door."

"Who was he?" When Joe shook his head, Mendenhall said, "Okay, then what did he look like?"

Joe shook his head again. "There was no light anywhere, and he came at me out of a dark door. Good-sized, solid. I didn't get any sense of great height. He was wearing dark clothes. I landed on the back of my head, and by the time I was on my feet and thinking, he was just footsteps. I didn't try to follow him; I came in to Cat." He paused to draw a deep breath. "I looked her over, and I tried to talk to her, and then I covered her up and called Dr. Brodhaus. And then I called you."

"How about you came in here and found her in bed with this other guy so you beat hell out of both of them?"

"No."

"Or maybe you were in bed with her, and this other guy came in, this great big guy we're looking for. . . ." As he paused, considering, there was the sound of a vehicle in the street, and Brodhaus moved to peer out the front door. "Here's the ambulance."

"I'm coming with you," said Joe, and Mendenhall moved toward him quickly.

"No, you're not; you're coming downtown with me."

"Oh no. No, Cat needs me with her." Joe could feel his temper slipping; his hands had made themselves into fists, and his face was hot.

"I'll get her friends." Kuisma was suddenly between the two glowering men. "I was out there today, remember? I'll go bring somebody, I promise."

Mendenhall had moved behind Joe and now snapped cuffs on before Joe realized what was happening. "Just a precaution, so you don't get yourself into trouble. You can call your lawyer from downtown."

CHAPTER 17

Cat lay on her back, two pillows under her head. Sheet and blanket were tucked smoothly across her breasts; her arms lay at her sides. Her body was clean and neat and carefully arranged, just like her mind. Blank. She could tell she was facing a window; sun was warm on her face and made interesting shapes inside her closed eyelids.

The hand clasping her right hand slipped free, and she grabbed, and opened her eyes. "No! Possum, don't go away!"

"Gotta go take a leak, lady, or ask the nurse to bring a bottle. Be right back, I promise."

She settled back into place, smoothed the sheet, closed her eyes. The right side of her head hurt, and her left cheek, and her right shoulder. And her belly, just below her ribs. She'd run Luz hard at a too-wide gully, and the little sorrel mare had landed scrambling in loose dirt, had fallen and rolled on her. She could still feel the saddle horn in her belly.

Stupid, stupid to risk not only her own neck but her horse's as well; she was angry and ashamed of herself. More than ashamed, disgusted, sick at the memory of her own blind and abject terror . . . "Possum?" she called.

He was there, taking her hand and settling into the low chair beside the bed. Last night he'd come, or early this morning; the hospital had said only one, he told her, and he'd threatened serious personal damage to any of the other three who disputed his right to be the one.

She blinked hard, made her eyes focus, and noted with a distant surprise that his hair was short and mouse-brown with only a few brassy spots. "You've had your hair cut."

"Yeah, Moose did it for me. Doctor's coming," he added.

"No!" She had a faint memory of a bearded face bending close, cool hands doing disagreeable things to her body.

"Yes," said a voice from the doorway, and the doctor strode in, his tunic a startling white above his faded Levi's. "You want Riley to stay, or go?"

"Stay."

"Okay by me," said the doctor, "so long as he makes a little room here."

A few minutes later Dr. Brodhaus clipped his little flashlight back into the pocket of his tunic. He pulled a plastic chair closer beside the bed, sank into it, cocked a moccasined foot on one knee, laced his fingers together behind his shaggy head.

"No evidence of concussion," he said cheerfully. "No broken bones. No indications of internal bleeding. No rape."

162

"I could have told you," muttered Cat.

"You weren't in any shape to do that, sweetie," Broadhaus said. "My apology for the indignity, which was certainly minor compared to what else had just happened to you. Anyway, so far as I am able to ascertain, you are a small but remarkably hardy person and should be okay in a day or two, except of course for some bruises that promise to be spectacular. Why didn't you eat your lunch?"

"I wasn't hungry."

"Why wouldn't you talk to the policeman?"

"I couldn't." Her voice was little more than a whisper; she slid lower on her pillow, hugging herself and pulling her knees up. "When can I . . . how long do I have to stay here?"

"Tell you what," he said as he stood up. ""I'm going to have the kitchen send you up a snack, some of that home-made vegetable soup from lunch. You eat that, drink some milk, take it easy. Then dinner, a good night's sleep, and we'll see tomorrow."

He ambled to the door, paused, and turned abruptly to fix her with a penetrating green gaze. "And don't stiff the cop again. Get it through your head that *nobody* has the right to beat you up."

Cat stared at the empty doorway. "Possum, what is he talking about?"

"I'm Eddie, remember? We're all gonna grow up and be real people; maybe I'll even get my teeth capped." He came to reclaim the bedside chair. "I guess the doctor thinks this is one of those classic cases; your old man likes to beat on you and you don't want to talk about it."

"Don't be ridiculous. I don't have an old man."

"Whatever you want to call him," he said with a shrug. "How come you haven't asked about Mancuso, why he hasn't been here?"

Because she had refused to let her mind wander in that direction. Cat pushed herself straighter against the pillow and cleared her throat. "He has more than enough trouble of his own, I guess he finally decided to keep clear of mine."

"Yeah? Well, one reason he's not here is he's in jail. The cops think he beat you up, and they think he killed that other girl."

"Don't be ridiculous," she repeated in a whisper.

"And don't you pass out!" he said, alarmed. "Here, take a drink."

"Eddie, it wasn't Joe." She sipped water through the bent straw and then handed the glass back. "It wasn't Joe; Joe chased Jimmy Three away."

"That's who it was? Your cousin?"

"He's not my cousin; he's my uncle. Step-uncle."

"You're sure it was him?"

"Yes," she said and shivered. "I keep thinking I'll grow out of it, but I'm still *so scared* of him."

"Maybe you just have to learn to live with that, lady." He sat back with a sigh. "That big bastard of a cop is gonna stomp in here anytime now. And unless you expect to see justice triumph all by its own self, like in fairy tales, you'd better be ready to talk to him. Hey, here comes food."

The nurse was a small woman with a round face and a single long braid of yellow hair. "I brought enough for your friend, too," she said to Cat, and tossed a smile at Eddie. "He's been here for hours, and the only food in the visitors' lounge comes out of machines."

"Nice girl," remarked Eddie a few moments later, settling into his chair with a cup of soup.

"Right," agreed Cat. Nice and round; Eddie liked women to be short but well-padded. "You take the bread," she added. "I can swallow, but hard chewing hurts. You get pretty friendly with her?"

164

"Sort of. She caught us at Miss Molly's, wanted to know where we were playing next."

Cat tipped the bowl and spooned up the last of her soup. "Could she get me some clothes?" He stared at her blankly, and she frowned. "Come on, I want to get out of here. I know what I had on last night, and this"—she gestured at the white cotton hospital gown—"isn't much better; it's too short and it's open down the back."

"Cat, the doctor said maybe tomorrow. And you gotta talk to the cops."

"I'll talk to them." She pushed the tray arm away and swung her legs over the edge of the bed. "It's high; help me down."

On her feet, she swayed, caught Eddie's arm, let it go, and took a few steps. "Okay, everything works. Please, *please* get me something to wear."

"Well, there's probably a pair of Levi's in the van."

Cat touched her belly in gingerly fashion, shook her head. "No. A bigger gown would do, and something to use for a belt."

Surgical greens proved to be even better, soft and loose. "I don't like this," Eddie said darkly. "What am I supposed to do if you pass out or something? That's a nice doctor; you should stay right here. And Abby was so nervous about getting this stuff for me that she says I shouldn't come around again, so there's another good thing down the tubes."

"I'm not going to pass out," she promised. "I want Joe out of jail *right now*. And I want to talk to Lieutenant Svoboda, not that Nazi who was here this morning. Eddie, what are you doing?"

"I just hope these are big enough," he muttered, pulling a pair of the baggy green trousers over his jeans. "There's a cop in the hall, down the corridor, kind of a dumb middle-aged guy. He sees us, he'll think we're a couple of surgical nurses. She didn't give me any of those bootie things; hope he doesn't notice your bare feet."

"Pray that he's nearsighted as well as dumb." Cat settled her trousers lower, to blouse out over her ankles. "And while you're praying, pray that Jimmy Three isn't out there waiting for us."

"You want prayers, you better send for Moose. Shit, I don't think I'd even recognize the guy." Eddie stuck his head out the door, muttered, "Clear, for the moment," and returned to take her hand.

"You real sure about this, Cat? It's safe here. And this time was different; this time the guy didn't just come across you by accident in a public park."

"That wasn't an accident," she told him. "I realized later, he must have learned about the birthday card I sent Aunt Eulalia. Mailed from Berkeley." And this time it must have been the band. Even under a different name, they were a noticeable lot, and Berkeley wasn't that far from Port Silva. Cat kept her mouth shut, but Eddie's mind was moving with hers.

"The posters show just five people, no girl. Except I guess anybody'd recognize Badger."

"Or Antelope."

"Right. Shit."

"It's not your fault," she whispered. She pressed her forehead against the doorjamb and closed her eyes. "And not mine either; it's his. Come on."

CHAPTER 18

"**G**oddamn it, you *can't* let him go!" Mendenhall stood in the center of the office, booted feet set wide. Clouds of smoke swung and swirled above him, as if he'd been bellowing flames.

"Keep your voice down!" snapped Gutierrez. "There are reporters all over the lot. And no more cigarettes; anybody who wants to smoke can climb up on a table and suck air!"

"D.A. says not enough evidence," offered Kuisma into the brief silence.

"The D.A. is a—" Mendenhall snapped his mouth shut. "Okay, it's not a whole lot of evidence, just a piece here, piece there, but what there is points to Mancuso. Christ's sake, how many guys like that you think we got in this little town? Son of a bitch not only rapes a girl but beats her until she's just a lump of meat! You didn't see this girl before, Chief; little bitty thing but she was real savvy and tough."

From a gray-faced Hank Svoboda came a throaty growl that he turned into a cough.

"Mendenhall, sit down." Gutierrez's voice was soft but very clear. He leaned back in his chair and waited until the other man had obeyed. "Duane, you're letting yourself get too involved with this. Maybe you need a few days off."

Mendenhall shook his head, then let his shoulders slump. "I liked Oakland. I mean, it was a pretty good force, interesting. But I finally decided my wife and my daughters should live someplace small and safe, you know? Where they could have horses and walk to band practice and shit like that. My girls are *big* girls and strong. I made 'em take lessons in self-defense, karate. And if even an average-size guy really wanted to, he could make any one of 'em look like that kid last night."

"I know that." Gutierrez's face was a mask of straight lines and hard angles and hooded black eyes. He set his hands palm-down on the litter of papers before him. "Duane, and all the rest of you, listen to me." Hank Svoboda, Val Kuisma, Ray Chang, and John Freund fixed eyes on the man behind the desk; Mendenhall kept his gaze on his own feet.

"I have the doctor's report here; I'll give you the highlights. First, Cat Smith was viciously beaten but she was not raped."

"Yeah, but what I think happened—"

"Shut up, Mendenhall, or you're on vacation!" Gutierrez took a deep breath and returned his attention to the papers. "Second, the beating was right-handed, and Mancuso is left-handed."

"Ambidextrous," grated Mendenhall, and Gutierrez nodded.

"Correct, but he favors his left. However, he had no split or bruised knuckles, not on either hand. The only marks on Mancuso are a bruise across his ribs and a lump on the back of his head . . . both consistent with what he told us, that the attacker hit him and knocked him backwards."

Silence. Svoboda put a cigarette in his mouth, caught Gutierrez's glance, and took it out again.

"Oh, for Christ's sake, go ahead; it's too late for my lungs anyway."

"Chief, what about the wrench?" Kuisma broke in. "That

big twelve-inch wrench we found under the bed? The doctor thought he hit her with that, her shoulder."

"Mancuso says it's not his, and in fact he has one just like it in his toolshed, hanging right where it obviously belongs." He glanced again at the intent, listening faces, then nodded. "Okay. In spite of all this, I'm not going to release him until we've had another talk with the girl. Duane, if you want to pass on this, Val could handle it."

Mendenhall's answer was a snort and an outraged glare. Gutierrez nodded again. "Okay. Treat her like one of your daughters. Dr. Brodhaus says she's in surprisingly good physical shape but pretty shaky emotionally. I may join you at the hospital later," he called after the retreating back.

Mendenhall slammed the door behind him; Gutierrez sighed and closed his eyes for a moment. "None of the others can prove where they were last night. Burns senior went to bed early; Burns junior decided to sleep alone on the beach; young George had a few beers and got back to the Burnses' house, where he's staying and went quietly to bed. Berggren was on his boat but chose not to answer the phone. The band members alibi each other, for what that's worth. Except of course for Grodnik. Val, what do you have on Grodnik?"

"Only negatives. No reports from other agencies on the Honda. No one on Lupine Road has seen him or heard the flute, not recently. There's no sign of disturbance at the burial site, nor in the woods near it. The guys at the farm, the other band members, insist he hasn't been back; and his stuff is still there, his clothes and his instruments and even his sleeping bag. You know, I saw Grodnik out at Miss Molly's, and it sure beats me how a guy who looks like that could wander around without *somebody* noticing him."

"Well, keep on it, you and Chang. I like Grodnik for all of

this a lot better than I like Mancuso." Gutierrez swiveled his chair to look at John Freund. "Johnny, what did you find out about Berggren?"

Freund's round face was solemn as he folded his hands on his belly. "What Berggren does is advise corporations on security for their computer systems, and people he's worked for think his high fees are a bargain. The company is privately held, just himself and his daughter, which makes financial investigation difficult. His local bank account is in the high six figures, with no financially unsettling activity; if you want to know more than that, the manager would like to see a subpoena."

Gutierrez sighed. "Not yet."

Freund nodded. "Berggren hires young guys right out of grad school, pays them well for a year or two, and then replaces them, which strikes me as a sharp way to keep current. It's also a good way to keep expenses down and profit high. His present employees think he's an eccentric genius; his former employees think he's a prick. One of the exes has just set up in business for himself, and the word is that he is beginning to provide serious competition for his former boss.

"All these guys had met Ilona; two of them took her out a few times; one of them took her to bed a few times. Nothing serious, no hurt feelings, or so they say." Freund glanced at the newspaper topping the stack on the corner of Gutierrez's desk. "Everyone's been following the story, of course. They all said Berggren was crazy about his daughter."

Ilona Berggren's half-smiling face gazed up from the folded-open newspaper. "Page nine yesterday, in spite of her mother's best efforts," Gutierrez murmured. "This latest attack means back to banner headlines, so watch your mouths, all of you. Anyone requesting information is to be referred to Hansen. Svoboda?"

"Yeah?" Hank Svoboda ran a hand over his flat-in-places crew cut. His eyes were red-rimmed; his left cheek and his upper lip bore razor nicks.

"Snap out of it, Hank." Gutierrez's voice was milder than his words. "You used your best judgment. You're not responsible for the beating."

"It sure as hell wouldn't have happened if I'd set up a stakeout instead of a patrol," he muttered. "So, anyway. I had a call yesterday afternoon from Mal Burns's second wife; her husband made her call. Present husband. Turns out Burns had a real bad temper, used to knock her around some. She left him after he broke her jaw. Her idea is that Nancy, his first wife, really screwed him up, turned him against women."

"We'll ask him in for another little chat," murmured Gutierrez, making a note. "It might be interesting to talk with his first wife, too."

"If we can find her," said Svoboda. "The kid, Aaron, says he hasn't seen her since he was sixteen. They'd been in Oregon; he decided to try it on his own and she dropped him off in Eureka."

"And went where?"

"He says he doesn't know. They'd lived all over the north state: Philo, Garberville, Willow Creek, Happy Camp."

"See if you can find her, Hank. You know people from here to the Oregon border; call some of them up. Or go see them."

"I'm looking for Grodnik."

"Kuisma and Chang are looking for Grodnik, and they'll have any help they need. You go digging for Nancy, and for whatever you can learn about Aaron. Now. Here's what I have from Englund, who's on his way back from San Francisco. According to a Mancuso aunt, George and several of his high school buddies used to amuse themselves by going fag-bashing. They finally hurt two men badly; they were

171

caught and convicted and put on probation. They were also underage at the time, so the records were later sealed."

"Little Georgy not so pure," murmured Svoboda.

"Right. The other thing is, I've got, or rather Meg got, a line on Lisa Haffner."

"Where?" came from Kuisma and "How?" from Svoboda.

"Meg drove to Willits, to talk to a lady she knows, another teacher. What she found out is that Lisa had belonged all her life to the First Southern Baptist Church there. The minister wouldn't reveal Lisa's current address, but he finally agreed to put Meg in touch with the minister of the girl's present church, in Santa Rosa—who has promised to talk to Lisa, and explain how important her help could be to us." Gutierrez's eyes narrowed and his hands gripped the edge of the desk, restraint against impatience. A knock at the door brought all heads around.

"Chief Gutierrez?" Dunnegan put his head in cautiously. "Sorry, but there's these two people want to see Svoboda. Couple of kids, a Cat Smith and an Eddie Riley."

The two of them came just over the threshold, the girl in front by a step. Woman, Gutierrez corrected himself at once. She was no more than five feet tall, and her dark hair was short and tousled, but there was nothing childlike in the remote gray-blue eyes. She surveyed the room, caught her breath, and half-turned, reaching a hand back to her companion. "I asked . . . I'd like to talk with Lieutenant Svoboda, please."

"I'm right here, Miss Cat." Svoboda got to his feet, glanced quickly at Gutierrez. "This here's the boss, Chief Gutierrez, Vince Gutierrez. I know he'll be pleased to help you, just like I am."

Gutierrez stood up slowly under her assessing gaze. In the greenish reflection from the baggy garment she wore, her face was a map of what had happened to her. He read the swinging blow that had raked her jaw and blacked her left eye, the brutal grip that had left finger-sized smears across her mouth. Son of a bitch.

"Chief Gutierrez. I knew some people named Gutierrez, before." The words were a kind of neutral acceptance, and Gutierrez bent his head in response.

"Hank will stay, but the rest of you can go," he told his men. "Somebody call the hospital, please. Tell the doctor, and Mendenhall, that Miss Smith is with us."

Cat stepped to one side and watched three uniformed men file past. Last in line was Val Kuisma, who smiled at her, nodded at Eddie, and closed the door behind him. She was holding her right shoulder stiffly high; Gutierrez remembered the wrench. "Miss, um, Cat," he murmured, and paused to clear his throat. "You look . . . uh, you should probably sit down."

"I want you to release Joe. Dr. Mancuso," she said, and stayed where she was.

Gutierrez pulled his padded chair out from behind the desk and gestured toward it. "Please. Sit down and tell us why you think we should release him."

She hesitated, then moved forward and perched herself in the middle of the chair. "Because it wasn't Joe who beat me up last night."

"Miss Smith, I understand that the room was completely dark and that you were asleep when the attack began."

"It was not Joe."

"But if you were asleep, dreaming." He saw a flicker of something, doubt, or fear, and decided to press her. "I'm not questioning your word, but people get disoriented when they're terrified, especially in the dark. And I know Dr. Mancuso has been a friend—"

"Don't be so *stupid*." She gripped the chair arms and spit

173

the last word at him. "I've been to bed with Joe; I know what he feels like, what he smells like. It wasn't Joe. For one thing, he doesn't smoke pot; I smelled pot last night. And my cat growled; he wouldn't growl at Joe.

"And his fingernails," she said desperately into the silence. "I forgot that. Joe keeps his filed to nothing, and I have deep scratches all down my back from fingernails. I didn't know they were there until Eddie was helping me dress. I'll show you."

"I'll take your word for it," Gutierrez told her. "Could it have been Grodnik?"

"Grod . . . Antelope? No!"

"Same question: how can you be sure?"

"Well, it's not the same answer," she said wearily. "Animal Fare was for music and friendship and surviving; fucking would have messed the whole thing up. But I'm sure I'd have known Antelope, he's so big. And his long frizzy hair; I couldn't have missed that."

Gutierrez watched her pull herself deeper into the chair, tuck her arms and legs tight. It was hard to detect a color change in the bruised face, but he thought her breathing was quicker. "So, Cat, who was it?"

After a long moment Eddie Riley spoke. "Tell him, Cat."

She shivered and twisted her hands together in her lap. "I'm sure it was Jimmy Three. No, not absolutely sure, but almost."

"And who is he?"

"His name is James Brown deKalb the Third. His sister is married to my father. Jimmy Three teased me and pushed me around and beat on me most of my life. Finally I could see it was a long mean story with just one ending; he was going to kill me some way, so I got away from there. That was two, no two and a half years ago. Then he found me in Berkeley."

"Berkeley."

"He and two of his buddies jumped us, jumped Cat really, in Provo Park, tried to drag her off to their truck," Eddie Riley said. "Turned into kind of a riot; the cops picked all of us up and then released us all, said they had no way to tell who started it. That's when Cat came up here; this was as much money as we had for a bus ticket."

Gutierrez pried the particulars from her, one sentence at a time. She was Catherine Eulalia Morrison, mother dead, father William Bryant Morrison of Oso Viejo Ranch at Corralitos, Arizona, southwest of Tucson. The ranch was half hers, in trust until her twenty-first birthday; she was presently nineteen. Jimmy Three was twenty-five years old, six feet one and slim, with dark brown hair and blue eyes; six months ago he had been driving a late-model Ford pickup truck, green, with Arizona plates.

"My father never believed anything I told him about Jimmy," she said bleakly. "But rape is the one thing Jimmy *didn't* do to me; probably it would have been hard to make that look like an accident."

"Probably," said Gutierrez. "Okay. Thank you, Cat, we'll look for him. Now I'll go arrange to have Dr. Mancuso released. He'll be with you in just a few minutes."

No charges had been filed against him, Gutierrez told Joe some fifteen minutes later. Cat Smith had insisted convincingly that Joseph Mancuso was not the man who attacked her. Joe was free to go, but should not leave town without notifying the police.

"I have no intention of leaving town," Joe said curtly. "I'm going home for a shower and a shave and clean clothes. After that you can find me at the hospital until Cat's well enough to come home."

"She's decided she's well enough now. They're waiting

175

for you in their van, she and Eddie Riley," Gutierrez told him. "She thinks last night's assailant was a man who has tormented her for years. She last saw him in Berkeley six months ago. We're looking into it."

"One thing for sure," offered Svoboda, "she's scared to death of the guy. She had to take a deep breath every time she said his name."

"What you'll need to remember, Mancuso," said Gutierrez, "is that a situation like that can make a person, a woman, feel like a participant, maybe like someone who deserves to be mistreated."

Joe stared at him. "Cat? I've never known anyone as spit-in-your-eye independent as Cat."

"Right now she's feeling very fragile. For which we can hardly blame her," Gutierrez added, drawing his lips tight against his teeth. "Anyway, give her time, and a good safe corner. And one way or another, I'll be in touch."

CHAPTER 19

Joe had read a poem once in which a skeleton moved about balancing its bones like a pile of plates. Cat was doing that now, carrying herself as if the slightest misstep would bring immediate disaster to body or spirit. He wanted to know about her old life but couldn't think how to ask, or even whether he should. He wanted to pick her up, cradle her, sing her soft and gentle songs.

176

He'd thought they might sit on the deck to enjoy the late-afternoon sun before the hovering fog settled in; but both of them were made uneasy by a steady stream of traffic in the street, car after car from which round white faces peered out at the scene of the crime, the victim, even perhaps the criminal. When Joe saw a man aiming a professional-looking camera from beyond the locked front gate, he urged Cat back inside, closed the door, and turned his sprinklers on high.

"Bunch of ghouls," he muttered. Cat limped into the half-dark living room and settled into the corner of the over-stuffed couch. "What we ought to do is get up on the roof with a rifle . . . no, maybe a basket of rocks." He tucked some loose cushions around her and nudged a hassock into place for her feet. "Or maybe a basket of eggs; wouldn't it be satisfying to lob eggs at all those goddamned wind-shields?"

"We could collect snails and slugs from the garden and use those. I would *love* to toss a big fat slug at somebody." Cat grinned, then gave a small squeak of pain as Arthur leapt into her lap. Watching, Joe gritted his teeth and wished he'd had a rifle last night, or a club, or even just a chance with his fists. "Cat, can I get you a Coke or something?"

"Yes . . . no." She slid lower against her cushions, adjusting Arthur. "Could I have a glass of beer? Or maybe several glasses. I have this boring life story to tell you; being drunk might make it easier. Probably for you, too."

"Right. I'll bring the cooler."

With a big thermal mug in one hand, her other hand stroking Arthur, Cat set the background. Francis Connolley and J. W. Brown, young men and poor but energetic, came to Arizona in the 1880s and established landholdings, ranches. Frank Jr. took his father's Oso Viejo ranch through bad times by hunkering down and living on chili and beans right along with his ranch hands; he kept his land and diversified into cotton along with cattle after World War II. James Jr. did less well with the J. W. Brown Cattle Co., and ultimately his three children split what was left and mostly sold it off.

"I'm a Connolley and Jimmy Three is a Brown, or our mothers were." Joe nodded that he understood, and Cat went on. "They were good friends when they were kids, my mother and Monica Brown deKalb. Anyway, Monica's husband went to jail; I think he was a stockbroker and stole money. So she divorced him, and she and Jimmy came to stay with us while a house they owned on a little piece of the old Brown ranch was being fixed up. Jimmy's sister Melanie, who was something like nineteen, was at the University of Arizona in Tucson."

Cat held her mug out; Joe poured it full and opened another bottle for himself. "Jimmy was twelve years old, I think, and he was beautiful; he always stood straight and never seemed to get dirty and he had wonderful manners with grown-ups. Women loved him. Especially his mother and his sister.

"For a while I liked him, too; I followed him around like a puppy. But to be Jimmy's friend, you had to do whatever he said right away. I was always, to quote my father, a recalcitrant brat; getting thrown in the cattle tank scared me, but it didn't stop me from fighting. And fighting Jimmy just made him meaner."

"Cat, how old were you?"

"Oh, I guess six."

"And this twelve-year-old was throwing you in cattle tanks? Where the hell were your parents?"

"See, mostly it was things like my guitar getting smashed or my puppy being put out at night so the coyotes got him. Things that could have been accidents. Even my mother thought I was being a baby; she felt sorry for Jimmy, with no father and no land and a mother who drank all the time."

178

The deKalbs eventually moved to their own house, Cat went on to explain, but Jimmy came to Oso Viejo frequently, and brought his school acquaintances. Jimmy smoked in the barns. Jimmy regarded the working horses as livery stable nags for his use, and the ranch people, whose families had lived and worked there for generations, as ignorant peons.

"Eventually my mother got onto him and made him leave me alone. Then she finally ordered him off the ranch for good, after he rode one of her Morgans to death."

"Morgans?" asked Joe before he could stop himself.

"Morgans. Horses! Morgans are small, sturdy, very intelligent horses."

"Sorry. Cat, I was born and raised in San Francisco; my idea of livestock is sea gulls and pigeons."

"Morgans are wonderful." Her mouth curved up softly. "Ours were my mother's special thing; she had horse breakers in for the working stock, but she trained the Morgans herself. I had my own; she was a sorrel and her name was Luz."

Cat's face tightened and she held her beer mug out once more. "I knew this was a drinking story," she muttered. "So after that, I'd see him now and then, in town, but he didn't dare bother me. Then my mother died when I was thirteen, and not long after that Melanie, Jimmy Three's big sister, got divorced and moved back to Corralitos. She's very pretty, and she and my father started going to the races all the time. My dad sold the Morgans and bought some quarter horses."

"So Jimmy Three had the run of the ranch again," Joe remarked.

"Oh yes, and I was his amusement when nothing else was happening. He'd pick me up and hug me, and I'd have big black handmarks on my arms for days. He'd play we were wrestling; that dislocated my shoulder once. A couple of times he sneaked after me when I rode out and watched until I dismounted. Then he took my horse away, so I had to get home across the desert on foot."

Joe had settled onto a hassock before the couch; now he stood up, gulped a deep breath, and rolled his shoulders loose. "And your father?"

"My father." Cat's voice was coldly reflective. "My father is considered a handsome man, and people say he's charming. I think he's a lot like Jimmy Three except that he's lazy instead of mean. My father wasn't interested in anything but racing his horses and fucking Melanie. Jimmy was just friendly and full of high spirits; I was spoiled and jealous and accident-prone. He sent me off to boarding school finally. Stupid expensive place for kids whose rich parents didn't want them or couldn't manage them."

Joe opened another bottle of beer and looked at Cat, who shook her head. "Not yet, thanks. What happened next was that my father and Melanie got married, and Jimmy found out about my grandfather's will. That the ranch was half mine, left to me in trust, and none of it could be sold until I was twenty-one and took control of my half."

"That was a heavy-duty load for your grandfather to lay on a kid."

"My grandfather was a fine man!" she snapped. "He was just trying to look after me. There was no way somebody like my grandfather could know there were people like Jimmy Three, people who think everybody else in the world is nothing but meat.

"You don't know either." She was breathing hard. "You wouldn't know about the man in the abandoned house with his ten-year-old son, only it was really his daughter or at least a little girl, and every night he'd rent her to one of the other squatters. He had his eye on me, too; that's when Moose came along."

180

"Cat . . ."

"Or the woman I met in the shelter with the cute little boy maybe two years old. She had this stash of something, I don't know what it was, in a plastic bag. The cops were coming through, and she hid it in her kid; she shoved that plastic bag up his ass. She said it always worked, no cops were going to touch a dirty diaper."

"Cat, I'm sorry."

"You can't imagine those people, even when you know." She leaned her head back and closed her eyes. "Back to my own soap opera. After Jimmy found out about the will, it got worse, more dangerous. Like the time that summer he locked me in an old feed shed miles from the main house and I was there all day and all night. Pablito Ortega finally found me."

Joe sat carefully down beside her, picked up her hand, and closed his fingers around it.

She rolled her head against the cushion and looked at him. "I told you about the Ortegas. Ortegas had worked the ranch from the beginning, Uncle Johnny the foreman and his brothers Uncle Pablo and Uncle Rosario. I grew up with their kids. Like one of their kids. By now they were all watching out for me, and one day Uncle Rosario saw Jimmy Three fooling around with the pickup I usually drove. He'd drained the brake fluid. So Uncle Rosario gave Pablito some money, and his old pickup, and told him to get me away."

"And where did you go?"

"To Glendale; that's near Phoenix. An Ortega cousin. Then to Denver, to Aunt Eulalia, my mother's best friend. She was an Ortega, but her married name is Ruiz. The thing was, all these people are poor, with lots of kids of their own, and I couldn't go out and get a job; I had to lie low because my father was looking for me. So Pablito went home, and

Aunt Eulalia sent me on a bus to L.A., to her oldest son, Rick."

A softening in her voice brought Joe's eyes to her face. She flushed. "Rick is a musician. He taught me to play electric guitar, on his big old Fender Telecaster. He bought me my little red guitar. Rick is a wonderful person, but he has serious trouble with drugs. Finally he had to go back to Denver, to a hospital. He was out for a while, but I think he's back in again.

"Anyway." She drained her glass and set it down. "He went to the hospital, and I hit the road north; actually I made it further north than I'd planned. And here I am, bloody but unbowed. That was a poem my mom read. I *think* I feel unbowed; do you suppose it's the beer?"

"I think it's character, but beer probably helps. Would you like some canned chili? That's about as close as I can come to a tribute to those Ortegas and Ruizes."

Cat remote-controlled the television set while Joe rattled pans and bustled back and forth. He cleared the coffee table and brought in placemats, spoons, napkins. He brought a basket of tortilla chips, a bowl of chopped onion, a bowl of grated cheese. He brought, finally, big bowls of steaming chili. "Maybe I'll make some from scratch tomorrow," he told her as he refilled the beer mugs. "I've got about six recipes; you can help me choose one. Do you want a lap tray?"

"No, I'll sit on the floor." She set Arthur aside, slid down carefully, picked up her spoon. Joe settled opposite her. They were scooping slowly from nearly empty bowls when the front door flew open and George burst in.

"Joey! I heard they'd let you go!" He snatched up a bottle of beer, gave the top a futile twist, then used a key-ring opener to flip the cap off and away. "Christ, that's terrific! I knew they'd come to their senses eventually; nobody could seriously suspect you of murder."

"Thanks for your confidence, George." Joe set his spoon down and wiped his mouth. "But the fact is, all they've cleared me of is attacking Cat last night. So far as I know, I'm still the murder suspect with the most counts against him. And still unemployed."

"But they can't . . . We were sure it was all right now, Aaron and me both."

George was standing next to a floor lamp. Cat, her mind washed blank by beer and confession, stared up at him, inspecting his handsome face. Not very clean. Pink fading with his excitement, a gray-green underneath that reminded her of something. The clothes she was wearing, hospital greens. Nobody had beaten poor George up, but he looked sick, beaten. Beer might help him, too. And confession.

"He should confess," she said aloud.

"What?" Two voices, two staring faces.

"George. You can tell by looking at him, he did . . . something." She watched, watched his forehead go shiny with sudden sweat, watched his eyes widen and stare. "Killed?" she wondered aloud and watched his head shake slowly and then more rapidly.

"No! No, I didn't, I never would, no way!"

Maybe, maybe not. "Okay. But something. Let's see, what would it be that George might do that would make him feel so guilty? Something to do with his brother."

Now Joe was looking up, too, and George took a step back, and another, and dropped his keys as he backed into a chair.

"Keys," said Cat, peering at them as if they bore magical signs. "George had keys; he was a watchman or whatever. That's what George would do."

"No."

"George would sneak a sexy lady into big brother's office for a quick fuck. When the lady turned up dead, George wouldn't tell anyone, but he'd be very very worried. And ashamed. Wouldn't you, George?"

Embarrassment was probably required of her, or at least acute discomfort. Cat listened to George's whine and Joe's angry roar, but found her own emotions unwilling to participate. Off duty. Besides, the whole thing had a rehearsed quality, same-old-family-fight. Quietly, quietly she edged from the floor to the couch, pushed herself to her feet. When Joe broke off in midbellow to reach for her, she brushed his hand away. "I'm going to the bathroom, thank you, and I believe I can do it myself."

"It wasn't *my fault*," George was insisting when she returned; he was sitting on a hassock holding his bottle of beer in both hands. "You saw how she was that night, shaking her boobs and twitching her ass all over the place. Burns and I were sitting on our bikes talking about it when she came out, and I bet him a six-pack I could nail her."

"You bet . . . ?" The words died, as if Joe's throat had clogged.

"Well, shit, Joey, we were just kidding around. Anyway, I followed her to campus and caught up with her in the parking lot of the computer science building."

"Where you had a job that you got on my recommendation," snapped Joe. "And presumably keys, which as I remember you're supposed to turn in when you go off duty."

"Look, Joey, I had in mind going somewhere nice and private, like her place. But she was determined to sneak a bomb into this guy's program, and she was very pissed at you. She just wasn't much interested in my moves until she found out that I had my keys on me and knew your password." He shrugged and took a gurgling swallow of beer.

"But it was you who made love to Ilona on my couch?"

"She let me fuck her on your couch, like a tip to the door-

184

man, wham bang, then she rolled me off and buttoned up her blouse and put her pants on." He cast a sideways glance at Cat. "Sorry. So help me God, Joey, she was okay when I left her; she was sitting at your desk combing her hair and she didn't even look up when I closed the door."

"And were you planning to tell anyone about this, ever?" Joe's voice was harsh. "Did you have a schedule, like, 'If they arrest Joe I'll confess, or if Joe gets convicted I'll confess, or maybe, if poor old Joey is sentenced to more than ten years I'll confess'?"

George huddled over his knees and looked miserable. "I was going to the cops, Joey; I made up my mind this morning." He dropped his head onto his crossed forearms. "*Jesus*, I was scared; I'm really scared of going to jail."

A long, heavy silence, until finally George muttered, "Yeah, I know what you both think," and lifted his head. "Joey, did you ever happen to notice all the grown-up places are taken in this family? Mama's in charge; she doesn't need any help, just somebody to pet. And ol' Joe's got the big brother slot; been holding down a job since he was twelve and he'll take care of things, don't worry; steady as a rock, just like his father. Here's the role for Georgy: he can look pretty and wag his tail."

Poor poor baby, thought Cat, but she managed to keep her mouth firmly shut. Joe shoved his hands into his hip pockets, rocked back on his heels, and fixed a level gaze on his brother, whose face was washed with sudden color as he stared back.

"So okay, I'm not much of a man by your standards," he said with a half shrug and a failed grin. "Not even by my own, if I had any. It's not a whole lot of fun being a coward, Joey. What do you want me to do?"

"What you should have done a week ago," Joe said in even tones. "Get on your bike and hustle downtown to see Chief Gutierrez."

"Now? Don't you think it's getting pretty late?" George glanced at the window, then at his watch.

"Police don't work eight-hour days," Joe told him. "Besides, it might be a good idea for you to get to him before somebody else does. Suppose Aaron Burns remembers your bet and decides the police should know about it?"

"Oh, Aaron knows the whole story, but he wouldn't rat on his buddy. Besides, he needs me, or he's never going to make it through basic algebra," George added. "Hey, maybe you'd come along downtown, give me a little moral support?"

"Sorry, George, not this time. I won't leave Cat alone."

George turned a hopeful glance on Cat, who stared calmly, silently back until he flushed and looked away. Damn right, she thought. And say hello to Chief Gutierrez for me. For us.

As George sighed and put on an expression of queasy resolution, she picked up her beer mug and then set it down again. She was pleasantly drowsy, her aches and pains buffered by what she suspected was just the right amount of alcohol. Be dumb to push it.

CHAPTER 20

Gutierrez obviously figured him for just another old fart who couldn't cut it anymore. Hank Svoboda took a swig of lukewarm bitter coffee and set the stained mug back in its gimbal-mounted holder. He resisted the urge to plant his booted foot harder against the pickup's accelerator; head-on a lumber truck in the fog, and his daughter and grandbabies would go hungry.

Vince might even be right; can't have cops going after suspects with a tire iron, or even wanting to. Funny thing, that a man should get angrier when he started to get old. Svoboda blinked in a patch of sunlight and turned his attention to the narrow green valley around him, the Anderson Valley. Nice little towns in here, not much fog. Cool down and ease off and talk, that's what Vince wanted him to do.

He had picked Philo as a logical jumping-off place because it was the first town Aaron Burns had mentioned. Svoboda pulled his truck into the gas station in that tiny town, put fifteen gallons of regular in his left tank, and got himself an early-morning Coke. No one at the station remembered anything about a Nancy Burns. No one in the small post office either, nor in the hardware store. But the store's owner suggested checking with old Mrs. Zimmer, and she remembered.

"Started out a bunch of women and a flock of kids, and they bought the old Loeller place west of here, maybe fifteen years ago. Take a little applejack in your coffee; it's my grandfather's recipe and can do you no harm whatsoever." A straight, spare old woman with a curly halo of white hair, she looked seventy and was probably, Svoboda thought, well into her eighties. "Two, three years later, two of the women and their kids left, and three men moved in, with *their* kids. It was the children that worried me."

"Misbehave, did they?"

"They didn't go to school. They didn't go *anywhere*. I complained to the county authorities, but they said this Ms. Burns had a teaching credential, and the children seemed healthy. One social worker said I was too old to understand alternative life-styles. I told her that four or five unrelated adults and maybe a dozen children living in that old three-room farmhouse wasn't a life-style, it was rural squalor. She said that for an old lady I had a very dirty mind."

Nancy Burns had finally left the communal farm some ten

years ago in the company of two men and six or seven children . . . headed, Mrs. Zimmer heard later, for Garberville. Nancy had pulled a battered Airstream trailer with an aged Cadillac sedan, and the men had traveled in an old school bus. Armed with this information and a bottle of applejack, Svoboda drove out of the Anderson Valley and headed north. In Garberville he found a police chief since retired who remembered Nancy Burns, her Airstream, and her companions.

"Whole bunch of them more or less camped out on a derelict farm. What they'd do, they'd leave the little kids on the farm, with one of the older ones babysitting, and the rest of the crew would go back in the woods where they were raising dope. Up here, we cooperate with the D.A. and the Feds when they come in. Otherwise, we generally don't mess with these people unless they mess with us.

"But this bunch kept catching folks' attention. Kids didn't go to school, or at least not very often. Then there was a couple of big boys out there playing patrol with shotguns, and they ventilated a tourist's nice new Mercedes when the fella drove up their driveway to ask directions. So we had to go clean the place out. Found two little kids who'd been kidnapped by their daddy. Found a pregnant fourteen-year-old. The Airstream lady's kid was probably the shooter, but he was only thirteen and we couldn't prove it, so we let them go. I heard they went to Dos Rios."

Backwards. Shit, he hated going backwards. But it was only fifty miles. Lunch first, he decided, and stopped in a coffee shop for a large hamburger, a plateful of home-fried potatoes, and another Coke.

By two P.M. he had left the highway and was piloting his rattling pickup along a bumpy road between two stony bluffs, a rock-bottomed river on one side. Chain-link fences, No Trespassing signs with the silhouette of a long gun be-

188

hind the letters. Dogs lying across driveways or pacing along fences, Dobermans and Rottweilers and one enormous mastiff. Finally he gave up on finding a friendly face and pulled to a stop before a heavy gate plastered with signs. No Trespassing. Trespassers Will Be Shot. Dogs. Honk Horn and Do Not Leave Car. Christ, he thought, and honked. Maybe after they shot him they'd let him call Gutierrez to say that he was on a thin and probably pointless but kind of interesting trail.

In fact, behind the barricades lurked a Pentecostal minister and his wife. The Burns woman and her mean-tempered son had lived in the area briefly, had even come to church for a while. Then the woman had taken up with one of those gangsters growing immoral crops out in the hills. When he, in his position as pastor, spoke to the son about the mother's behavior, the boy knocked him down.

"Miz Burns come by right after that to apologize," said the bony old man, shaking his head. "I do believe she had a wish to be saved. But like most women she needed the rule of a man, and she couldn't seem to come by a good one. I told her to seek Christian guidance from our church in Weaverville, from our brother Pastor Veach."

Weaverville! thought Svoboda, as he rattled his dusty way back toward Highway 101. Sweet Jesus, Weaverville was, what, a hundred miles north and another hundred miles east, unless you were a crow. He guided the old truck with absent-minded care, trying to decide what he should do next. Interesting story: female, maybe lesbian, farm to rampantly heterosexual dope farm with a fling at a church or two along the way. With a boy, apparently her only child, who grew large and mean and carried a shotgun.

At the highway Svoboda stopped at a gas station to get himself another Coke, then headed back for Garberville. He'd make some phone calls from there, and maybe look up an old navy buddy. Jake Delucca ran an air charter service with a couple of little Cessnas. If Weaverville was necessary, be a lot nicer to fly there than drive.

"Joe, I feel good," Cat insisted when she limped into the kitchen midmorning Wednesday. "I borrowed another T-shirt, okay? Just what I needed; it's not tight and it's not green."

"Sit down and I'll scramble you some eggs." Joe followed her to the table and set a glass of tomato juice before her. "Tell you what, I'll have George bring you something from downtown, maybe a sundress? He has a better eye for things like that than I have."

"That would be nice. Something that hangs easy. Not green. What happened with George?"

"He called late last night, breathing hard and probably dripping sweat. Gutierrez grilled him, according to George, for hours. I almost felt sorry for him; Vince Gutierrez angry makes a man want to stand straight and tuck it all in tight."

"But he let him go."

Joe nodded. "He's on the list, like the rest of us."

"And what's in the paper?"

"Nothing personal about you or about Jimmy Three," he assured her and set a steaming plate on the table. "Toast in a minute."

"Then where *is* the paper?"

He sighed, retrieved it from a stack beside the door. "You really don't want to see this picture." After a moment he set it beside her plate. The two of them, Joe and Cat, stood beside the van, with Eddie Riley's face peering down at them. Cat looked like a battered child about to burst into tears; Joe wore a black frown on his unshaven face as he stretched a muscled arm toward her.

Cat gasped, then giggled. "'Ooooh, Daddy, don't hit me

again.' Let's find that photographer. I want to throw a slug at him."

"Or a lawsuit," said Joe glumly. "The story doesn't say much, just that you occupy a cottage belonging to Dr. Joseph Mancuso of Shasta Road, and so forth, and were attacked while you slept last night; police working on several leads."

"Maybe I should call the paper and tell them about Jimmy Three."

"No."

She nodded and sighed. "Has Chief Gutierrez found him? Or do you think he's looking?"

"I think he's looking, but he hasn't called this morning. I've put an . . ." The phone rang, she started, and he shook his head at her. "I've put an answering machine on it."

She started again as Joe's recorded voice announced that he was unavailable but would appreciate a message. A brief silence and then Ed Berggren identified himself. "Mancuso. I'm beginning to think I made a mistake about you. For the time being anyway, you can forget the job offer." Click.

"Joe, were you really planning to go to work for that gringo sumbeesh?"

"He'd made me something of an offer, which I was planning to refuse with thanks. I guess he saw the paper."

The phone rang and they both turned to stare at it. Another ring, Joe's message, and then, "Dr. Mancuso, this is Madalyn Stanley, from Dean Schwartz's office. In light of the amount of media attention the campus is presently receiving, the dean feels it would be advisable for you to avoid your office entirely until further notice and to refrain from any contact with your former students. Thank you."

"That wasn't a person, that had to be a robot," said Cat. "Built in Japan and learned English there, too."

"She was probably quoting Schwartz exactly; that's the way he talks."

Cat pushed her nearly empty plate away. "I think this is worse than just answering the phone. Next thing, I'll hear Jimmy Three asking if I'm busy tonight. In fact," she went on as Joe moved to turn the speaker off, "why are we here, in the middle of all this shit? We were going to the mountains, remember?"

"Cat, I don't think Gutierrez will let me leave town. And I don't think you're in shape for the mountains, not quite yet."

"I'm not in shape for anything; I'm useless." Cat blinked hard, sniffed once. "Well, nothing better to do, I guess I'll take my electric wheelchair out on the sidewalk and run down a few pedestrians."

Vince Gutierrez drained the Orange-Crush can and tossed it toward a wastebasket half-full of Styrofoam cups. "Okay, I'm out of here in fifteen minutes; Meg and I are driving to Santa Rosa to talk with Lisa Haffner. Mendenhall, would you set up frequent patrols by Mancuso's place and by the Burnses' place for tonight? And whoever you send, tell them not to be aggressive about it; Mal Burns is yelling harassment and Joe Mancuso is ready to blow."

"Right. Anything from Arizona on deKalb?"

"The Pima County sheriff has had a warrant out on de-Kalb for more than two months. He roughed up a Corralitos girl, claimed he thought she was a prostitute. She has a lot of angry brothers, so deKalb disappeared. Deputy Obregon thinks the family, Morrison and his wife, are hiding him. DeKalb has an arrest record back to his high school days, in Corralitos and later in Tucson, violence and drunk driving and drug dealing; no convictions.

"And we've called the ranch several times," Gutierrez

went on with a frown. "A maid answers the phone, says the family is away, and that's *all* she'll say. So far as Cat Smith is concerned, I think Mancuso will prevent another attack on her."

"What about young Mancuso? George?" asked Kuisma. "Shall we pick him up again?"

"For what, fornication and cowardice?"

Bob Englund grunted as he let his back-tilted chair settle to all four feet. "George Mancuso has an IQ somewhere around 150 and made straight A's when he bothered to go to school. And he's about as much use in the world as a flea. But no gaps have turned up; nobody's memory suddenly improved. You remember that Georgy did have a date on June 9; he met the girl as she got off work not much more than an hour after Annie Willis was found. I talked to her again, and she insists he seemed perfectly normal. Whatever that is for George."

"Aaron Burns corroborates George's story about Ilona," said Gutierrez, "about sitting outside Mancuso's house after the party and betting on George's chances. Burns says he guesses he owes George a six-pack. Val, nothing yet on Grodnik?" he asked before his listeners could comment.

"Nothing," said Kuisma. "And I feel really bad about this; I must be doing it wrong. The only thing I can see . . ." He paused, gave a palms-out shrug. "I'm beginning to think either he's in L.A., just went zoom down the freeway the night he disappeared. Or he's dead.

"Suppose, see, Grodnik's our rapist. And he's crazy, we know that. So he attacks Cat Smith and gets chased off and then comes to realize that he's nearly killed his friend. So he maybe kills himself? Anyway, I'll do hospitals and morgues and like that again tomorrow, on a wider circle. And the Coast Guard."

"Fine." Gutierrez rose, opened his desk drawer, and

pulled out a manila envelope. "Pictures of all our suspects and the other band members and of several of you as well, to show Lisa Haffner. Wish me luck. Oh, Duane, be sure to stick around until Hank calls again. He's out in the woods somewhere, looking up background on Aaron Burns. I'll see you all tomorrow."

CHAPTER 21

"I don't have anything to fix for dinner." Joe slammed the door of the refrigerator. "Maybe we should just go out to eat."

Cat, playing solitaire at the kitchen table, eyed her reflection in the glass of the open deck door for a moment before lifting her glance to Joe's. "I don't think so."

"Ah. No, of course not. I'll go to the market. Could you manage a steak, if it's a very tender steak?"

"Hey, Joey, I sure as hell could." George came around the corner of the house, stepped through the open door, and gave the two of them a tentative smile. "Sorry, I should have knocked."

"True," said Joe. "You look harried, little brother."

"Every place I go, I get the feeling people are looking at me. In a different way from usual, you know; none of this 'Who's that handsome guy?' stuff. More like, 'Who's that creep?' The police aren't supposed to repeat what a citizen tells them, are they? Wouldn't that be a violation of my civil rights or something?"

"Policemen probably gossip like everybody else."

"Well, shit. Maybe I'll just move back to San Francisco. Cat, this was the best I could do for you." He set a large white paper bag on the table. "Not a lot to choose from in this dump, but I think they'll fit."

Cat slid two tissue-wrapped bundles from the bag, folded the tissue open. One dress was simply a tube of rose pink crinkly cotton gathered onto a piece of elastic; the other, made of slightly heavier fabric striped in varied blues, had shoulder straps that buttoned.

She stared at the garments in silence, lifted a fold of the pink stuff and let it fall, traced a blue stripe with one finger. "I haven't had a dress since . . . I don't remember when I wore a dress. I'll look funny."

"No, you won't," George said cheerfully. "You'll look fine. Go try them on."

"Not yet. Not until I've had a shower. Thank you." She tucked the paper tight, put the packages back in their bag.

"My pleasure." George opened the refrigerator, found an open carton of milk, and tipped it to his mouth. "Joe, I have this little problem you could help me with. No, I didn't do anything, I swear," he added quickly as Joe's face darkened. "See, Aaron's dad booted me out."

"*Booted* you? Mal Burns?"

"Well, not physically, but for a minute or two I did think he was gonna get tough about it, and I had a vision of myself back in jail for hitting this older guy."

"You should probably revise your definition of 'older,'" Joe suggested. "Why did he ask you to leave?"

George shrugged. "He was drunk, for one thing. First time I've seen him take more than a beer or two; he generally prefers grass to booze. He said I was a butterfly brain and a moral imbecile." His voice rose, aggrieved. "He said Aaron needed to study instead of chasing around with a jerk whose brains were all in his cock. Now that I'm remembering it, I wish I *had* hit him!"

"What was Aaron doing during this lecture?"

George shrugged. "Listening, watching. I've been thinking Aaron was repressed, from too long out in the woods, but I guess he's just a dull dog all the way. Anyway, Joey, I am once again without a bed; okay if I crash on your couch?"

Joe shook his head. "I'm using the couch."

George raised one eyebrow. "Sorry, I thought you . . . well, look, maybe . . ."

"Joe isn't sleeping with me until I look better," said Cat.

"Cat!"

"Sorry, just kidding." She disciplined her mouth into a straight line, reaching across the table to touch his arm. "But *I* wouldn't want to wake up beside this face."

"You need a bed to yourself, not somebody rolling and snoring beside you." Joe's voice was stiff. "And we need food. I'll let George stay here with you while I go . . ."

"No!" Cat took a deep breath, loosed her sudden grip on his arm, sat back. "Sorry. Go ahead, I'll be fine."

"No, George can go."

The phone on Gutierrez's desk buzzed, and Duane Mendenhall picked up the receiver. "Mendenhall here."

"Duane. This is Hank Svoboda. Vince not around?"

"He's in Santa Rosa, talking to Haffner. He asked me to cover. Hansen's downtown having supper with the mayor, explaining our traffic and patrol plans for the Festival."

"Good for Hansen. Anything going on up there I should know about?"

"Minor stuff. No new murders or assaults; nothing going down on the old ones. Just watching, watching everybody. Goddamned boring."

"Okay. I'm in, let's see, yeah, Garberville. Jesus, I spent

half the day running my truck up and down 101, hard to remember just where I am." He outlined the information he'd turned up earlier. "Then I stopped here and spent an hour on the phone, just finished talking to this reverend in Weaverville who knew Nancy Burns. She came to town seven, eight years ago with a man and her kid, and the guy got shot, killed; apparently a dope deal gone bad. She stayed on for maybe a year with the kid; he was sixteen or seventeen. Then she met a man at the church and married him, moved on up to Weed.

"That's where I'm headed now; an old navy buddy is gonna fly me up there, then we'll fly back tomorrow. Tell Vince I'm spending a little money, saving some time and my kidneys."

This is cruel, thought Meg Halloran. And it's not going to accomplish anything; she simply can't do it. Lisa Haffner's brown hair stood up in stray wisps, and freckles made greenish splotches on the skim-milk pallor of her face. The girl shifted her weight on the sofa, set her feet flat; one foot promptly began to shake, its heel playing a muted tattoo against the floor. She clutched her knees, pressed them together.

Gutierrez bent over the low table laying out photographs one by one. Probably not a cocktail table here, not in a Baptist minister's study, but a coffee table. It sounded like a slow card game: slap, space, breathe, slap. Lisa was looking; she was putting her eyes on each picture the way Meg's mother used to put a spitty finger on a hot iron.

"See, I didn't really *see* him." The girl's voice was startling in the quiet room. "It was getting dark, and I was kinda sick; I really needed a ride and he looked like just an ordinary guy. Then he pulled me in the back and I thought he wanted, you know, and there wasn't anything I could do; he was big and I was sick. But he didn't do that, not then; he just started beating on me and saying bad things."

"What did he say?" asked Gutierrez softly.

"Bad words. I didn't listen. I was just saying, 'I love you Jesus, save me Jesus,' and then he hit my mouth and said shut up so I squeezed my eyes shut and kept saying it in my head real loud: I love you Jesus, save me Jesus. And he did." She lifted her head. "See, I'm alive, Jesus saved me. Praise the Lord."

Gutierrez scooped the photographs into a stack and got to his feet. "Thanks, Lisa. If you should remember anything, please call me. Two other girls weren't saved, you know. And a third was beaten Monday night."

"I'm sorry," she said in a quavering voice, and the Rev. Art Burrus, sitting beside her, patted her hand.

"Lisa and I have prayed over this, Chief Gutierrez. And we'll continue to pray."

"Lisa." Meg sat forward and waited for the girl to meet her eyes. "What do you think of as ordinary?"

"Well, he wasn't black or Mexican." Lisa glanced at Gutierrez and went scarlet. "And he wasn't a hippie after all," she added quickly. "He didn't have long hair or a beard."

"What made you think he might be a hippie?" asked Meg.

"I don't know. It was just the van, I guess."

"Van. A hippie van. Did it have pictures on it or something like that?"

"Isn't that dumb, I just now remembered what kind of van it was." The girl smiled her pleasure at being some help after all. "No pictures, but it was one of those old Volkswagen things hippies always drove, real old with dents and stuff."

"A Volks van. Do you remember what color?"

She shook her head. "Dark, fairly dark, maybe green or blue. Well, except for the door. The big door on the passenger side, the one that slides. Somebody must have hit him, and he had to put a new door on, and it was light, like tan."

"Not a lot of information, for the pain and effort," Meg said as she settled into the Porsche and fastened her shoulder harness.

"The guy who said every little bit helps was probably a cop," said Gutierrez grimly. "Unfortunately, the only Volks van we've turned up belongs to Animal Fare and I remember it as tan and not recently painted. Son of a *bitch*, I want to find this guy!"

"Or guys."

"Or guys." He started the engine, eased the little car out into traffic. "Now there's a restaurant not far from here. Let's have a drink and some dinner and let the evening commute work itself out."

CHAPTER 22

The sun banished the last few patches of morning haze and the temperature on the deck edged past warm and headed for hot. Two leftover pieces of toast curled their edges up on a small plate; a single fried egg congealed on a larger one. A blue jay screamed hungry threats from the nearest tree, but he knew Arthur and would not swoop down while the cat was in sight.

Which he wouldn't be for long; he had already slid from Cat's lap to the cushion beside her and would soon abandon the lounge entirely in search of shade. Cat stroked the wedge-shaped head, marveling at the precision of nature's design scheme. Dark orange against light, from delicate tracery on the face to broad sweeps across either flank, Arthur had matching sides, like the two wings of a butterfly. Magical.

Arthur said "grrmph" and rolled off the edge of the lounge to disappear beneath it. Cat slid lower against the sun-warmed cushions, let her hands fall to her sides. There was a steamy, damp-earth smell from the garden and a rich sweet-ness from petunias massed in a planter box. The jay had gone; something smaller twittered nearby. Nearer still, Joe's breathing was deep and slow, with a faint rasp; he'd be snor-ing in another minute.

She turned just her head to look at Joe. For the past two nights he had caught sleep in snatches on the couch; she'd often sensed his watchful presence when her own sleep thinned. Even now his pose was less than relaxed, with his pillowed head straight, arms crossed on his chest, hands tucked under his biceps. Men's arms were wonderful to look at, Joe's especially: all hard purpose in the forearm, with its heavy planes of bone, and above it the reserve power of the massive biceps. Would it wake him, she wondered, if she were to reach across to run one finger very gently over the silky brown skin of his upper arm?

Joe's head turned and his eyes opened.

"Hi. I guess you're vain," she told him.

"What?"

"I was merely looking at you and thinking your arm was beautiful, and you woke up. What could that be but vanity?"

200

"Lust," he said, and then yawned widely, and stretched.

"Yeah, I can see that. Joe, I've been lying around so long I'm twitchy, and I'm not talking about lust. Can I work on the paint-stripping or something?"

He yawned again, sat up, felt around under the lounge for his sneakers. "If *you* get started, the six months' work I had in mind around here won't last three."

"You'll be able to get back to real work soon."

He concentrated on a shoestring. "Depends on your definition. I think maybe I'm becoming a hippie, twenty-five years too late." The other shoe and the second shoestring. "I can design a good computer. I can build a good computer. I can program it, talk to it, play games with it, teach it to . . . whatever. But it's just a machine; I don't love it, didn't even when I was in school."

He stood up and stretched again. "And now they have taken my machine away, or my place as its acolyte, and I'm not sad. Maybe that's sad. Come on, let's go burn off a little paint."

There was a two-beat rap, then the door opened and Mendenhall stuck his head in. Gutierrez gestured him in and returned his own attention to the telephone. "I'm sorry, Mr. Mayor. I realize it's inconvenient and discouraging, but an arrest is *not* in the immediate future." A lengthy drone from the receiver, and then, "No, sir, I don't plan to arrest Dr. Mancuso again soon. The police in Tucson are holding a man we're interested in, but I'm afraid that information is not for release."

Gutierrez closed his eyes and pressed his lips tight for another long moment. "Yes, sir, unless something breaks on this particular case, I'll be there. Two P.M., Port Silva Municipal Park."

"So His Honor Mayor Wirkkala wants an arrest yesterday,

and he also wants his chief of police on hand for the opening of the Art Festival. Hope you've got your boots shined," said Mendenhall as he dropped heavily into a chair. His face was red and dust-streaked, his hair rumpled; half-moons of sweat darkened the armpits of his uniform shirt.

"You can see your face in them," Gutierrez assured him.

"Tucson has deKalb?" At Gutierrez's nod, Mendenhall grinned. "Need a volunteer to go get him?"

"I think I'll go myself tomorrow. A Lieutenant Morales in Tucson is questioning him, and it seems he'll be there awhile. The family is not pressing for bail, figuring he's safer in jail than he would be on the street. So far deKalb refuses to say *where* he's been for the past two months, except to insist that he wasn't in Port Silva."

"Well, it'd probably be too hot for me in Tucson, anyway. In fact, it's hot as hell *here* today. There's not a parking place left in town; I've got two men at the Art Center sending people out to the shuttle lots. And I need a man out there, too; be hell to pay if the tourists get back to their cars tonight and find they've been broken into. Or ain't there at all."

"Svoboda should be back before long," Gutierrez said.

"Okay, but where's Kuisma? I need him downtown; kid manages to move people around without pissing them off."

"He called in, said he'd just talked with the Coast Guard. A fishing boat took a body from the water this morning, down around Point Arena, that might fit the description of Lawrence Grodnik. Kuisma was going down to check."

"Hey, what about Kuisma's idea that Grodnik committed suicide?" With a grunt of effort, Mendenhall got to his feet. "Tying the murders up nice and tight, and leaving the whole force free to direct traffic and bust dopers and drunks."

Gutierrez shrugged. "Nice. Probably too neat."

"Yeah. Well, when Kuisma gets back, I could use him."

"Mendenhall."

The sergeant turned smartly at the door and stood straighter. "Yessir?"

"Forget about the guy in Tucson. Just assume that there's a murderer running loose, a real bastard who is not careful but who seems to be very lucky. Remind everyone, every single uniform."

"Yessir."

Assigned to priming rather than paint-stripping because the little propane tank was too heavy for her sore shoulder, Cat headed for the cottage in search of her oldest shirt. George, who had slept there last night, would surely be awake by now. George was in fact standing at the curb beside the borrowed van talking with Aaron Burns. Buddies again, thought Cat, the dull dog and the . . . What was it Aaron's father had called George? Moral imbecile.

George muttered something about keys and set off for the house. Aaron saw Cat and grinned at her; she nodded and stepped into the cottage, closing the front door behind her and then wishing for a moment that she hadn't. No one had put the big table back in its place, and there was a dark stain on the wooden floor that she knew had to be from her blood. She breathed deeply, wondered if she caught a hint of sweetish smoke. Breathed again and decided that the room smelled a little like George, like coconutty hair conditioner and beer. Three empty brown bottles beside the bed, and he could pick them up himself.

In the closet she discovered a forgotten garment, a pair of overalls she had fallen heir to when they shrank too much for Moose. Still plenty roomy for her, certainly, and she could wear just a tank top underneath. She changed quickly, went out the back door, turned as someone called her name.

Two vans at the curb now. The second shuddered to silence, old clanky sewing machine, and all of the Animals spilled out, looking washed and pressed and barbered. All except Antelope.

"Hey, Cat." Moose took her shoulders carefully between his big hands and leaned forward to kiss her; Badger followed with a cool brush of dry lips, Squirrel with a hug and a hearty smack. No. Walt, and Bruce, and Danny. Eddie Riley stood to one side, frowning.

"What's up?" she asked. "Are you going someplace?"

"Hey, Cat." Danny grinned and tipped his head as he looked her over. "Pretty good, you look pretty good. Yeah, we're losing the old farm; Badger's mom has a buyer. So we decided to head back to the Bay Area; we're leaving tomorrow morning. We stopped by to find out if you want to come along."

She managed a wavery version of his grin. "Thanks, but I don't think so. I like it here."

"I'm staying, too," said Eddie, with a shrug. "Got a room downtown, and a job. I'll probably visit you sometimes, if that's okay."

"What it is, Cat," said Walt, producing a duffle bag, "we brought you Antelope's stuff. His books and notebooks, and his tools and his flute. The sax, too; it's in the van. See, if he comes back to town, he'll know where to find you. And if . . ." Walt spread his hands sadly. "If he don't come back, he'd want you to have his stuff anyway."

". . . Maybe some cashew chicken and an order of sweet and sour spare ribs," Gutierrez told Dunnegan. "I don't care, whatever Johnny Wing can deliver right now."

"Never mind, Vince," called Svoboda from the front door. "I got some barbecue here, and some kind of interesting stuff to tell you."

"Go on in, I'll get Cokes," Gutierrez directed.

Svoboda spread newspaper for placemats and set out two thick packages whose wrappings bore greasy red smears. He dropped a handful of paper napkins on the desk as Gutierrez entered, then accepted a can of Coke and sat down with a sigh. His Levi's and shirt were wrinkled, his boots dusty, but his gray eyes were clear and bright.

"Sure would taste better with beer," Svoboda observed sadly as he unwrapped a corner of his sandwich and took a bite. "I was noticing the pictures," he remarked a moment later, gesturing to a fanned-out sheaf of photographs beside Gutierrez's blotter. "You getting set to go see Lisa Haffner?"

"I've been." Gutierrez scooped up the photos and dropped them into the center drawer of his desk.

"She didn't make anybody?"

"Nope." Gutierrez sank his teeth into the thick sandwich, tore off a chunk, chewed for a moment. "She says she didn't really look at him because she was too scared. He was just ordinary, not black or Mexican or a hippie. So, white guy, no beard, short hair—big and mean and more interested in beating than raping."

Svoboda grunted and Gutierrez worked on his sandwich for a few moments. "One thing. She's definite now that it was a Volks van, an old dented one. Dark, maybe green or blue, with an odd door; the door on the passenger side was white or light tan."

Svoboda frowned. "I don't remember seeing anything like that."

"I don't either, but we're sure as hell looking around." Gutierrez crumpled the greasy paper, wiped his mouth. "Now, what did you bring me besides a good sandwich?"

"Vince, I think we ought to take a real good 'nother look at Aaron Burns."

"Okay. Why?"

"Because he had a mean, rough time as a kid and got to

be a hard case practically before he hit his teens. He used to beat on his ma, and he maybe shotgunned, killed, a boyfriend of hers.''

Gutierrez's eyes narrowed to slits and he said softly, ''Go on.''

''Last two days I been tracking Nancy Burns all over God's creation, and what I find out, she was a lady looking real hard for the way to go. She tried plain dirt-farming; she tried dope-growing; seems like she tried sex with women and sex with men and sex with groups. She tried religion, several kinds. She lived in communes; she lived solitary in the woods in a tent. Most times she took her kid along; now and then she parked him with other folks.''

Svoboda sighed, leaned back in his chair, and lit a cigarette. ''By the time Aaron was thirteen or so, he was big as a man and working like one. His ma says he did the heavy work, drove the machines, smoked and drank what he liked. Chased off men who bothered her.

''And then she'd find a new man and move him in, and it's back to little boy for sonny. Nancy Burns was real straightforward about this part, says she was a wicked woman and a bad mother. She lives in a kind of church compound, just outside Weed. Fundamentalist Christians and probably survivalists, I didn't inquire. Got two little kids now, and she moves fast when her husband says; only reason she talked to me is he told her she had to.''

Svoboda took a last long drag and butted his cigarette. ''The husband, name's Melvin Earl Archer, he says Aaron had been working outside and coming back and making trouble ever since Archer and Nancy got married. The men in the church voted to boot him out for good two years ago, the last time he took his fists to his ma. Archer also told me— this was after he'd sent Nancy out of the room—he told me Aaron shot her last boyfriend, guy I'd heard was killed in a

206

dope deal. He says Nancy won't admit it, and the law never found it out, but that's what happened."

Gutierrez drew a long breath and expelled it slowly through pursed lips. "When was that? The killing?"

"Five years ago, in Weaverville. I talked to a minister there yesterday, and two cops, but they didn't figure the kid for it, not at the time. They remember it as bad blood between drug types."

"Okay, Hank, let's go pick him up. Don't bother about the uniform, but get your side arm—" Gutierrez broke off and instructed whoever had just knocked to come in.

"Chief Gutierrez." Val Kuisma wore a spotless uniform and shiny black boots. His tan had a greenish undertone and his eyes were somber.

"Val. Was it Grodnik?"

"Yessir. It'll take awhile to get fingerprints, but I'm sure. There just aren't that many guys that big, and he had that kinky light brown hair I remembered, long and real thick."

"No indication what had happened to him?"

Sweat glistened on Kuisma's forehead. "No, sir, apart from what fish and water did. Coast Guard says there are no obvious injuries inconsistent with a plain drowning death. We'll have to wait for the postmortem. But Grodnik didn't beat up Cat Smith Monday night; everybody is sure he's been in the water longer than two days, more like four or five."

"Good work, Val," said Gutierrez. "You can do the paperwork later. Mendenhall needs you downtown, to help with directing traffic."

"Yessir."

"Wait a minute, Val," said Svoboda. "You're a noticin' kind of fella, might be you could help us with something else. We're looking for a dark old Volkswagen van with one light door, the sliding door on the passenger side. That ring any bells with you?"

"Wait, I saw one someplace. Yeah, out at Dr. Mancuso's house. The night we went out there after Cat Smith got beaten up. It was parked on the street just beyond his carport; his truck was in the carport."

Gutierrez frowned. "I had Mancuso checked out when we impounded his truck. He doesn't own any other vehicles."

"It wasn't his. I asked him about it later, and he said he hadn't gotten around to returning it yet; he'd borrowed it from Mal Burns while we had his truck."

CHAPTER 23

"Sal, Sal, my heart is broke today, broke in two forever when they laid you in the clay." The song was a favorite of her grandfather's; he had loved sad or gory tales set to bouncy melodies. Cat dipped her brush in dark brown primer and finished the top of the window frame in three smooth strokes. Her progress was slow, with the small brush, but it was progress. And the sky was blue, and the sun was warm, hot even, on her back. And Jimmy Three was in jail in Tucson; the sergeant had told her so when she called.

"I would give creation to be walkin' with my gal," she sang, "strollin' down through Laramie with Snag-tooth Sal." She had primed one double-casement frame, had perhaps half an hour's work to do on this one. Then she'd put the gear away and have a nice long shower. By the time she was through, Joe should be back.

Another dip, tap, another sweep. Cat searched her repertoire for a love song, grinned to herself, and took a deep breath. "My lover was a logger," she caroled, "there's none like him today. If you poured whiskey on it, he'd eat a bale of hay."

"You sure know some weird songs," said a voice from below the scaffold. Cat started and felt primer splash on her overalled leg. "You must be getting tired," George went on. "Anything I can get you?"

Yes, get me Joe. "No, thank you," she replied, "unless you want to clean the brushes when I'm finished."

"Actually, I'd kind of hate to get dirty," said George, and looked down complacently at his blue madras shirt and off-white jeans. "Soon as Joe gives Mama a good lunch and gets her settled at the Whale Watch Inn, she'll send him home and expect to see me, all spruced up."

Cat closed her teeth on a rude remark about mothers who flew to town with an hour's notice expecting to be met and wined and dined.

Watching her face, George grinned. "The old girl's not so bad; she just likes to make a fuss now and then. If she stays long enough so you get to meet her, all you have to remember is to act like a lady. Mama's big on ladies."

An unladylike reply was drowned in a burst of engine noise from the street, and the two of them watched Aaron Burns's bike come to a gravel-scattering halt in the driveway. "Now what?" muttered George.

"George, it's fine with me if you want to go someplace; Joe will be back before long."

"No way, lady! My brother may have peculiar taste in chicks, but he's my brother, and he very definitely said I was to stay with you until he got home." He gave her a nod and then ambled off toward the street, hands in his hip pockets.

She had slowed her work during the exchange with George, and her shoulder was beginning to stiffen. She finished the window less neatly than its fellow, pausing now and then to wipe smears of brown from the glass; then she climbed wearily down from the scaffolding and set off for the cottage.

Aaron and George were leaning on their bikes, talking in low voices. At her approach they fell silent. "Hello, Aaron," she said. "George, I've quit for the day. I'm going to have a shower."

Cat hung the overalls in the closet and realized with mild irritation that her dresses, her beautiful new dresses that she had not yet worn, were in the house. Living in two places at once was awkward and confusing. Maybe she should move everything to the house; did she want to do that? Did Joe want her to?

Anyway, this was the best shower, much nicer than the tub-shower in the house. She closed the glass door and dreamily watched it fog over as hot hot water pounded down.

She had toweled her hair and was combing it when she heard a thump from somewhere else in the cottage. "George?" She pulled on panties, yanked a T-shirt over her head, and hurried into the outer room. "George, I'd like a little privacy if you don't mind!" The only answer was a rustle of movement from the walk-in closet, where the light was burning.

"Hey! What do you think you're doing?" She pulled the closet door wider, shoved the few hanging clothes aside, and found herself face to face with Aaron. "What are you doing? Where's George?"

"We kinda agreed it was my turn, and ol' George decided to wait outside. This the stuff that belonged to that hippie flute player?"

"That's Antelope's. You have no right . . ." Cat closed her mouth and backed out of the closet. The overhead bulb threw heavy shadows on Aaron's face; she saw a rocky slab of forehead, broad, flaring nose, thrust-out lower lip with a slick shine. His eyes were mere glints under stubby lowered lashes. She caught the sour tang of sweat and an edge of something sweeter: pot?

"You have no right to be in here. Your turn at what?" She took slow steps back, toward the open front door.

He set the duffle bag down without taking his eyes from her face. "I saw your friends give you his stuff; thought I might take a look. Flutes are interesting." In a quick move he flanked her, moved between her and the front door, pushed it shut behind him.

"What's in there, besides the flute?" he asked softly. "Papers, notes? See, I remembered you said he writes. Wrote."

"Only music; he writes music. Songs." She was backing toward the kitchen now, making herself move slowly while nerves and muscles screamed for flight. Aaron the other night, not Jimmy Three? She could see his hands, his long-ish fingernails, and the skin crawled on her back. But what was this about Antelope? "Why?"

"No. What you said was he writes stories for songs, like about that bust in Berkeley. See, he was out there that night, playing his flute down by the bridge. I thought he might have written something about it." Aaron's face was smoothly bland as he followed her across the big room. "Crazy bastard, had me thinking *I* was crazy, you know? Like, I tossed her on the beach, and where'd she *go*? Then I saw him out at Miss Molly's; I mean, he *freaked* when he saw it on TV, where the body was found. And then he switched from sax to flute, so I knew for sure who he was. And *then* he took off, so— Hey!" He lunged, reaching, but she slid past

211

the stove and hit the screen door and nearly tripped over the step down.

Cat recovered her balance and spun to her left, to make for the street, but he cut her off easily and began another slow stalk. Where was George anyway, was he part of this, was he waiting somewhere behind her? She dropped her jaw to listen, to gulp deep breaths as she took one step, another.

Aaron grinned, shrugged. "Might as well take it easy; you're not going anywhere. And no need to yell, either; there's nobody home on the whole block. Everybody not at work's downtown at the Festival."

"Antelope is dead, isn't he?" Bright orange through a blur of tears, her canvas chair. She blinked and shook her head once, hard. Garden close behind; she stepped back and sideways as if her feet had memorized the ground. "You lump of shit, you killed him."

"Lady, lady, you oughtta watch who you're calling names! Anyway, I didn't, not exactly. He kept trying to outrun me, which was dumb because I had a lot more bike. So finally I got close, nudged him just a little touch; he gunned that Honda right off the cliff." Aaron flicked a long arm out; his fingers just missed her shoulder, and he sighed. "For all I know, the crazy bastard is still swimming."

In her mind's eye she saw the jumbled pile of logs beside the deck, close behind her now. She stepped sideways to skirt them, sensed their bulk and a splotch of color, Joe's old blue shirt on the ground where he must have dropped it. Aaron was standing still and watching her, half-smiling.

"You didn't have to kill Antelope," she said in a voice that wobbled. "He wouldn't have hurt you; he wouldn't hurt anyone."

"Come *on* now; I read in the paper where he hurt his own daddy. Not that I think offing your old man is such a bad idea," he remarked thoughtfully. "So what about it, you want to stop to give first aid to good ol' George?"

A keening sound that must have come from her, from between her clenched teeth as she stumbled backwards and snatched a look at the blue shirt. George was stretched out on his face beside the log pile; she saw slack limbs, splayed feet, a smear of red in fair hair. "What did you do to him?" she whispered.

"Ol' George fell down and hit his head on a log. You wouldn't think anybody as classy as ol' George would be so clumsy. I *think* he's still breathing. Tell you what, you want to check, I'll give you ten seconds, how's that?

"One," he drawled. She cast another hopeless look at George. The only way she could help him or herself was by getting away from here. "Two." Something dark and upright loomed at the edge of her peripheral vision: the corner of the shed. "Three." Between the shed and her cottage a grassy opening beckoned, green pathway to the low, thorn-armed fence and the empty street beyond. "Four." She glanced once more at George's motionless body, then darted the other way.

His left arm caught her, flung her back. She saw the next blow coming, a full swing with his right arm; the back of his hand met the side of her head and sent her crashing against the rough wood of the shed, to fall in its open doorway.

"Well, shit, that's not the most terrific place . . ." He bent swiftly, grabbed her by an arm and a leg, slung her inside. "What the hell, it's out of sight of the street."

Cat pushed herself from her belly to her hands and knees, got her feet under her, and lurched upright. Her head rang from his blow, her whole body was running with sweat; her own raw odor caught at her throat, sweat and fear.

For just a moment the board and batten walls were adobe,

the tin roof wavery with heat from the desert sun. She gulped air and tasted paint, damp soil, engines. Joe's shed, every inch of it familiar. Maybe ten feet square. Pegboard hung with tools on one wall, shelves on the other, workbench along the back wall, with two small windows there set high. The windows didn't open; she'd have to break the glass and she wouldn't get halfway through before Aaron caught her.

Aaron stood wide-legged in the doorway, a massive silhouette in a flood of sunlight. "So now I can finish what I started the other night," he growled. "You twitch around in little shorts with your tits bouncing, push yourself up against me on the bike. You're past due."

"I didn't, I didn't mean to." An old table stood across the center of the room, for potting; pots on top, and trowels and a small pruning knife. More pots underneath, a bag of potting soil, bundles of slim and fragile bamboo stakes. She huddled behind the table, gripped its edge with her left hand, curled her right around the handle of the knife. Rape wasn't the end of the world; women survived rape all the time. Her thumb tested the blade, thin but very sharp. She looked down and could barely see it through the glitter of tears; a wound from such a tiny thing would be a mosquito bite to someone Aaron's size.

"And that blond bitch," he said, speaking from low in his throat; "she sat there at dinner with her shirt unbuttoned and leaned over and said, 'Pass the salt,' like I was a goddamn gelding." He found the light switch, and the single bulb over the table blazed; his worn jeans did little to conceal a massive hard-on. "Took off her pants for old George, and then said, sure, she'd love a ride on my bike."

He stepped inside, rolling his shoulders and shaking his hands loose. "No," said Cat softly. Not fair not now you can't you set this up somehow didn't you some way you're in

214

jail they told me *not fair*! She pressed her thumb against the tiny blade and thought she heard her skin part to release a slippery smear of blood. Joe's tools on the wall, the sledge and the rake and the long-handled pruners closest. Toward the front the smaller things—wrenches, hammers, big pliers. She could lift and wield those, her hand knew them, but she'd have to come out from behind the table.

Aaron seized the edge of the table and tilted it quickly toward her, sending pots crashing around her feet. "Then it was no, who do you think you are, leave me alone. So I did, I left her alone for good."

And Antelope. And George. And me. And and and and. From behind the fragile barricade of the now-empty table, Cat did an instant's inventory of the left wall, floor-to-roof shelves of paint, brushes and rollers, putty and glue, cans of oil and transmission fluid. A big tin can of paint stripper, wonderfully caustic, and she would give anything to throw it into that glowering face, but it was the thick stuff, slow as glue. Near the door, a tin of lacquer thinner.

Aaron followed her glance, hawked, and spat. "Want to try for that, be my guest."

I'd like to try for it, and light it; I'd like to burn you to black bloody meat. Breathe, and think. On the top shelves were the power tools: drills, the little chain saw, the electric pruning shears. They were about as much use to her as the gluey stripper, with their long orange cords to be plugged in. Just hang on a minute, Aaron, while I get this thing ready to take your head off.

"One time I read in the paper that in Iran, if a woman gets a man excited, they punish *her*, they beat her. Sometimes they beat her to *death*." He seized the table and flung it sideways against the shelves, to set off a rattling spill of cans and tools. "See, it's not my fault if some dumb cunt waves it

215

in my face and I get a hard-on. I didn't ask to have that happen to me; it's not my *fault*."

Cat launched herself at the open door, but he caught her in midair, caught her left forearm and flung her back against the workbench. Her knife was gone, knocked from her hand; and she'd felt something snap in her left arm.

Aaron stood across the doorway with his head forward, eyes heavy-lidded in a face blank of expression. After a moment he extended his right hand, fingers curling inward in a slow beckoning motion. "Here, kitty kitty," he called softly.

Hard wooden edge of the bench against her spine, smell of grease from the vise, scarred oily wood under her exploring hand, and a clutter of small pieces of something. Metal. Carburetor parts, that accounted for the other, acrid smell; Joe was cleaning a used carburetor. Aaron's beckoning fingers mesmerized her, curling and curling. Thick fingers on broad meaty hands. She took a deep breath. Antelope had long, narrow fingers; she remembered how they'd felt gripping hers, linked fingers between their two chairs.

Aaron was moving toward her very slowly, knees bent. "Come on, kitty kitty," he whispered. "What does it matter anyhow? You're nothing, you know that? Less than nothing, all of you."

Cat's elbow bumped cold metal; she heard the slosh of liquid. Aaron took another step. She grabbed at the wall, pulled loose the heavy metal rake amid a rain of smaller tools. Aaron dodged, grunted, came fast at her with both hands out. She thrust the rake between his feet and he tripped and went down.

Roaring wordlessly, he rolled and reached for her. She threw herself up and back, crooked her arm around the pan and swept it sloshing forward, to drench his upturned face, his open eyes and gaping mouth, with carburetor cleaning fluid.

The roar was a high-pitched wail now, and the meaty hands clawed at his face, pawed his eyes as Cat leaped across his rolling body and bolted through the door. "Help!" he wailed and coughed and spat and coughed again. "Oh, God, my eyes! I can't see!"

Cat slammed the door shut, leaned all her weight against it. "Oh shit, oh shit," she muttered as the fingers of her left hand fumbled the padlock and nearly dropped it. Hasp in place, put the lock through with the other hand, there!

She didn't think George had moved. She knelt beside him, heard his slow breathing, touched the pulse point in his neck but couldn't find anything; her one good hand was shaky. Did his eyelids flutter? "Wait, George, okay? Just wait."

Phone in the cottage; she dialed the police, screamed that she needed a doctor and an ambulance right now! And Chief Gutierrez, and Joe Mancuso! She slammed the receiver down, grabbed a blanket from the bed, turned at the door, and ran back to her closet to kneel and pry up the loose board. Possum's gun.

Maybe George had moved; maybe his breathing was deeper. Cat dropped the blanket over him, brushed the fair hair away from an ugly scrape just above his temple. Something wrong with the air, sound . . . Aaron's screams had stopped. On her knees still, she turned to look at the shed door and saw it shiver.

"Stop that!" she howled. "Stay there. Stay where you are!"

There was a thud, and she saw the door shake and bulge, she thought it bulged.

All right. Cat turned and sat on the ground, rested her useless left forearm across raised knees, braced her right wrist, pulled the trigger of the small black revolver. Click. Pulled the trigger again and saw an explosion of dust and splinters from the center of the door. Felt the sound of the shot slap at her ears. Heard a scream.

"Stay there, I said."

CHAPTER 24

". . . Basement." The word was hanging in the air as he flung himself away from the hospital's information desk into a broad corridor where people and furniture were simply bright smears against the edges of his eyes. Banks of elevators, people waiting, so screw that. Heavy door, loud metal stairs, down and hard left and down again and through another door. Narrow hall, closed and silent rooms to either side and a bright rectangle down there, at the far end. Joe blinked at the figure planted in the doorway, tucked his chin down, and dropped his right shoulder: one last barrier, take it *out*.

"Easy, Joe." Gutierrez's voice against his ear, Gutierrez's hand clamped like a hook over his shoulder. Joe lurched to a halt, noted and dismissed the outraged face now almost nose to nose with his own, stepped sideways to look past Dr. Brodhaus into a long white room coldly bright under banks of fluorescent lights.

And there she was, in a wheelchair pulled close against a high, gleaming table, watching a nurse shape plaster on her arm with quick, sure strokes.

"And where the fuck were you *this* time, Mancuso?"

Brodhaus's low-voiced but angry question finally penetrated, and Joe shook his head without taking his eyes from Cat.

"George was with her, I thought. . . . Gutierrez found me. He says she has a broken arm."

"A broken arm, and a whole new crop of world-class bruises and abrasions and even *splinters*, for God's sake." Brodhaus spoke the last words through clenched teeth. "Just listen here, and you, too, Gutierrez; you stay right where you are!"

"I wasn't going anywhere," said Gutierrez mildly.

"Good, because nobody talks to Cat Smith until I say so." He settled back on his heels and jammed his fists into the pockets of his tunic. "The break itself isn't bad: simple fracture of the radius and her bones are young. But somebody had better get that little girl out of the combat zone pretty quick, because she's had about all she can handle."

"Agreed," said Gutierrez quickly. "But I need a statement from her. Maybe after a good night's sleep here—"

In the casting room the nurse gave a final admiring pat to her handiwork, murmured something to her patient, and came toward the door, peeling off her plastic gloves. Joe pushed past Brodhaus and veered around the nurse, who said something he didn't hear. "Cat?" he said, and crouched beside her chair to pick up her right hand, which lay limp in his grasp.

"Joe, I keep asking them about George and they keep saying he's fine. But he didn't look very fine the last time I saw him."

"He has a concussion, and they're keeping him here overnight for observation, but basically he *is* fine. George has a hard head."

"Okay. Is Aaron Burns dead?"

"No, he just has a big hole below his collarbone."

"Too bad. He killed Antelope." Her voice was slow and thick.

"I know. Cat, we're going to the mountains."

"I have to see Antelope."

"Let's ask Eddie Riley to do that. Let him say good-bye for both of you."

She closed her eyes and then moved her head in a single nod.

"My mother will stay and look after George. I'm going home now to put the shell on the truck and toss in what we need, gas up. It won't take, oh, two hours at most. I'll fix a bed for you in back and you can sleep while I drive."

"Where are we going?" A gleam of light from beneath the lowered lashes.

"Plumas County. A guy I know has a cabin there he lets me use. Not fancy, but quiet, and right in the middle of some spectacular scenery. Cat, can you talk to Chief Gutierrez now and get it over with?"

She produced a glimmer of a smile. "He'll probably fine me. For having an unlicensed handgun."

"I'm taking her out of here in two hours," Joe said to Gutierrez in the hall a few minutes later. "She's clear-headed; you can get a statement from her while I'm pulling gear together. I'm sure you can find a stenographer and a typewriter in a hospital," he added.

"I'll manage."

"What do you think, can she handle traveling?" Joe asked the doctor. "I've got a cabin in the mountains for a couple of weeks."

Gutierrez cocked a doubting eyebrow, but Brodhaus nodded. "I'll get her some pain pills for the first few days. Lots of clean air and hardly any people, just what she needs. Come to the emergency entrance when you're ready and have them ring for me. I'll bring her down."

"Her father has been trying to reach her," Gutierrez said quietly. "He's called the station three times, and we've just put him off."

"Tell her father to go fuck himself," said Joe.

"Okay, Vince, thanks." Joe hung up the phone, scooped up the remains of his stock of quarters, and stepped out into the brisk air of the little mountain town of Quincy, California. He glanced up and down the broad main street, and sighed. In a single week Cat had progressed from wan silence to a ruddy vigor that had her cursing the restrictions her cast imposed. If he went looking for her, she'd accuse him of hovering.

"Hi."

He turned quickly to face a mirror image of himself, smaller: hiking boots, Levi's, blue shirt, blue down vest. The black sling cradling her left arm was different, of course, and the yellow traces of old bruises on her face.

"I found the Forest Service," she told him. She glanced at the telephone booth and quickly away again. "The ranger says it feels like cold weather coming; they sometimes have snow this early in September. He says if we didn't bring chains with us, we should get some."

They'd come to town to do laundry and pick up supplies. But the truck didn't have four-wheel drive, and the cabin was several miles from the highway on a graveled forest road. Joe pulled his vest closer, noting that the air had a distinct bite and there was a sharp wind rising. "Maybe we should head for home, Cat, what do you think? Or we could stay in town tonight, in a motel, and decide tomorrow."

The briefest moment of absolute stillness. Then she turned and grinned, and he thought, No, she's fine.

"You mean beds with sheets? And hot showers? And maybe even TV?"

* * *

221

But she wasn't fine, not quite. Beneath tousled damp hair her face was pink from heat and scrubbing, but her mouth was a tight straight line. The giant-size T-shirt he'd bought at the local Penney's hung to her knees and wasn't funny after all; it made her look like a starving child on a refugee poster.

"Well, sit down," he said in hearty tones, "and let's eat this before it gets cold." Cat settled herself into a nest of pillows against the headboard of the big bed; Joe moved the bedside table closer and handed her a triangle of pizza on a paper plate, and then a glass of wine.

"So," she said as he sat down in the room's only chair, "tell me why we have to go back. Did they let Aaron Burns go?"

Joe set his paper plate back on the dresser and picked up his glass of wine. "We don't have to go back unless we want to. Aaron Burns is dead." He saw her face go chalk-white and realized his mistake. "Oh, shit, you didn't do it, Cat! No, listen to me; he was killed trying to escape."

"Trying to escape," she whispered, and coughed to clear her throat. "Trying to escape? That's too neat, like a set-up. Something Ed Berggren might have arranged, to get even for Ilona."

Joe shook his head. "Ed Berggren is above all else a practical man. He'd have risked his life to protect Ilona, but not to avenge her. What happened to Aaron is that he tricked a policeman, got his gun, and then forced three others into a shootout. Vince Gutierrez says he effectively committed suicide."

Color was seeping back into Cat's cheeks. She picked up her slice of pizza, looked at it for a moment, then took a bite and chewed thoughtfully. "Okay. But Joe, that's truly strange. I've been thinking about it all week, and there wasn't that much of a case against Aaron. *I* say he beat me

222

up, and *I* say he told me about killing Ilona and Antelope. But that's all there is, just my word against his. So why would he do such a dumb thing?"

"You were supposed to be healing and enjoying, not thinking," he admonished her. "As a matter of fact, Vince says the case was coming together. They found physical evidence at the Burnses' house, and an earlier victim had agreed to testify."

"Oh."

Joe slid lower in his chair and took a slow sip of wine. "But Vince says he thinks Aaron's mother precipitated his action. She came to see him with a Bible, prayed with him, and—"

"And convinced him he was a doomed sinner? Bullshit."

"Let me finish. Aaron's mother said *she* was the sinner. She told Vince Gutierrez, and the press, that her son was not competent to stand trial. She said it was all her fault; he'd been so damaged by serious and repeated abuse during his childhood that he couldn't be held responsible for anything he'd done. She said she would produce witnesses to support her claims."

"She told all this to the newspapers?"

Joe nodded, his face somber. "Probably thought publicity would aid her cause. There was an interview with Mal, too. Aaron had lied to him right down the line, about finishing the junior college courses, about being accepted at the universities. Fantasy, inability to accept reality."

"Whose, I wonder?"

"Good question. Anyway, the day after all these stories appeared, Aaron managed to get himself shot and killed."

Cat blew a long, slow breath through pursed lips. "Joe, you probably have a way you think I ought to feel about this. Never mind," she said sharply as he leaned forward to speak. "Let me tell you how I do feel. I think that whatever makes people into monsters, once that's what they are they don't belong out here where other people are walking around. So I'm glad I didn't kill Aaron Burns, but don't expect me to be sorry he's dead."

"I don't. I don't expect anything, I haven't said a word."

"Moose will," she said with a sigh. "We, the Animals, used to argue about things like this. Moose was at one end, Possum at the other, Squirrel and I back and forth in between. You're more like Moose, which makes you lovable but . . ."

"Lovable but irritating?" he suggested.

"Irritating. Yes. Is there any more pizza?"

For several minutes they ate slowly and didn't look at each other. Finally Joe collected the empty plates and refilled wineglasses. "Are you really so reluctant to go back? To Port Silva, I mean." He settled back into his chair and watched her face.

"Actually, I'm getting homesick for Arthur."

"Ah. That's good, because George, who is fully recovered and living in the cottage, says Arthur is very unhappy. Turning down Friskies but hunting with fervor. George says there's a little row of corpses on your back step every morning."

"I rescued Arthur when he was a half-grown kitten, so he thinks I'm his very own private property. He's bringing me presents to coax me back. Joe, you look like that doctor when he says the needle will hurt but it's good for me. What's the rest of the news from Port Silva?"

"The rest is actually news from Arizona. First thing is that Jimmy Three is apparently going to plead guilty to a lesser charge than attempted rape. He probably won't serve much time, Vince says."

"That's too bad, but I'm not afraid of him, not anymore." She lifted her head suddenly, as if listening to the echo of her own words; then a grin stretched her mouth wide, and still wider. "Not anymore."

"And your father has been trying to get in touch with you. He was trying the day we left, but I didn't think you needed to know then."

She shrugged. "I'll call him when we get back, but he'll be sorry. I think he owes me money; I'm going to talk to your lawyer about that. I mean, I know I can't sell my half of the ranch yet, but I bet I'm entitled to what it earns."

"Oh." Joe tipped his wineglass back and forth, watching reflections and colors. Cat healthy or near enough, Cat with no one to fear, Cat able to support herself comfortably. And old Joe Mancuso sitting here on the sharp edge of self-pity. "So, Cat, what do you want to do?"

"Nothing. Stay right here in this nice soft bed."

"With money from your father you can do. . . . Well, somebody suggested you might like to go to school, to college."

"What somebody, your mother?"

He shook his head. "Alice, actually. She said a bright person your age should probably be in school. She mentioned Humboldt State College, in Eureka."

"Eureka. Do you want me to go to Eureka?"

"Jesus Christ! Of course not." Joe leapt to his feet and stood glaring down at her. "The worst thing in life . . . No, let me get this right. *If* you're warm and dry and not hungry, the worst thing in life is being bored. I haven't been bored for five minutes since I found you. Met you."

Cat slid down against the pillows and pulled the covers to her chin. "Here's the thing. It's been a long while since I sat in a regular classroom, and I didn't like it all that much at the time. I might take some courses at the Builders' School in Port Silva. Moose—Walt, I mean—says that's a good

225

place. Then Walt and I, and probably Eddie, too, could set up a little construction and woodworking business. In Port Silva."

Joe grinned widely. "Terrific. I think that's wonderful."

"Me, too. But right now I'm getting very lonesome in this big bed. Maybe I should go out and catch you some mice."